WIGHT CHRISTMAS

Holiday Horror
and Seasonal Subversion

Edited by Martin Munks

Wight Christmas:
Holiday Horror and Seasonal Subversion

Cover Illustration by Eran Fowler
Interior Illustrations by Sam Agro and Marco Marin
Published by TDotSpec Inc.

Illustration Acknowledgements:
"The Wrong Prey" Cover Illustration Copyright © 2017 Eran Fowler
"Snowman" Illustration Copyright © 2021 Sam Agro
"The Santas" Illustration Copyright © 2021 Sam Agro
"Red Grow the Rushes, O!" Illustration Copyright © 2021 Marco Marin
"Have a Holly, Jolly Nuclear Winter" Illustration Copyright © 2021 Sam Agro
"Harry and Samir Are Still Asleep" Illustration Copyright © 2021 Sam Agro
"The Holly King" Illustration Copyright © 2021 Sam Agro
"I Still Believe in Santa Claus" Illustration Copyright © 2021 Sam Agro
"The Battle of Hitchens' Bridge" Illustration Copyright © 2021 Marco Marin

TDOTSPEC

Wight Christmas Team

Lead Editor
Martin Munks

Managing and Copy Editors
David F. Shultz
Don Miasek
Andy Dibble

Submissions Editors

Adam St. Pierre
Andy Dibble
Anna P.L.
Brian Wheeler
David F. Shultz
Don Miasek

Jesse McMinn
Emil Terziev
Ernie Earon
Justin Dill
Karl Dandenell
Marlaina Stocco
Martin Munks

Melissa Terry
Mitchell Harris
Nujhat Tabassum
Rio Murphy
Wayne Cusack
Whitney Black

Kickstarter Contributors

Aaron Turko
Andy Dibble
April Neal
Arne Radtke
Bart Kuiper
Bryan Dawe
Carolyn Rock
Chris Griffin
Chuck Robinson
Claire Rosser
Damon & Peni Griffin
Don

Ernesto
Guillermo Sanchez
Irwing Nieto
Ivan Radovic
Jordan
Kayla O'Hare
Lilly Ibelo
Marley Stocco
Mubarak Al-Naemi
Peter Vroomen
Phil Shultz
Richard Parker
Robert Claney

Ryan
Sally Fung
Sara
Sarah Olmstead
Sean B
Stewie
Tania
The Creative Fund by
BackerKit
Theric Jepson
tvest
Y.M. Pang

Introduction
Martin Munks

Christmas has a rich tradition of being terrifying.

The secular hero of the holiday is an ancient, all-knowing beast master who *sees you when you're sleeping*. He lives in the coldest and most desolate place on Earth. He commands small elves to work their fingers to the bone building toys for soon-to-be-spoiled children. And you'd better both watch out and not cry, because on one night of the year he commits billions of after-hours B&Es all around the world.

That's how the story goes, at least.

The reality is no better. We force our kids to sit on the laps of strange old men and share their deepest wishes and desires. We use threats of giftlessness to coax little boys and girls into being on their best behaviour. We post plastic elves high atop shelves where views are unobstructed, telling our children not to worry—he's only an agent of Santa's thought police, there to closely monitor their behaviour in the privacy of their bedrooms.

And don't get me started on the plastic clamshell packaging.

But that's really just the tip of the terror iceberg, as these 30 festive and frightening pieces prove. Each one aims to subvert the classic holiday tropes in order to uncover the true meaning behind the darkest season of them all, spinning new traditions around murder and monsters, cannibalism and the occult, hostile takeovers and indentured servitude, and yes, even wights.

I hope you enjoy *Wight Christmas!* Let us know what you think of the stories by social media, especially on Twitter @tdotspec. And if you enjoy a story, let the author know! I'm sure they would love to hear from you.

—Martin

Contents

The Island in the North
Andrew Majors

I have beheld all the cosmos holds of jollity; with goodwill and peace on Earth, I am now assuaged. The sweet-smelling, candied embrace of those ultimate latitudes has seen completed the vilest circuit of my life, and nothing will entice me further to brave such accursed climes. I finish this narrative tonight and contemplate a long journey to the tropics, whereat if fate is kind there will be no further horrors. Amidst palm trees and hot white sand, all the merry ministrations I witnessed on that far-flung, frozen island in the north will be forgotten, never again to haunt any but the dimmest corridors of my memory.

To relay everything would be too much. Know only that several months ago, in the search for quick passage from Davis Strait to the Bering, the vessel I was ensign aboard struck an uncharted shoal in the vicinity of 74 north by 100 west. Though well-provisioned, we deduced quickly the ship was aground, and that it would do little good to remain there. Thus five men struck out in the lifeboat—the captain Croker, Villiers, Prescott, Pruett, and I—to reach the Mountie station at Craig Harbour to the northwest. Almost upon our departure the weather worsened precipitously, and it was three hours in rough seas before we alighted, weary and storm-battered, upon the shore of that misfit isle whose name is forever lost to man.

Andrew Majors

The striking features of the place remain clear to me. Its peaks stretched for leagues to either side of shore, high and cold, with crags and crenellations that grasped the sky like black talons. Sheets of snow and ice reached from the coastline to the base of those dark mountains, a *malpaís* of winter that would prove difficult to navigate on foot. After some deliberation, we decided to press inland, for we had little recourse other than to return and be battered to bits in the sea. It was Villiers, during our search, who found a thin, flat escarpment which trailed away from the beach toward the heart of the landmass, and after stripping the dory of supplies we climbed upon it and set off.

As we travelled we began to notice things out of sorts with the nature of the arctic as we had come to know it. Prescott, an avid biologist, marveled that the ice surrounding us was thinly stained and striped both red and white in places—no doubt, he surmised, due to some chance agglomeration of the local algae. Pruett, once a stevedore at Lake Erie, suggested the ice's curious colourations were due to the same unnatural force that had shaped it into long rods, which in several places reached the height of a man. These rods—he so laughingly noted—often sported a curved crick at the end like a longshoreman's hook. Fatigued as we were, we contested little of this at the time, and sought only to overnight in a suitable alcove sheltered from the cold.

The escarpment ended at the base of a natural stairway that led into the foothills. All hope of returning to shore without difficulty abandoned, we started a precipitous climb to the rim of that weird place. Then and there, its true nature began to reveal itself in force, though none of us would admit anything until later. Whether altitude sickness or exposure to the raw elements caused our maladies I cannot say, for none of us stopped to ponder from whence they came, as in the ever-worsening weather there was no opportunity to do so. All I recall is that our faculties became overwhelmed in turn by the queerest of sensations, each of them intensifying as we plied our way up the rough trail, drawn onward as if by some ever-increasing magnetism toward that icy crown of rock.

I can only hope to describe the symptoms adequately. First, the air began to writhe with colors not unlike those of the northern lights, albeit more fractious and intense; long-banded ribbons of red, green, and gold in equal measure spilled round the sides of my vision, then crossed it as I started to gasp for breath. Villiers claimed he heard ringing in his ears—a hysterical chorus of bells, atonal and gibbering, their intensity almost enough to loosen his grip upon the rock and send him careening into the abyss below. On the brutal winds which tore about us the smell of fresh-baked gingerbread lingered as if the lot of us stood in some grand-dam's kitchen, and when that departed there came the acid and pungent smell of pine needles.

"Good King Wenceslas," I whispered. I do not know if anyone heard me; I hope not.

The ridgetop's perimeter made a large bowl that curved inward to form a chasm-like depression. There the five of us made camp for some time, unwilling to sleep, for the storm grew even worse, and the place we had landed in gifted us not only hallucinations but evil thoughts; Croker became morose at the thought of swindling his first mate out of a bottle of liquor, while Pruett wept about some mischief he'd practiced at the age of seven when he'd cut off most of his sister's hair before school-time. At last, exhaustion overtook us and we slumbered. For how long I do not know, save that when we regained consciousness the storm had passed and the day was gone, replaced by nighttime and the crystal majesty of the heavens. Glistering stars smiled down in weird constellations, their radiance almost blinding in the eerie perfection of that northern aerie.

It was apt that Villiers, the youngest among us at nineteen, first took note of what lay on the floor of the valley below. Eyes wide, mouth gibbering in awe and dread, he beckoned us to look through his field glasses at the occult realm he had discovered. The valley bottom seemed twice as distant to us as the climb from the outer shore, and if not for the starlight that lanced upon it there would be no way at all to judge its chthonic depths. That selfsame light, bolstered by that of a newly ascended gibbous moon, illuminated a scene I wish never to revisit, a cavorting grotesquery the like of which Fuseli or Goya would have painted only in their most tumultuous fevers—though perhaps with far fewer white spruces.

The floor of that hideous vale was covered in spotless snowfall. Dotted here and there were small huts, crudely erected, their tilting sides and eaves and rooftops seeming to swirl and crinkle into forests of arabesques. The center of the motley village held a tiny plaza where a hundred or so denizens gathered, a race of stunted half-men with ruddy countenances and spindly limbs protruding from bulbous torsos, their cheeks wet with blood, their mouths fluttering with razor teeth. Loitering at the center of the throng were eight monstrously fat albino reindeer, blind eyes milky with rheum, struggling in cruel harnesses chained to a sled yet twenty times their size, its innards loaded with an innumerable supply of colored boxes.

Around this fane the half-men stood hand in hand, overawed looks directed at the architect of their reverie. The omnipresent bells which now assailed all of us were joined by a strange chorus of repetitive chanting whose lyrics surpassed me, something akin to endless repetitions of "fa-la-la" and "very-merry," a scene of saccharine decadence we watched with bemusement and disgust. Pruett took sick, Croker moaned and held his head in both hands, while I stood aghast at the proceedings as they took on a new and more frightening dimension of horror.

At the center of that unholy gathering stood a creature who had haunted my compatriots since the days of their youths—bloated like a tick, barely shrouded by a red cloak, emerald head awry with albescent tentacles of hair. 'Twas he who filled the nights of winter—perhaps those of every season—with sublime dread at the prospect of finding anthracite placed within various articles of clothing as one slumbered. A creature whose blind idiot gaze somehow knew when one slept and when one woke, knew one's every thought for good or ill, and commanded only good—but oh! What good could exist coterminous in a universe where such a hideous thing was unleashed to do its wont? To invade one's home, consume sweets, and leave nightmares festively wrapped near hearths and beneath so many trees?

Andrew Majors

I stood listening to the repetitive music, swaying deliriously on my feet as the half-men capered and cavorted in their wintertime bacchanalia. I began to see children—*human children* —file steadily through the throng to genuflect before this being, this Elder God of giving. With bells a-gong and sanity frayed to the last stocking thread, the final shrieking chorus came and all childhood fears were realized in a single instant of caliginous cheer—

Hö! Hö! Hö! Santhulhu fhtagn!

Then I and my four crewmates knew nothing more till we awoke again, and the sergeant at Craig Harbour told us four weeks had passed. Our dory was spotted drifting nearly fifty miles west of its last recorded position by a trawler whose crew had radioed our ship's distress to the authorities. Embarrassed though I was by the mistakes made in my post, for it was obvious by the light of day and the circumstances of our return I had led us awry in the storm, we were all nonetheless glad to be rescued.

It was only later upon chance inspection of that boat that my exuberance faded. In the bow there sat a small package wrapped in gauzy, gaudy, gilded red and green paper and topped with the most gossamer golden ribbon I have ever seen—a simple present. Yet it was enough for me to know the strange place we had visited, and the things we had seen there, had been no fanciful dream but a distinct reality.

I picked the thing up and inspected it. A small card was affixed to the top. It read, in outlandish cursive—

To David G. – From Mr. C.

I briefly considered giving it to Villiers but wished to spare him any relapse in horrid memories, and the same went for the others. To leave the thing unattended would be no good either; someone would chance upon the evil and ensure it followed me to the ends of the earth. With no further recourse, I elected to rid mankind of it altogether. A packing crate emptied of its contents became the box's tomb, and the next week I pitched it over the ship's railing when we got underway for York Factory. As I watched the far horizon of the lonely north disappear in our wake, before we sailed out of eyeshot I swear I saw the crate bob up from the depths, though perhaps it was a shimmer of *fata morgana* and nothing more.

Regardless, I have planned my departure altogether from this country and shall give this letter alongside my resignation. They will think me mad; it no longer matters. Nevermore will I look out across frigid waters in anticipation—in terror—of some unholy artifact floating down from the Arctic to come to rest upon the shore of Hudson Bay, or even to Toronto's wharves where I write this by way of the Saint Lawrence. I sail tomorrow on a tramp freighter, my ultimate end the South Seas. It will do me good to be subsumed by warm air, clear skies, and the sand— but, I think, there will be no little seaside bungalow. For even in a tropic realm I would fear going out upon its deck one evening to spy, washed up on the farthest beach of the smallest atoll of any archipelago, a small black sea-worn crate with an unwelcome gift waiting inside for me.

With condolences,

David Goldberg, ex-navigator, *S.S. Bishop-of-Myra (H.B.C.)*

23 December, 192-

Andrew Majors

•

This document is Mr. Goldberg's last known correspondence before his departure aboard *S.S. Dead Morrows*. His former crew wishes to be contacted at once if he may be found, as he is missing a Christmas package arrived for him from Craig Harbour with postage due.

    –Mgmt.

Snowman
Rainie Zenith

A hard-packed snowball caught young Zoe squarely between the eyes. She reeled from the impact, icy shockwaves reverberating across her forehead.

"You did that on purpose!" Zoe's brother Mason roared, leaving a half-finished snowman to stomp over to Lucy with his hands on his hips. Despite being the younger sibling, Mason was very protective of his sister Zoe.

Behind them, the farmhouse twinkled with fairy lights, standing out like fireworks against the dull white-coated surrounds.

Lucy's cherubic face contorted into a scowl.

"So what if I did it on purpose? Zoe deserved it—she won't play with me."

Lucy's older brother Dylan stepped in, looking like a marshmallow in his white puffer jacket. "Zoe won't play with you because you keep tripping her over. Try being nice for a change—it is Christmas, after all."

Lucy flipped him the bird and busied herself forming another snowball.

"Honestly, I don't know how you put up with her," Mason said.

"With great difficulty," said Dylan.

Thwack!

A cold hard lump of snow collided with the back of his head. "Lucy! You little jerk!"

She gave him the finger again, then set upon Zoe and Mason's snowman-in-progress with her hands and feet, reducing it to a pathetic hump.

Zoe started to bawl.

"Well, she's not gonna want to play with you now, is she?" Dylan said to Lucy.

Mason put his arm around his sister, barely feeling her through her thickly insulated jacket. "Don't worry, we'll build another one," he said.

"I'll keep the little witch away while you do it," Dylan said.

Lucy pelted another snowball at them from across the yard.

"I've got a better idea," Mason said.

•

Inside the farmhouse, the fire roared, the wine flowed and the cheesy Christmas carols played. Garish strands of tinsel strangled a limp fir tree in the corner, its branches sagging beneath the weight of too many dime-store baubles. Balding brothers Alec and Toby aligned a mass of gifts beneath the tree, most of them intended for the children. Their respective wives, Julie and Francis, bustled back and forth from the kitchen with platters of turkey and ham and potatoes. The extended dining table was already heaving with food and they were having trouble finding room for more.

Scattered around the room was a mass of parents, grandparents, and cousins, plus Toby's ex-wife's boyfriend's nephew and the elderly lady from down the road with her fluffy white dog, Cindy. Cindy was stuffed into a hideous hand knitted Christmas jumper.

"Dinner's ready," Julie announced. "Alec, go call the children."

"I hope they've been playing nicely together," Francis said. "My Lucy can be quite beastly at times."

"It's the season of goodwill—I'm sure they've been getting on just fine," Julie said, taking up a glass of wine. "Cheers! To health and happiness!"

Francis raised her glass and took a deep swig.

The focus was firmly on food when the children finally scuttled in and took seats at the table alongside the adults.

"Nice and warm in here," said Mason, shedding his down jacket. "It's freezing outside!"

Toby carved the turkey and Alec the ham, while Francis made sure everyone was kitted out with a drink. Bright chatter and tipsy laughter drowned out Bing Crosby crooning away about a White Christmas.

They got all the way to plum pudding time before Francis suddenly realised her daughter wasn't there. "Where's Lucy?" she said.

"Yes, come to think of it, I haven't seen her at all," said Julie. "Kids, where's Lucy?"

Dylan, Mason and Zoe shrugged their shoulders in unison.

"Did she come inside with you?"

They shrugged again.

"Oh, hell." Francis pushed back her chair. "We have to find her!"

She raced out with Julie on her heels, followed by Alec and Toby, then the three children.

Rainie Zenith

Francis hugged herself and shivered in the biting wind.

"It's so cold out here! Thank god she was wearing her jacket. Should we spread out?"

Julie tapped her on the shoulder and pointed to the snowman in the center of the yard. It was dressed in Lucy's beanie, Lucy's scarf and Lucy's jacket. Lucy's shoes sat at its base.

The three children stood with their hands in their pockets, shoulders hunched, heads down, eyes guilt-ridden.

"Oh no..." Julie said.

She and Francis tore at the snowman with their naked hands, blue fingers numb to the cold as they hauled away handfuls of ice.

A shock of blonde hair emerged at the top.

A purpling hand at the side.

A naked girl with a scowl frozen permanently on her face.

A Christmas Cake
Kara Race-Moore

Natalie lay back in a post-coital glow, enjoying the moment. She and Josh were on the futon he used as both couch and bed in his studio, both of them naked under a snow patterned throw blanket. They had gotten Chinese take out for dinner and then had rich slices of the cake she had brought for dessert. The rest of the decadent cake and the remains of the Chinese food in their white cartons littered the coffee table next to the futon. Their Christmas feast had been followed by a round of sex, illuminated by the gentle glow of the Burning Yule Log on the TV screen. This, Natalie reflected, might be her best Christmas Eve ever.

"I think we should break up."

Josh's words hung in the air like tinsel decorations.

Natalie frowned, trying to process what he had just said. "What?" she finally asked, confused.

Josh shifted, stretching his arms out from under the blanket. "This is all becoming, like, too intense, babe. We said we didn't want anything serious."

"We'd said we'd go slow," she corrected. She clearly remembered all their conversations about why it was too soon to be exclusive, of why they needed a few more months before deciding this was official, of letting everything grow 'organically,' as he had put it. She had agreed, thinking they were on the same path of letting intimacy build up over time to something real and long lasting.

"Yeah, but you're, like, totally turning into a Christmas cake." He waved at her gift on the coffee table.

"A Christmas cake?" Natalie repeated, her voice scaling up into an undignified screech.

"You know, women who are just, like, desperate to get married and have babies and have that whole white picket experience. That's what you've become, babe. It's so not a good look."

"That's not what a Christmas cake means," she told him, latching onto facts in her shock. "Calling a woman a 'Christmas cake' is an old-fashioned Japanese term for a single woman over the age of 25."

"And you're way over 25," Josh said, reaching forwards to drag the container of chow mein towards himself.

"I'm only 29, same as you. And the term is an insult. What kind of guy has sex with a woman and then insults her?"

He grimaced briefly, looking guilty for about a second. "Yeah, but you were the one who showed up with that... cake. It put a lot of pressure on me, you know? I'm not ready for that kind of seriousness."

"I brought you a present," she said flatly. "That's all. A Christmas present. People give Christmas presents at Christmas time! It's just a cake!" Inwardly she winced, thinking of how long she had spent on making it. "It was just some dessert! It's not like I showed up with a ring and demands for some Pintrest-perfect winter wedding!"

"But you were talking about wanting us to do more stuff with your friends. Maybe even meet your family soon. *I* haven't told people we're seeing each other. And now it's all going just so fast, you know?"

As Josh went on about how things weren't 'chill' or 'cool' between them anymore, Natalie's gaze fell on the cake that apparently set this turn of events in motion.

She had made him a traditional Irish Christmas cake, using her great-grandmother's recipe, and spending almost the full traditional month of prep time required to "feed" the cake the obligatory amount of cherry brandy a few teaspoons at a time every day for three weeks.

The result was a dark, moist cake bursting with spices and filled with enough brandy to get tipsy on from just one slice, the outside frosted carefully with a smooth coating of white icing and a perfect, preciously cut fondant triangle of three red berries and three green leaves arranged in the center. Properly stored, it could last up to three months, due to the alcoholic content. She hadn't realized her relationship wasn't going to last past the first serving.

Natalie got up, flinging off the blanket. She shivered as the air hit her naked skin. Josh yipped as her movement left him cold and exposed, and he quickly tugged the blanket back around him.

"I'm gonna go," she said, trying to sound calm, but her voice quavering slightly with the anger that was now taking over the shock.

"Aw, don't be like that," he said, barely putting in the effort to object as he concentrated on digging a forkful of noodles out of the white container. "Stay the night. I'm not kicking you out. I wouldn't do that to you." He slurped the noodles and said, mouth full, "We can have goodbye pancakes in the morning."

She stared at him, incredulous. "I said *I* would make pancakes."

"Yeah? So?" Hastily he swallowed and added, "I mean, I'd make the pancakes, no problem. After, like, some goodbye sex?"

Shaking her head as she picked up her scattered clothes, she told him, "We've had the goodbye sex." She snapped her bra back on in record time. "Clearly. I just would have liked to have known that ahead of time." She practically hopped into her underwear. Bra and underwear had been a matched set bought for the occasion, snow white satin with lots of little red bows.

"Then you wouldn't have been in the mood," pointed out Josh.

"Aw, gee, I wonder why?" she asked sarcastically as she pulled on her bright red sweater dress. Even though the plan had been to stay in, she had still dressed up for the occasion. Josh had not, in his usual jeans and The Darkness concert t-shirt, something she now looked on as a sign of things to come.

She jammed her boots on and just stuffed her green leggings into her purse to be able to leave faster, figuring rage would keep her warm, grabbing her coat and exiting as quickly as possible.

Rage did not, it turned out, keep her warm. The cold bit her legs as she stepped outside Josh's apartment building. He hadn't even bothered to get off the couch as she left, mumbling he was sorry it had to end like this as he helped himself to more cake.

Standing on the sidewalk, Natalie didn't know what to do. She was reluctant to call an Uber; she had thought she would be at Josh's all night, and she had let her roommate know that. Sarah and her latest girlfriend were probably still up watching old stop-motion Christmas movies, or something nauseatingly cute like that. No way she was going to show up to interrupt and have to explain. Natalie determined she would just have to stay out late enough until they were likely asleep. Until not a mouse is stirring, she thought bitterly.

Luckily, she was in New York, so she was sure to find something open. If she was already at her parents' house out in the suburbs, everything would be closed. Of course, if she'd gone home for Christmas Eve, instead of promising just to come over for dinner on Christmas Day, she'd now be asleep in her boy band poster-bedecked childhood bedroom, with sugar plum dreams about Josh in her head, blissfully unaware he wanted to end things.

Spinning out on all the other ways this Christmas could have turned out, she walked down the sidewalk, doing her best to avoid tripping on the piles of frozen brown-gray snow while moving quickly to try and keep her legs warm.

She started in the direction of the restaurants nearest Josh's place. She then turned in the opposite direction as she decided quite firmly that she never again wanted to set foot in any of the places she had frequented with Josh.

Natalie marched down several more streets, grumbling at the endless apartment buildings she passed. The whole point of New York rent prices was so you could be steps away from any type of cuisine at all times, right? She glared as she passed endless displays of cheerful Christmas decorations in windows and propped up in postage stamp yard spaces, put up by happy couples and families, all probably blissfully asleep and cuddled up together.

Thinking of couples snuggled together in warm beds made her feel even colder. She rubbed her gloved hands together, her fingers stinging inside the thin nylon fabric, her cheeks prickling as she blew out dragon clouds onto her hands.

The scent of a raft of cinnamon and sugar hit her; she looked up to see she was outside a bakery-café. The sign hanging over the door proclaimed it: 'Celestial Cakes n' Coffee.' Even better, there was an 'Open 24 hours' neon sign lit in the window. The bright lights inside the restaurant made the windows glow with the promise of warmth and Natalie dashed in.

A blast of heat enveloped her as she entered, the little bell above the door jangling merrily as she sighed in pleasure at the sensation of her body wrapped in hot air. The bakery smelled of sugar and spices and the always-enticing evil carbs.

There was a glass fronted shelf in front of her loaded with cakes and cookies, and behind the counter a tall rack of metal baskets filled with rolls, donuts, and all sorts of other pastries. One corner of the black and white tiled floor was dedicated to a few rickety looking round tables. No one was at the register, but she heard a radio playing Christmas carols from what was probably the back kitchen.

Natalie sank into a chair at one of the little tables, the adrenaline of righteous anger suddenly wearing off, and her whole body sagged in relief to be warm and sitting down. She closed her eyes for a moment and breathed deeply, trying to remember the meditation exercise she had seen on YouTube, but all she could think was how good everything smelled.

"Something to drink?" asked a voice.

Natalie's eyes flew open. Standing in front of her was an older woman, an ageing Boomer in probably her early 70's. She was tall and thin, dressed in black slacks and black shirt covered with a white apron. Her pixie cut hair would be called silver rather than gray and she wore cat eye style glasses. "Coffee? Latte? Hot chocolate? Tea?" She squinted suspiciously at Natalie through her glasses. "You're not one of those crazy New Englanders who like everything iced, even in December?"

"Uh, no, no, I'm from New Jersey," Natalie hastily reassured her. "Hot coffee would be great. With skim milk please."

"Hhmm," the waitress pursed her lips disapprovingly. "I'll see if we have any of that watery stuff. You might have to settle for 2%." She strode through a swinging door off to the side before Natalie could respond.

A tinny version of 'Hark the Herald Angels Sing' warbled from the back kitchen and Natalie sighed in relief at the relative quiet. Tomorrow would mean all sorts of awkward conversations with her extended family at Christmas dinner, and then she would have to spend New Year's single, but for now she could put everything on hold and enjoy not talking to anyone or having to try and do anything.

She looked around at her temporary refuge from the world, in every way just a typical bakery. It took her a minute, but she realized there wasn't a single holiday decoration in sight. No strings of light, no mini-Christmas tree, and no fake holly swathed about. No menorah placed in pride of place on a countertop or windowsill, or paper dreidel decorating the wall.

As far as the bakery was concerned, it could have easily been that period of late winter or early spring, that brief point in the year when it's weeks in between any sort of major calendar event and there are no holiday items in any of the stores. Natalie smiled. She liked it. Even if whoever was in charge was a real Scrooge and hated Christmas, they weren't stingy with the thermostat, and the delicious smells promised good quality food and drink.

The waitress bustled back out, bearing a tray loaded with all sorts of food and two steaming mugs. "You are in luck," the waitress told her. "You have arrived just when we do the switchover of what didn't sell in the past day and start to replace it with fresh batches. The guy from the homeless shelter already did his daily pick up of our leftovers, but I held a few things back for a snack. Enjoy it with me, dear, it's been dead quiet and I could use the company. It'll go to waste, otherwise."

Natalie looked at the tray and saw one of the items was a slice of promisingly decadent looking torte, looking much like her dessert, and she burst into tears.

The woman put the tray down on the table and sat in the other chair to take her hand and pat it while Natalie cried hot tears of shame and misery.

"He called me a Christmas cake!" Natalie sobbed, and then choked out the whole sorry story. Talking helped her get back under control and, once done with describing the horrid night, she took several deep breaths. She began silently repeating mantras of being enough that her therapist had taught her. Soon her breathing returned to normal, and the tears ceased.

"Here, drink." The waitress pushed one of the mugs into her hands and Natalie gratefully sipped from it, embarrassed to have cried in front of a stranger. It was coffee, but with all sorts of spices added to it. She couldn't put her finger on what, but it tasted better than any seasonal drink from Starbucks.

Natalie drank some more as the waitress took her time considering the plate of goodies, seemingly absorbed in her choice of cookies and pastries. Natalie was grateful for the woman giving her the space to compose herself.

The waitress finally decided on a large gingerbread man, picking it up with long fingers with bright pink polish on the nails.

Natalie blurted out, "You don't have a lot of Christmas stuff in here."

The waitress gave her a grim smile as she waved her gingerbread man, "Too patriarchal for my taste, dear. Like everything else, the patriarchy has co-opted Christmas and made it a 'boy's only' space. Santa Claus and his male elves, his male reindeer. The baby Jesus and the three wise men. The Nutcracker Prince and the Mouse King. Saint Nicholas and Black Peter. It's an almost all-male cast with just a few women regulated to walk on roles." She bit off one of the gingerbread man's legs with obvious satisfaction. "Mrs. Claus serves the boys snacks like a good den mother," she gestured with a wry smile at the plate of goodies on the table between them, "and the Virgin Mary sits to the side mutely, an unattainable standard of post-partum beauty."

Natalie shrugged. "The patriarchy sucks, what else is new?" She took a large gulp of the coffee.

"But it *is* new, that's the point. It wasn't always this way."

"Yeah, I know, it was just a Roman feast day until the

Christians turned into a day of prayer, and then the capitalists turned into a season of spending money," said Natalie, pleased with her podcast knowledge coming in handy.

The woman snorted derisively. "Oh, there's a lot more to it than that. Almost all aspects of Christmas come from matriarchal cultures that have been stolen or paved over. For example, the Christmas Tree started as a Nordic tradition of a pole decorated with ribbons and ivy. The pole represented the magical staff of the traveling winter goddess Thorbjorg, who blessed all the houses that worshiped her with songs of praise that became the first carols."

The waitress cheerfully bit off one of gingerbread man's arms, swallowed, and then continued, "At the solstice, the Teutonic practice was to decorate the home with boughs of evergreens to welcome Hertha, goddess of eternal renewal. She would arrive on the longest night of the year from the divine realms to bless the house through the smoke in the fireplace coming from the fir branches lit to honor her. Children baked her little cakes, and she would leave gifts for them when they were asleep."

She put the half-eaten cookie down and took a sip of her coffee. "And there was the Scandinavian goddess Nerthus, their Mother Earth, who would mark the turning point of the year by driving through the land in a sleigh pulled by milky white cows, going so fast over the snow she seemed to fly as she spread blessings of peace, so there would be no battles wherever she went."

Natalie blinked, surprised. "Why... why isn't this talked about?"

"Why should it be? Those in power find it easy to keep holding onto to power if everyone thinks this is 'the way it's always been.'"

"But…" Natalie said, her voice trailing off, not knowing what to say.

"And there's lots more. Cailleach, Santa Lucia, Mother Carey, Frau Gode, the Snow Maiden, Budelfrau, Befana. Powerful female figures from all over the world, worshiped for centuries, goddess and saints and legends, wiped out and rewritten to suit the patriarchy. Female becomes male, and the holiday becomes a dominant event."

"Well, that sucks," said Natalie, taking a bite of the apple cake. It was delicious.

"And still so prominent. Like this Josh—having his cake and eating it too, so to speak."

Natalie felt her checks burn in humiliation. "I wish I could do something about that," she muttered. She picked up her mug to have another sip of the divine coffee.

"Like what?" asked the waitress, eyes sparkling, looking amused.

"I don't know. Like, revenge?"

"Do you mean it?"

Natalie thought about it and decided she wanted to speak the truth, even just once to a stranger. She put down her mug and said firmly, "Yes. I wish something terrible would happen to Josh. I wish he could feel used. Experience being thrown away for having passed some invisible expiration date!" It was freeing to speak her desire; her limbs were limp as if she were drunk, but her mind was stone cold sober.

The waitress grinned and shook her head ruefully. "I'm always surprised by who comes through my door each Christmas Eve."

"What do you mean?"

"I'll tell you. Even though you won't believe me yet. My store calls to those who have been wronged on Christmas Eve and I see what I can do to help—although this is the first time I've gotten an actual Christmas cake!" She chuckled. "Did you just turn thirty?"

"I'm still 29!" said Natalie hotly. "My birthday isn't until January 7!"

"There's no shame in being in your thirties. I'm centuries old, and you don't see me apologizing for it."

"It's just that—wait. What? Uh, you mean, poetically, that's how you feel? Like an old soul?" Natalie took enough gulp of the coffee to try and steady herself, wondering if this woman was assigned to the night shift because she was too mentally unstable to handle customers and how she could make a quick and safe exit.

"No, I mean literally. I'd tell you my name, but you wouldn't recognize it. My married name, before the divorce, was Mrs. Claus. But I go by 'Joanne' these days. And I use the surname 'Winter' just for paperwork, since even all my magic isn't enough to get around the forms the New York Board of Health requires these days."

As she spoke, she waved her hand at the plate of goodies and the gingerbread men sprang up and ran around, assembling a small pyramid of fudge squares. Her half eaten gingerbread man sat halfway up and twitched his remaining arm and leg feebly, silently expressing deep despair. The others ran in a circle around the table and then all fell back down.

Natalie looked at the now still cookies and then at her mug. "What's in this coffee?"

"Cream. Some cinnamon. And a few other harmless spices." Joanne smiled wickedly. "As well as a dose of magic to shut up whatever little Jiminy Cricket you've got in your brain holding you back. I want you to let your Id out. I want to know what you really want, not what this oppressive society tells you what you want. My ex only cares about those little innocents who are still untouched. To balance things, I choose tonight to help those who have been roughed up by the world and could use a little help getting their own back."

Words spilled out before Natalie could stop herself. "Could you really make Josh feel like I do? Feel like he's now too old to succeed? Missed all opportunities to 'have it all'? Hell, could you even make him come close to comprehending the idea of both being expected to 'have it all' and yet never able to have it?"

Joanne gazed at her with speculation. "I think so. Yes, I think I could arrange to have him feel quite the gauntlet of emotions. And, as a Christmas bonus, I could put a little power in your hands as well; help even things out, cosmically."

"What kind of power?"

"Have you ever seen the bumper sticker: 'Lord, grant me the confidence of a mediocre white man'?"

"Yes."

"I can inflate you with that confidence. Help you start the

new year fresh and on a course for success."

"How?" Natalie was sure her ego had never been flatter in her life.

"Don't you know how Christmas magic works? You have to be"—Joanne raised a hand, palm up—"*asleep!*" And she blew a handful of some sparkly powder into Natalie's face, making everything go black as she fell into unconsciousness.

Natalie blinked as she woke up. The light from the windows suggested it was late morning. She was in Josh's apartment on the futon. The Chinese take-out cartons were still on the coffee table, as well as the much reduced remains of the cake. Her body felt heavy. Was being dumped and the magic bakery all just a dream from too much MSG and brandy-soaked cake?

She felt around the mattress but there was no sign of Josh. Her blood froze when she caught sight of the hand that she was patting the mattress with. It was bigger, had more hair, and overall just looked wrong. She held both hands in front of her. The hands and arms were not hers.

Painful spikes of fear shot through her whole body, which still felt too heavy and awkward. She scrambled out of the blankets and realized she was naked. She slapped at her bare chest, now too flat and with too much hair, as she ran towards the bathroom. In the mirror above the sink, Josh stared back at her, eyes wide with panic, mouth open in a shock. She touched her face, watching Josh touch his.

Natalie pivoted Josh's body to vomit into the toilet. Luckily, he had left the seat up and she was able to let forth an uninterrupted torrent of regurgitated Chinese food and cake into the bowl. When she was empty, Natalie ran the tap to clean her mouth out, trying to spit out the acrid taste. Stumbling out of the bathroom, she saw a note on the coffee table next to the Christmas cake, the handwriting large and in an elegant, old fashioned script:

You now have the power of a white man. You can walk into a job or relationship and demand anything. Merry Christmas!

Natalie listened to her breath become panicky in Josh's deeper tone. No, no, this wasn't right! This wasn't what she wanted! Her pronouns were she / her! She was very happy with her gender and sexuality! This was a terrible mistake. She had to make Joanne undo this!

She threw on some of Josh's clothes and began walking briskly all over the neighborhood, trying to retrace her steps, desperate to find that bakery again. There was no sign of it as she went in wider and wider circles around the neighborhood, tracing and retracing her steps.

She walked for hours, with no sign of that strange bakery. She had a bad feeling that if she were ever able to find that bakery again, it would probably only be on a Christmas Eve. She might be stuck in this body for a year. Or forever. Natalie realized she was going to have to think carefully of what to do next.

As she walked, now slower and calmer, she noticed no one brushed past her, that people made way for her without her even having to say 'excuse me.' She was given her personal space in a way she never had before. People saw her now that she was in Josh's body. And, consciously or unconsciously, were deferring to that perceived power. She began walking back to Josh's apartment.

She was going to have her Christmas cake for breakfast, and then she was going to start making plans.

She grinned with all of Josh's teeth, imagining Josh waking up in her bed and having a screaming fit at the unexpected change. Her roommate would probably think "Natalie" was having some sort of psychotic break and call the police. Natalie chuckled to herself and hoped the mental hospitals were open on Christmas Day.

The Child
Carson Buckingham

The three men rode across the night desert, traveling as fast as their steeds could carry them, but not fast enough for any of their riders. With them, they carried many rare gifts.

Gifts for the Child.

"It's a miracle," Malchior cried for the third or fourth time since they set out on their journey. "Oh, the impossibility! And yet, it happened."

The other two wept silently, for they never believed that this day would come and they repented their lack of faith.

"We had the dream—all three of us. The same dream down to the finest detail," Gespir whispered.

"The prophecy has come to pass in our lifetimes," Belthazir said. "All hail the Child."

"All hail the Child," Gespir and Malchior echoed.

"The sun will soon rise. We must escape the heat and rest the animals."

"Yes, Belthazir, and ourselves, as well," Malchior said.

In an hour's time, they came upon one of the many oases that were sprinkled over the otherwise desolate landscape. The three travelers saw to their mounts first, then removed their tents and slipped into the trees to set them up and sleep through the hottest part of the day, planning to resume the last leg of their journey after dark, when travel was, if not comfortable, at least more bearable.

"Sleep well, my brethren, sleep well," Gespir mumbled as he closed his eyes.

•

After sunset, the three awoke, saddled their steeds and set out once again.

"I have naught but a single handful of grain to give to you this morning, loyal friend," Gespir said to his camel.

"Once we reach our journey's end, there will be grain aplenty," Belthazir said.

"And much to drink," Malchior added.

They traveled silently this day, the gravity and awe of the phenomenon they were soon to witness stilling their tongues. They passed the time lost in thought.

When the star they were following suddenly winked out and lights appeared in the distance, they knew they had arrived at last.

In a scant half hour, they were dismounting among fellow travelers and friends.

"Here, let me take your camels for feed and water."

"Refreshments for the Wise Ones! Hurry! Be quick!"

The three basked in the pleasure of the company of their fellows but for a few moments, then Belthazir held up a hand to still the crowd that had gathered at their arrival.

"We humbly thank you for your kind attention, but our needs must be put aside until we have seen the Child and visited the site of this miraculous birth. Please take us to the Mother and Child."

The group parted and a young man with an arrestingly beautiful face led them to the miracle.

The Mother had made a crude bed for her Child by creating a depression in a nearby mound of hay. The Child was calm and wide awake to greet the three. The Mother nestled the child in her arms, then rose and approached the Wise Ones so that they could view Him more closely.

She handed the Child to Gespir, who gazed down, awestruck. In an effort to shield the infant from the chill of the desert night, he cupped his large hand around His tiny head. Belthazir and Malchior each followed suit when their turn to hold the Child came.

The striking young man was summoned once more. He seemed dazed—almost disconnected from his surroundings. The Mother gently passed the Child to him and he held Him close. The infant nuzzled into his neck for the warmth there, and the two remained that way until the beautiful young man slowly crumpled to the ground—but not before the Mother plucked the Child from his arms.

The Mother tenderly wiped the Child's face and dropped the bloody cloth into the haymow. "Isn't it amazing?" she exclaimed. "Only one day old and he's already feeding himself!"

The Santas
David F. Shultz

Jacob stood in the pale glow of the tinseled tree. Christmas Eve. A time when the loneliest among us, in the quiet solitude of their homes, can reflect on their emptiness.

A blizzard outside. Cold as death. It was like this when the officers came to Jacob's door. Their words were a blur. Something about a transport truck, and a slippery highway, and how the paramedics did everything they could. Either Jacob asked about it, or they offered, but he didn't need to identify the bodies. Or he wouldn't want to. Then he thought of the strawberry-rhubarb jam his grandma used to make at Christmas.

He gripped the wooden rail of his stairway. Coloured lights wound along its length. They glowed like nothing had changed, mockingly oblivious. Stockings hung lifeless over an empty fireplace, quiet and somber.

Jacob found himself in the bathroom. The bathtub was full, ready. There was his straight razor on the counter, ready, only ever used once. He'd bled everywhere. "Not yet," he said. "Advil first."

One Advil, two Advil, three Advil, four. Five Advil, six Advil, seven Advil, more. And the caps and bottles floated like little boats on the bathwater. Then the lights went out in the bathroom, and the background hum of the house went dead.

"God damnit," Jacob said. *A powerout in the middle of a fucking blizzard*, he thought. *I'll freeze to death!* "Christ almighty," he muttered, then fumbled through the dark house.

David F. Shultz

Jacob put on pajamas. He lit the fireplace, grabbed a blanket, and bundled on the couch next to the fire. Then he went to sleep.

Jacob awoke to a creaking floorboard. A gangly silhouette stood in front of the fireplace. The figure turned its head slowly towards him. In the flicker of the dying fire, Jacob saw a sickly-green face with a strange rash.

"I know when you're awake," the man said in a raspy voice, then snickered.

Jacob screamed, and the man scrambled away. Wet footsteps slapped the floor towards the stairs. Emboldened by the stranger's retreat, Jacob leapt from the couch, grabbed a firepoker, and pursued.

"Come here, ya bastard," Jacob yelled. He nearly slipped on the slick floorboards. Then he heard a loud thud, and a groan. There was the man, no longer fleeing, but curled in the darkness at the base of the stairs. Tripped on the cord of the Christmas lights.

Jacob approached slowly. "Who the hell are you?"

"I'm Santa—"

"Don't fucking tell me you're Santa Claus."

"Santa *Claus?*" said the man. "That fat asshole? No, I'm Santa Murggis."

And just then, the power came back on. The skinny stranger was lit by the glow of a hundred coloured lights. He wore something like a Santa Claus costume, but blue and green instead of the usual red and white. His face had green scales, like a fish, two holes in place of a nose, and enormous yellow eyes.

"Are you just gonna stand there," the creature said, "or are you going to help me with these lights?" It fumbled with the cord caught around its leg.

"What are you?" Jacob said.

"I just told you. I'm Santa-fucking-Murggis." Then he stood, drops falling from his sopping costume. "You weren't expecting Claus, or you wouldn't have lit the fire, am I right?"

"I wasn't expecting anyone."

"Well, here I am. Now are we gonna do this, or what?"

"Do what?"

"What do you think? You're the one who summoned me."

"What in God's name are you talking about?"

Santa Murggis sighed. "Santa Claus comes to give presents to good kids, right?"

"Right."

"And Santa Piotr comes to give coal to bad kids, right?"

"I thought that was Santa Claus."

"You don't even know about Piotr? What are they teaching in schools these days?"

Jacob shrugged, still wielding the firepoker like a baseball bat.

"You mind putting that thing away?" Murggis said.

"Not until you tell me what you're doing in my house."

"Why don't I just show you?" Then Murggis started slowly up the stairs. "Come on."

Jacob followed with firepoker raised. "Where the hell do you think you're going?"

"Everyone knows about Claus," Murggis said. "Stockings by the fireplace, milk and cookies, all that shit. But they never teach you about the other Santas."

"Other Santas?"

"Like Santa Piotr. And Santa Tobias. And me."

"Santa Murggis."

"You remembered," Murggis said with a grin, and made his way into the bathroom. He motioned to the bathtub, full of water. "Claus uses chimneys. I use the bath. So of course you understand, when we saw the chimney was lit and the tub was full, we thought it was my turn."

"I don't know what to tell you. I don't believe in Santa Claus, and I've never even heard of you. I wasn't trying to invite you in."

"Well, I'm here now." Murggis dipped his hand into the water. "So you want your gift or not?"

Jacob shuddered at the thought of what sort of gift this freakshow might have in mind. "I'll pass."

Murggis squinted his big yellow eyes. "We Santas have a sort of power-sharing agreement, you know. Division of responsibilities and such. Claus gets the good kids. Piotr gets the bad kids." Murggis waited awkwardly for his prompt.

"And you?"

"Single adults with suicidal ideation."

"You get a lot of work?"

"Not as much as Claus. But it's still busy this time of year. Anyway, Claus has his bag of gifts. Stupid toys and bullshit, because he's got to deal with kids. But me, I give the gift of clairaudience."

Jacob stared blankly.

"It means," Murggis said, "that I can let you hear things from the spirit world. Like, for instance, your family. You want to hear from them, don't you?"

Jacob lowered his poker.

Murggis swirled the water. It bubbled. Then Jacob thought he heard, from somewhere in the gurgling water, the faintest trace of a voice. No words, just a distorted murmuring.

"Sorry," said Murggis. "That doesn't sound quite right."

"It's them," Jacob said. It was unmistakable now, even without words. His wife and daughter. Their voices bubbled up from the tub.

"But no words," Murggis said. "No, no. This isn't right. You deserve better, don't you? You should get to talk to them. Come. Come with me and we'll fix this."

"Come with you where?"

"To my workshop," Murggis said. "Through the tub." Then he grabbed Jacob by the wrist with a cold and wet clamp of reptilian fingers.

Jacob yanked his arm away and lifted the poker. "Don't touch me, you creepy shit."

"I'm creepy? What about Claus? He's the one who 'sees you when you're sleeping'. Why would he watch you while you're sleeping? Can't be to figure out if you're good or bad, now could it? That's creepy if you ask me."

"You really have it in for Claus, don't you?"

"He gets all the credit," Murggis said. "Sorry I got so upset about it. I just want to do my part, you know? And then the water didn't work, and you didn't get to talk to your family. I just want to make it right. So what do you say? Will you go with me?"

"Into the tub?"

"It's like a magic sleigh. Just a little more wet. And no reindeer."

"You first."

"Of course," Murggis said, and splashed into the tub. "Room for one more. Then we can get you in touch with your family."

Jacob thought about his family, how he would do anything for just one more minute with them. Maybe even get in a bath with Murggis. And besides, what did he have to lose? So he joined Murggis in the tub, cold water soaking into his pajamas, with the two of them facing each other, and Murggis grinning widely.

"Here we go," Murggis said, and the walls of the house melted away like waterfalls. A blur of coloured lights raced by faster and faster, and suddenly stopped.

They were in the middle of a cave with smooth polished walls, brightly lit with coloured lanterns. A large wooden table spanned the room, surrounded by strange people. Jacob recognized only Santa Claus, the white-bearded fat man in the red suit. But there were many others there. In a green suit, a purple skinned newt-faced man. In a yellow suit, an apparent burn-victim. And all the other Santas, staring at Jacob in the tub.

"You brought him here?" roared an enormous yeti Santa in an orange suit.

"My gift wasn't working," Murggis said.

"Murggis, Murggis, Murggis," said the newt Santa, "when will you pull it together?"

"Ho, ho, ho," said Claus.

"Now's not the time," Murggis said. "Are you going to help me or not?"

The Santas looked at each other.

"Alright then." An impish Santa in brown hopped from his seat. "Let's figure this out." He walked over to the tub and put his ear to the water. It bubbled and gurgled and hummed. The imp nodded at the sound. "So your family's all dead, right?"

The bluntness caught Jacob by surprise.

"Yeah," Murggis answered for Jacob. "On the way home from Christmas shopping."

"Ho, ho, ho," said Claus. "Merry Christmas." And the other Santas laughed.

"Yes, yes," said the imp, "but how?"

"Car accident," Jacob said.

"I see, I see," said the imp. "And how long did it take them to die?"

"Instantaneous," Jacob said. That's what the officers had told him.

"No, no, I don't think so," said the imp. "That's not how water-talking works. They get to use their voice from before their death. They must have been alive for at least a few minutes."

Then Jacob heard the murmuring again. The distorted, tortured gurgling of the bubbles in the water. And he felt a stabbing pain, like his intestines were being eaten from the inside.

"Jacob," Murggis said, and hopped out of the bath. "Are you okay?"

Jacob sat alone in the tub. The water was filling with brown and red, leaking from Jacob's body.

"You're shitting blood, man," Murggis said. "How much Advil did you take?"

"Eight or nine," Jacob said. And he clutched his gut.

"Eight or nine pills won't do it," Murggis said. Then he turned to the other Santas. "He's still mine."

"Bottles," Jacob said. "Eight or nine bottles."

The Santas murmured to each other. Then a white-robed Santa stood. He had translucent flesh, giving a clear view to organs and bones.

"This one is mine," the translucent Santa said.

Murggis looked at Jacob. "Sorry, buddy. He's right. I only deal with people who fuck up their suicide attempts. Santa Sephtis will take over from here."

Jacob could only groan as the pain intensified. Sephtis loomed over him.

"Are you ready for your gift?" Santa Sephtis said.

"No," Jacob said.

Sephtis placed slimy hands on Jacob's head. "I will send you now to see your family." Jacob thought of the strawberry-rhubarb jam his grandma used to make at Christmas. Then Sephtis pushed his head below the water.

Santa's Little Helpers
Donna J. W. Munro

That damned poem set us all up. Painted a picture of a jolly old man with red cheeks and a bushy beard and presents. Mostly it's true. True enough for us to recognize him when he comes for us.

No trees for me.

No presents or carols. No cards and twinkling lights.

All of those things, so pagan and visceral under the modern glamour, are sacrifices. He's no saint, damn it!

Fairies paint the world with a cocoon of beauty and joy, so you'll sit on their laps, stroke their beards, smile into their hunger. But the real underneath, the peeled away scab, shows big eyes and gnashing teeth in the mouth smiling behind the beard.

For me, Christmas is Halloween.

•

"Daddy, can't we have just a little tree? Just for me? All my friends —"

"—are idiots," I finished for her. My poor baby girl was bright as the dawn and sharp as an edge, but she didn't see through the Santa Claus glamour. The neighbors, her friends, the whole damned world spends months paving the way for him. Melodic carols played in stores, sparkling lights on street poles, fucking displays out before the Thanksgiving turkey is even dead —his little helpers are thorough beasts.

My poor girl cried when I wouldn't let her light the beacon

for him by decorating. She knew how I felt, but still thought just a little Christmas cheer wouldn't hurt.

"Lisa, look at these," I said each morning of November, trying to break the spell. I leafed through pages of clippings I've kept my whole life, showed her the diary entries from fathers going back generations to the old country. They all spoke of the same horrific sacrifices the little helpers made to the old god of the fairies—the collector of names and one-eyed wizard—all captured in the grainy images and the breathless written accounts I'd saved. I showed her the crime scene photos I pay dearly for each Christmas, the only present I give myself. The bodies always look the same in the stark prints.

Dead humans, teeth marks, spilled bowels, all on Christmas Day. All with signs no one else sees. Patterns they're blind to. Exsanguinated. Dribbles of blood where there should be slicks and gouts. X shaped cuts down the center, entrails exposed. Dangling. Body hanging from a noose wrapped above the deep throat slash like a yawning mouth. A wreath of evergreen branches on their heads. Facing northeast.

I'd found hundreds of recorded cases around the world throughout history. The attacks happened in any place that practices Christmas. Any people with trees and lights and presents and stockings invited him in. It's all Odin/Father Christmas/St. Nick bait. He didn't take enough for the police to get wise, but the pattern was there.

My family had traced it through generations.

Maybe that's why he hunted for us and why we hid.

"No, Daddy, don't make me look again."

But I did. She took it like the tough little warrior I raised her to be. Kept her eyes open, even if they ran with tears.

"We can't let them in, Lisa. They're monsters."

"But none of my friends—"

"It's like a lottery. They gamble every year and mostly they win. They worship him with their greenery and their feasts after the winter solstice, but then don't see the cost. The Christians didn't tame the god. He fooled them. He and his little demon helpers."

She rolled her eyes at that. Thirteen is such an asshole age. They know everything and nothing at the same time. Lisa had listened long enough to me to know better, but her friends, the advertisements, the colors of the season hummed in her head like a summer pop song. I knew it. It had done the same for me when I was her age. Treacherous times. My girl was coming into her own power, filled with doubt. I had to work twice as hard to keep her safe.

Because Santa's little helpers have big eyes. They see everything.

•

December 24th.

Winter solstice passed, but that day doesn't hold the potency of Christmas Eve. Anxiety crushed my stomach into a chunk so dense and sharp, I imagined a lump of coal rolling around in my gut. Poor Lisa had been in her room crying for hours. She wanted to escape to her friend's house, to take part in their celebrations and leave me here to my "crazy ideas." That's what she'd called our family traditions.

I sent her to her room, the only place she'd be safe.

Our house, the only dark one on the street, was thick with sage smoke and blessed by my mumbled prayers against the halfway places and the openings Santa's little helpers might use to get in. I climbed the steps, setting protections on each stair. As I smudged my way through the second floor, I heard her singing. The chink in our armor.

"Silent night, holy night. All is calm, all is…"

She must have heard my tread outside her door because she fell silent. I heard her leap up, scamper with soft socked feet around the room, the thump of a drawer forcibly closing, then she opened her door.

"What, Daddy?" She asked, cheeks red and gaze sliding off of mine.

"What are you doing, Lisa?"

She shook her head. "Nothing."

I pushed gently past her.

"No! My room is private, Daddy. Please stay out!" She wailed, tugging on my elbow.

The biting smell of forest found my nose. I went to the closet first. Inside, the smallest tree stood decorated in the corner. Paper links and an origami star brightened the twig branches. I didn't want to know what was hidden in her drawer. The tree and the song she'd sung negated all I'd done to protect us.

"Lisa, they'll see us now and they'll come."

"Daddy, don't be ridiculous. That's what they call you, you know!" She bit down on the words as she said them, grinding and spitting them out. "You're crazy! Just Christmas crazy! After Mom, you—"

I grabbed her and shook her to shut her up. "Don't say another word! They'll find us now and if you talk about her—"

"Mom died. Someone killed her on Christmas. I can't change that and neither can you. We need to—"

Something downstairs crashed, then a rolling, spiraling, clattering sound wound up the stairs. Shuffling. I could hear it. I crushed Lisa to me so hard she squirmed.

"You're hurting me, Daddy."

"Get in the closet. Don't come out, no matter what. Okay?"

She looked up into the panic crowding my eyes, my panting breaths puffed against her cheeks, hot and desperate. She nodded.

I hoped this time she'd do as I asked.

The door opened with a creak and I winced. Above my head, the thump and clatter of hooves rattled the roof. As I eased my way down the steps, the hooves scattered, seeming to thunder down every wall, every side of the house, scrabbling at windows, pecking at doors.

The chimney. I hadn't smudged it.

When I turned the corner into the living room, he crawled out of the flue as sooty and red as the poem promised. He turned to face me, muscled and bulky instead of fat in the red fur trimmed jacket. Hat over one eye, beard smeared with blood, he set down his bag and looked at me.

"All-father," I said. Now that he was here, knowing what he came for, I had to convince him not to take Lisa. I needed to save my baby from the horror that had happened to my wife. "All-father, please…"

He opened his mouth and screeched an ancient spell,

evaporating the clouds of sage and shattering my weak protections. Every window slid open to let his little helpers in. White-skinned, baggy creatures with dark pie eyes and saw-toothed maws. Hooves for feet, gangly hands. Naked but for the bags slung on their backs.

I couldn't move as they crawled in. My heart convulsed. My mind begged me to run. My skin pricked, but he held me there with his one coal black eye.

Behind me, hooves ticked on hardwood while they searched from room to room. In front of me, the old god opened his bag, drawing out a copper pot and a seax dagger.

Gurgling around my fear, I begged, "Not again. Please. We've already paid. You took Dora from us."

The father of winter, many-named beast, lay a finger aside his nose, weaving a curse.

A scream. Of course, they would take Lisa first. They dragged her down the stairs and laid her head over his bowl where he held his dagger ready.

"Please no, please. Not my daughter. Not my baby, too," I wheezed, fighting the geas that held me. "Why me?"

His finger, stubby and fat with a sharp, ragged nail pointed at her then me, back and forth licking his lips. That's when I understood that those of us who knew him best were the tastiest sacrifices. That he took some random folks unknowingly practicing the old ways here and there, but the ones who questioned or who knew he wasn't the jolly elf of the poem—we had to go first.

"Me," I said. "Please, me."

47

For a minute, I saw the twinkle—a bit of holiday wishing on my part? I hoped in that second maybe he'd take me instead. Maybe he'd spare her. But then he laughed, booming down the scale into deep, bone rattling notes. There'd be no substitution.

He nodded, though not at me. To one of his helpers.

Her last word was, "Daddy?"

The shriveled bastard ran the blade across her throat. The blood gushed into the pot as her heart pumped. Beat-gush... beat-gush. The little helpers leaned in, stirring the blood with their fingers, then sucking them clean.

Odin All-father lifted the copper pot and sipped from it as his creatures strung rope around Lisa's neck and hung her from the stair's handrail. She was dead, but seeing her there hanging like a broken puppet crushed me down into a fragment. I wanted to scream and kick, but he held me frozen.

They cut a swift x through her belly and her intestines flopped to the floor. Helpers scrambled over them, prodding. Scrying like the books said they did in the old times.

No, I muttered inside my mind. *No, no, nonononono...* because that was my daughter and she couldn't be dead. Not her, too.

Then the white-skinned, hooved helpers pointed her body toward Odin, squatting on my hearth. They bowed and began to hum. Their songs, disincorporated, might have been carols sung by children at a mall. Woven together in their discordant round of voices, they were a terrible prayer. Tribute to the god. Part of the sacrifice.

As they sang, Lisa's body shuddered. It bent on the end of

her rope, flexing out at all angles like a bow. Her abdomen's ripped edges fluttered.

One of the creatures broke ranks, stumbling through the slippery intestines to Lisa's body. It dug in the flapping maw of the cut, spilling drops of fluid on the floor. The helper gurgled, a happy sound, then stuck its other hand in. Slowly, it pulled out a tiny white creature. One of them.

The helper clutched the thing pulled from Lisa tight to its chest, patting and rocking. It moved close to me, black eyes watching. Patting and rocking. Patting and rocking. The thing reached out with slick, stretched fingers to stroke my chin.

Just like my wife had done before *she* died.

Before they took her.

Looking down at this thing clutching a baby monster to it, patting and rocking, my muscles loosened against the geas. I knew. That knowing freed me.

My body collapsed at her feet. I couldn't touch her, but I knew. The helper was what was left of my Dora. My beautiful wife.

She'd come for Lisa.

Given her to the All-father so he'd keep her, too.

And now, she stood in front of me, eyes full of dark but something else. A question? An invitation? Something I couldn't understand in that moment of terror.

Odin laughed, booming through my skin cells and shattering my grip on reason.

I fell into blissful dark.

•

When I woke in the hospital, they had me chained to a gurney. No forensic evidence connected me directly to Lisa's murder, but they did find me bawling incoherently under her swinging feet. Every time they bring in a lawyer or a cop to question me, I tell the truth. That's enough to send them away, heads shaking.

They found my scrapbook. My research room with all the maps and written accounts. They talked to my neighbors. They'll build a case against me this time. There will be no tolerance for my lawyer's defense from last time: random wacko with a Santa complex. No. Our family history is against me. Lightning doesn't strike twice and I'm the only constant in the cases of my wife and daughter.

Even if they can't convict me, they'll put me away for good in a loony bin.

That's fine.

Next year, when Christmas rolls around, I'm going to get a little tree and some tinsel. I'm going to sing tunelessly all year, carol after carol, in the sitting room of the asylum. Next year, I'm going to say yes when he shuffles down the chimney and lays his finger aside his nose.

Merry Christmas to all and to all a good night.

Frankenclaus
Rhian Bowley

The bodies of the Reindeer Liberation Front swung merrily from the antlers of the herd as they crashed home through the starlit night.

•

Hunched over a bourbon on her front porch, Ma Claus heard the jingle bells and swore. They were back too soon. She stubbed her cigarette out on the crisp white snow, grabbed her sewing bag from under the rocking chair, and strapped on an old, stained apron.

•

The reindeer landed in a flurry of blood and tipped the sleigh's corpse onto the ground in front of her. A snapped-off placard —'Free the Lapland Nine'—jutted from Santa's belly at an ugly angle.

"Again? Those damn protestors." Ma Claus poked at the figures impaled on the antlers and nodded approvingly at their frozen entrails, stiff like stalactites.

"Make another," howled the herd, eager to continue their Wild Hunt. Foam sparkled around Blitzen's slavering jaws.

Grunting, Ma C. lifted the bodies from the antlers and dragged them next to her erstwhile husband.

Rhian Bowley

Straddling Santa's corpse, she pulled a well-worn sewing pattern from the bag and signalled the reindeer to begin. Diamond-sharp hooves sliced the protestors into careful pieces, ready for Ma Claus's needles. Red flecks seasoned her steel-grey curls as she worked her magic. Generations had performed this ritual, preserving the legend of the original Claus.

A sprinkle of elf dust and the spell was complete. The sleigh launched into the air once again, a fresh twinkle in New Santa's eyes.

The Selfless Gift
Rio Murphy

He kissed the old woman's cheek. They'd put her in the housecoat he'd given her for Christmas. Her naked, boney ankles stuck out from under it, above the socks they gave everyone, with the sticky bottoms to prevent slipping.

He leaned over to adjust the catheter tube that had gotten twisted on a knob on her wheelchair.

His mother settled back and seemed to shrink. "I can see the line very clearly. Yes!" She drew an imaginary line between herself and her son, and then, in a sort of lasso, indicated perhaps the whole world beyond her.

The care home had the smooth cleanliness of a hospital despite the few nods to the Christmas season—an artificial tree with lights and decorations, a bit of plastic holly strung around the windows. There was a constant hum of something or other, the heating system or monitors and the frequent squeak of rubber soled shoes on polished tile floors—the occasional clang of doors that locked in but not out. When they opened, the sound of Bing Crosby crooning, "I'm dreaming of a White Christmas" spilled into the room.

Sitting alone in a wheelchair, a grey skeleton of a man started to wail, "Oh, oh, oh! OH! OH!!"

"Shut up or it'll find you!" The old woman waved a boney arm at him.

One of the attendants gradually got up from behind his station. He wore hospital fatigues that looked like pajamas with pictures of fruit all over them, and a Santa hat on his head. He wheeled the wailing man away, saying, "Let's go watch the movie, buddy!"

Outside the snow was falling softly.

Her son noticed that her eyes were gummy, crusted around the edges, cloudy tears hanging on the few spare lashes of her lower lids.

They need to give her the eye drops, he thought. The sunken area around her eyes was purplish. *Is that normal?* He wondered.

"Are you warm enough, mom? You want me to get a blanket? Your bare legs are hanging out." He wandered off in search of one.

"Watch out for the line. When you cross it, everything changes," she called after him.

He came back without a blanket feeling desperate for a cigarette.

He tried to pull her housecoat closer around her legs, and grew frustrated.

She said: "It's too late now. I am on the other side of the line. You don't want to cross it."

"I *would*. I would cross it for you mom."

She touched his hand. "Well, don't."

It had been snowing steadily all day. He could see his car and he wondered why they put the visitors lounge here instead of at the back overlooking the garden. Perhaps they thought that families who put their elderly in a place like this cared more about their cars.

"Mom, I have to get going now. I'll come back on New Year's Day."

She looked blank.

He managed the awkward business of kissing her goodbye. He tilted his head this way and that to reach her cheek. On contact it was so soft she seemed as if she was made of mist.

Outside he cupped his hands around a flame and lit a smoke. Stamped his feet to keep warm. Looked up and saw the "No Smoking for 20 meters" sign and trudged to his car. He sat behind the wheel and just watched the snowflakes falling steadily for a while. He wiped his eyes, blinking against the smoke that stung them and made them tear. Then he started up the car.

It crept out of the parking lot, slowly the headlights formed an arc in the wall of snowflakes, beyond that, nothing could be seen except for the procession of pools of light formed by the street lamps.

It was a two-hour drive on the highway to get to the cottage. The trunk was full of presents and extras that Bonnie, his wife, had forgotten to take up there. He was tired and dreaded facing the crush of so much family "home for the holidays."

He rolled down the window and pitched out the cigarette butt, the red embers bouncing against the side of his car. He adjusted his seat, straining to see the road. The concentration it took was wearing. The blast of the heater made him sleepy—he opened the window. The cold wind was bracing.

•

Rio Murphy

Now, as far as she is concerned, she is not in the assisted living hospital. She is in what was once her childhood home. She wanders around the empty house, listening to the sounds of unseen children playing and the distant thunder of a storm— thunder in a snowstorm, unique to this land of lakes.

She turns a corner and comes to the large room with the white line drawn down the middle.

On the other side of the line everything is in full colour. There is a Christmas tree brightly decorated, and a stack of presents spilling out from under it onto the rug, a brilliant fire in the fireplace, a table all dressed with sparkling china and crystal laid out beneath boughs of holly and ivy hanging from the ceiling.

She can't join in. She can't cross the line and they can't come to her. She wants to leave gifts for them but on her side of the line, there is nothing she can share. Where she is, it is all grey.

The line is White. The deadly presence with her, "The Thing" as she calls it, is an absence of light, a darker than black emptiness. It makes her watch as it plays with those who still have lives.

Only the white line keeps the emptiness from reaching those she loves. But they can stumble. When they come too close to the emptiness, it can grab them.

Sometimes The Thing grows bored and lies flat and just looks like a polished floor.

"DON'T CROSS IT! DON'T CROSS IT!" she yells at the fools who stumble, like that boney old man who refuses to eat. She's seen it, the inky thing, which rises up in a flash and slurps them up and then they are gone.

"Too late! You're done for!"

Once she heard her son talking to her, *not long ago,* she thinks. "Don't cross the line!" she warned him. The thing slurped at her naked legs under her robe. "Don't try to find me, son. I'm alright. You stay over there."

Suddenly she's sitting beside him in his car. He is driving. She's thrilled to feel the wind and the snow coming in through his window. Thrilled to be out of that grey house with the Thing, but then she sees he's dropping off to sleep at the wheel. There are headlights coming straight at them. "WAKE UP!" She screams but he won't. She has to turn the steering wheel and she doesn't know if she has the strength. But she's resolute. This is one gift she can give him.

•

He was in the ditch. He didn't even know what had happened. He'd fallen asleep—yes, he was certain of that. He did a quick inventory and found he was uninjured. *What a nightmare this Christmas is turning out to be.*

Fortunately, the truck he'd almost hit was a tow truck and the driver was also unhurt. He even offered to pull him out of the ditch.

He followed the tow truck to the gas station/motel which just happened to belong to the driver—a lucky break.

Once inside the office of the motel, he called his wife Bonny and explained he was going to stay overnight. He was exhausted.

As soon as he fell into the lumpy motel bed, he was asleep.

An hour later he woke from a violent dream to the dim light of the unfamiliar motel room. He had a vague recollection of a dream that his mother was sitting next to him—but she and the dream evaporated as soon as he reached towards her.

He sat for a while in the velvet silence of the snow falling outside, undisturbed by traffic on the lonely road. It was Christmas Eve, and he was haunted by the feeling that he had barely escaped something horrifying, how if he hadn't turned into the ditch, if instead he'd slid across the line...

He managed something close to sleep and woke later that morning. He paid the guy for the room and the tow and gratefully downed several cups of coffee, apologizing for disturbing the man's Christmas.

He got back in his car. The snow had stopped falling and the remaining drive was uneventful. He'd forgotten how beautiful it was up here this time of year.

When he entered the cottage that had been his mother's childhood home, all the faces of the family sitting at the breakfast table turned at once. They looked like they'd been up all night, some with faces swollen from crying.

Bonny ran and threw her arms around him. "They called from the home, just after you called—last night—I didn't want you to drive anymore so I didn't call you back—it was about an hour after you left her—John—oh John—your mother—"

Red Grow the Rushes, O!

Alice Loweecey

Mallory sipped her third cup of Smoking Bishop and invented new curses for bloodsucking CEOs who worshiped at the altar of "lean and mean." She'd been one of fifty-seven employees sacrificed on their altar last month, forcing her back to the podunk town she'd escaped the moment she turned eighteen.

Ten Christmases later, the place still looked like a Thomas Kinkade painting come to life. Six inches of snow sparkled under a star-studded sky. Most of the town's adult population had gathered in the square, singing carols as they decorated a twenty-foot tree and the larger than life illuminated Nativity scene. Decades ago the town council had decreed this as the traditional end to a Black Friday spent in frenzied shopping in the genuine 1950s era Main Street stores.

Nostalgia meant tourism dollars. The marketing VP in her acknowledged the smart decision. The rest of her hated it like poison.

These perky, wholesome adults had tormented her since fifth grade. They'd jeered and excluded her when she was a fat, awkward pre-teen. They'd sabotaged her locker and played keep-away with her granny-panties underwear in the gym showers when she was a fat, shy teenager. They'd painted "Good riddance" in fluorescent finger paint on her car when she left for college.

Now she was a toned, confident adult and they acted as though the years of torment had been harmless fun between friends.

Mallory wished the Krampus would appear and whip them straight into hell.

A tall, blond, muscled guy in jeans and a plaid flannel jacket shouted, "Mallory, come help me with the Baby Jesus!"

Mallory also wished the guy she'd secretly adored in high school wasn't still single. Ryan had taken her home to dinner three times already and her inner teenager remained in a state of swooning ecstasy. It would be much too easy to let him whisk her off to his horse farm for life.

She would not succumb. She was not going to wake up five years from now saddled with a life of changing diapers and mucking out stables. Especially not in nostalgia-ville.

The Bar and Grille's proprietor dressed as Bob Cratchit for the festivities. He presided over one urn of hot mulled cider and another of the Dickensian concoction of wine, port, sugar, citrus, and spices. It went down smooth with a helluva kick. Mallory tossed back the rest of her drink and plastered on a smile.

She and Ryan wrestled the three-foot long plastic baby into a manger, feeding its electric cord into the power strip behind the eight-foot tall stable. Mary and Joseph already knelt on either side of the manger, simpering pink smiles on their faces.

"Light 'er up," Ryan shouted.

The display flickered and went dark. The sheriff called from his spot near the urns, "Check the plugs, horse boy."

Mallory unplugged and replugged everything. "Try now."

This time the crèche population stayed lit. Ryan jumped

onto the stable roof and sang four bars of the Hallelujah chorus. Despite herself, Mallory laughed.

"That's my girl." Ryan scrambled down and kissed her with a loud smack.

"Christmas is for lovers," Ryan's brother said. He grabbed her left hand, Ryan grabbed her right, and they started to dance around the giant Christmas tree. Within a minute twenty people had joined them. As if on cue, the dancers stopped and burst into the Whoville song from the Grinch TV show.

Swaying back and forth alongside her teenage crush, singing in the kaleidoscopic glow from dozens of strings of retro-style lights, the spiky ball of anger in Mallory's chest eased a trifle. Or maybe it was the booze.

"Got a surprise," Ryan breathed into her ear. He and his brother backed her out of the circle. When they reached the ranch's pickup truck, they placed her by the tailgate. "Three. Two. One." They flipped up the tarp.

A scream lodged in Mallory's throat. For a moment she couldn't breathe.

The men high-fived each other. "Meet the Mari Lwyd."

"It's a skull." She stared at a snout of gleaming white bone with teeth as long as her index finger.

"To be specific, it's a horse's skull." Ryan flicked the brow. "Notice the sparkly ornaments she has for eyes?"

"The better to see you with, my dear," his brother cackled.

Ryan wiggled the skull's beribboned headdress. "She's all decked out for the holiday."

"Jingle bells, jingle bells," his brother sang.

"Why do you have a dressed-up horse's skull in your truck?" She glanced around. "Thank God this is an adults-only event."

The Main Street decorating crew had returned and surrounded the Smoking Bishop urn. While they imbibed, Ryan sweet-talked Mallory. "Grandma visited the Olde Country last Christmas and came home full of Welsh traditions." He tickled the skull under its chin. "You know how American carolers go from house to house singing and people give them cookies and cocoa? My ancestors were hard core. The Mari Lwyd and her companions come to your house and sing a verse of a song. You have to sing the next verse, and so on. If you forget, she bites you or steals food. If you reach the end, she comes in and you celebrate together."

"More or less," his brother said.

Ryan finished with, "We're going to take her to all the good townsfolk here in the square and make them sing or pay the penalty."

Mallory wrested her gaze from the bedecked skull. "What's the penalty?"

The brothers grinned. "We demand a kiss from the pretty girls."

"Sexual harassment, guys."

"All in good fun, you corporate drone." Both brothers batted their eyes at her.

Mallory crossed her arms. "Drop the other shoe."

Ryan put on his most charming smile. "We designed her with you in mind."

"Oh, hell, no."

The brothers cozied up to her. "You could nip the sheriff's fat ass for giving you that speeding ticket," Ryan said.

"It's a dead horse's skull, you numbskulls." As she said it, the thought of disappearing into something both terrifying and gaudy tempted her.

"You could give the paper factory mogul a concussion," his brother said.

Ryan winked. "As a stand-in for all CEOs everywhere."

Mallory wanted to terrify someone. To know their guts were twisting in fear the way hers did when everything was stolen from her. To pay them all back for years of "Porky piggy Mallory can't see her own feet" and hundreds of nights sobbing herself to sleep while other girls were necking at the drive-in.

"It'd only be for an hour or so?"

"Max."

She held out her hands. "Gimme."

"Yes." They high-fived each other and her.

She crouched so they could fit the skull over her head. "How big was this horse?"

"We hollowed it out some," Ryan said. "It's supposed to be on a pole, but we knew you'd get into the holiday spirit. Fit your lower jaw into the hinge we added."

Mallory wriggled her face into the thankfully clean bone and clacked the jaws together. "Let me practice on you two." Her voice sounded as hollow as the skull.

They stepped back. "Save it for your neighbors." They covered her with the attached sheet and draped the ribbons and bells to their full effect.

"Ready?" Ryan said. "We'll do all the talking. You're the silent threat."

The horse's teeth partly obstructed her vision, but she could see bits of people and colored lights with her peripheral vision. Her guides led her to the tree and shouted.

"Listen up!"

Screams and laughter answered them.

"Meet the Mari Lwyd, the hard-core Christmas caroler from Wales here to sing with you! We'll only give you the verses once, so pay attention! Miss a verse and pay the price!"

They shouted the first verse and the essential lines to "Green Grow the Rushes, O."

Four people pulled out their phones. The brothers pounced. "Any cell phone cheaters automatically lose."

They stopped in front of the Bar and Grille owner and the brothers sang the first verse, ending with a gesture to him to continue.

He sang, "I'll sing you two, O!"

They sang, "Green grow the rushes, O! What is your two, O?"

A pause. "Two, the, uh, boy-oy-oys clothed in green, O?"

Ryan laughed. "Close enough."

All three men sang, "One is one and all alone, and evermore shall be it so!"

"Come join the Mari Lywd on her rounds," Ryan said.

They circled the Christmas displays, gathering townspeople in their wake. The sheriff forgot verse three and Mallory nipped the back of his neck. He cursed and slapped his meaty hand over the spot.

The brothers said, "The Mari Lwyd takes no prisoners, people! Better practice those verses." Mallory clacked the bloodied jaws in emphasis.

The head of the school board shone a flashlight on the sheriff's neck. "He's really bleeding. What kind of game is this?"

A bandage appeared in Ryan's hand. "All in good fun! We promise the Mari Lwyd is sparkling clean and sanitized." He covered the wound. "Smoking Bishop cures all ills. Am I right, Bob Cratchit?"

"God bless us, everyone." A full cup appeared in Cratchit's hand. "Drink up, Sheriff."

The sheriff's blood dribbled onto Mallory's lips. She tried to spit it out, but her jaws were trapped in the skull. She reached for Ryan to ask for a napkin, but the high school music teacher was arguing drunkenly with him about the correct verses to the song. Mallory's gag reflex deserted her and the blood slid down her throat.

The tang of copper filled her mouth while someone on the outside of the skull mangled verse three. Ryan pushed her against the mangler's neck and she bit.

"Hey!" A fist connected with the skull.

Ryan's brother pulled a bandage out of his back pocket. "No biggie, it's just a scratch. I'll cover it up."

The voice was as hard as the punch. "If this gets infected, I'll sue your farm out from under you."

The brothers' reassurances were insects buzzing in Mallory's ears. She felt the skull for cracks, caressing the silky bone. The aroma of fresh blood caressed her nose. She tried to induce a sneeze as the thick liquid coated her teeth. The bone was smooth and warm under her chilled hands. Her fingers tingled with its heat. The blood sparkled on her tongue.

The grade school principal palmed her phone as they approached and nailed verse four. Ryan's brother wanted to date her so he pretended not to see. She demanded a kiss from him in tribute.

The next verse was sung correctly but the prize was spoiled by the four-person Chamber of Commerce's attempt to halt the fun.

"It's dangerous."

"Did you get a permit?"

"It's unsanitary."

"Did a veterinarian check the skull?"

Their coup failed thanks to the crowd's state of happy inebriation from Smoking Bishop. The procession called out the name of their next target and left the town officials to fuss to each other.

"I'll sing you six, O!"

"Green grow the rushes, O! What is your six, O?"

"Six for the six proud walkers."

This correct soccer mom also demanded a kiss.

Mallory almost nipped her anyway. A fading voice in her head scolded her. A louder voice quoted an obscure piece of history about drinking from the skulls of conquered enemies. She fluttered the bells and ribbons. Ryan kissed the side of the skull. "You're doing great."

She snapped the teeth at him but came away empty. She wanted rich, fragrant blood. The blood of her lifelong enemies. The bells jingled in her ears, urging her on.

Red Grow the Rushes, O!

After failure at verses seven and eight from two men too smashed to react when the skull exacted its payment, the Mari Lwyd's conga line reached halfway around the massive Christmas tree.

"I'll sing you nine, O!"

"Green grow the rushes, O! What is your nine, O?"

"Nine for the nine bright shiners."

Ten and eleven also gave the correct responses. Mallory fumed. Her throat screamed for blood. Her head throbbed with need.

The Mari Lwyd's followers surrounded the gym teacher for the final verse. He looked at the ground. At last he mumbled, "I'll sing you twelve."

Several voices corrected him: "I'll sing you twelve, O! Green grow the rushes, O!"

Ryan sang, "What is your twelve, O?"

Another silence. "I don't know."

Crows of triumph. A ragged chorus assailed him.

"Twelve for the twelve Apostles,

Eleven for the eleven who went to heaven,

Ten for the ten commandments,

Nine for the nine bright shiners,

Eight for the April Rainers,

Seven for the seven stars in the sky,

Six for the six proud walkers,

Five for the symbols at your door,

Four for the Gospel makers,

Three, three, the rivals,

Alice Loweecey

Two, two, the lily-white boys,
Clothed all in green, O,
One is one and all alone," a deep collective breath, "And evermore shall be… it… so!"

Many hands pushed the Mari Lwyd into the gym teacher. She opened her strong, hungry jaws. He threw up his arm to block her. Her sharp teeth ripped through his fleece jacket and fed.

The Christmas revelers laughed at his curses. They clapped the brothers on their backs. "Great work. Last one to the punch is a Scrooge!"

Ryan and his brother led Mallory back to their pickup.

"Dude," Ryan's brother said, "you were right. Shooting that vindictive old mare and selling her meat was the only good we ever got out of her."

"Don't forget boiling her skull for the Mari Lwyd. We should make this our new Christmas tradition. Right, Mallory?"

Silence.

"Mallory? You okay? Let me give you a hand." Ryan grasped the sides of the skull. He jerked back from its reeking breath.

A voice like and unlike Mallory's said, "You took everything from me. You ignored my terror." Another charnel exhalation. "You profited from my pain."

The ornaments popped out of the skull's eye sockets and shattered on the asphalt with a musical tinkle. Mallory's green eyes appeared in their place. The jaws opened.

Ryan's brother won his fight with the tailgate. "Costume off yet?"

A headless body in a plaid flannel jacket fell at his feet.

A skull crowned with ribbons writhing like Medusa's snakes filled his vision. Its three-inch teeth ripped out his throat and he collapsed on top of his brother in a geyser of blood.

The Mari Lywd closed the final thread of its cocoon around Mallory's brain, uniting their hate and hunger. It turned toward the humans drinking hot liquid. They laughed and sang, smiles on their faces and joy in their hearts.

It took the fat one with a gold badge on his lapel first. His blood raged through its new body. The songs and laughter became screams. Some ran. Some fainted. It caught them all, stuffing its muzzle in hot, slippery guts, snapping bones to suck the marrow, savoring the delicate whorls of brains. It howled in joy at last, at last.

A word reached it from their assimilated brain: Decorations.

The moon rose on a new Christmas display. Skins draped over the Nativity figures changed their yellow glare to a rosy glow. Loops of intestinal garland circled the branches from the trunk to the tip, gleaming in the colorful lights. Dripping blood sizzled as it hit their glass surfaces. Hands sprouted from the sturdiest branches, fingers clutching heads by the hair. Dozens of stiff needles pierced eyes and tongues. A skirt of shattered glass baubles circled the base.

The Mari Lwyd crowned the tree. Its new arms and legs wrapped around the tallest branch. The star twinkled against its chest. Its green eyes shone in the wide white sockets. From its open mouth came Christmas carols. The heads joined in the choruses.

Satan's Whispers
Stephen Howard

Satan hovered above the schoolyard as the children fled their parents' sides. His form was that of a large muscular man, naked, his skin a scorched red, eyes glittering red like rubies, jet black wings bursting from his back. Curved horns protruded from the side of his otherwise bald head.

Christmas lights decorated the school building, holly wreaths hung on the various entrances. Most of the local children attended St Jude's, a mid-sized primary school in a town outside Manchester, built from red brick. Crucifixes adorned the hallways, but Satan could do his work here in the grounds, beyond the glare of Christ. Drifting among the children unseen, he pressed his mouth to their ears and, one by one, whispered his demands.

It was a grey, dry morning. Clare Sanderson, ever the doting mother, kissed her son, Michael, and daughter, Melissa, goodbye and watched her two cherubic babies run off towards their friends. A gust of cold wind whipped the hood of her parka coat, and Clare shivered. The invisible hand of Satan caressed her hair as he passed, pursuing her two children. First, he whispered into Melissa's ear. Second, into Michael's. Michael stumbled and fell to the ground, grazing his hands as he tried to catch himself.

As Clare rushed to her son's side, Satan grinned. "A particularly susceptible boy, a promising omen."

Children flooded into the safety of the building, to be greeted by Santa and his elves, but not before Satan had spoken to each of them, planting his devilish demands into their young minds.

71

•

Clare, coat pulled around her slim frame, straight dark hair plastered across her face, walked into a headwind as she passed the church adjoining the school. It stood out as a modern design. With a slanted pale green roof, glass façade, and yellowish brickwork, it was significantly newer than the school buildings. Spots of rain fell as she turned the street corner. Trees flanked the road, erupting from the pavement with belligerence. A car horn beeped and Clare's friend, Sally, pulled over in her Range Rover. Dyed blonde hair, perfectly manicured nails, immaculate make-up, Sally often gave Clare a lift home.

"Get in you poor thing," Sally shouted.

Clambering in and passing through the veil of heat, Clare muttered a thank you and did up her seatbelt.

"It's truly Christmas in Manchester when it gets this cold and grim," Sally said cheerfully.

"It's hotter than the sun in here, Sal," Clare replied, unzipping her coat awkwardly under her seatbelt. "Are you off somewhere? You look ready for a night out," Clare asked.

"I run hot, you know that. And nowhere in particular. I've got a personal training session in an hour, so I'll be heading to the gym," Sally replied, her eyes fixed on the road as she came up to the mini-roundabout, just before the motorway bridge.

Clare nodded in response but stayed quiet.

It was a short drive, but a torrid walk in the cold and the rain. They pulled up outside Clare's home. Sally turned to her friend, a serious expression on her face.

"How are you doing, Clare? Have you and Tom… you know, are you spending time together?" she said, her countenance that of one attending a funeral.

Clare blushed. "He leaves for work early and gets home late. You know how it is, you've said the same about Dan. It's just one of those things. Two kids, bills to pay, all of that."

"But you can't just do the housework then sit at home alone every day waiting for Tom to remember you're there, honey," Sally said, her hand reaching over and patting Clare's. "You have to talk to him. Men are like that. They don't notice something's wrong unless you slap them in the face with the problem," she added with a laugh.

Clare offered a weak smile in response.

"It's just hard. I mean, look at us. You look a million dollars and here I am, tired, pale, grey hairs coming through at the roots, there'll be more grey than brown before you know it. Tom barely looks at me anymore."

"Honey, look, let's go out on Christmas Eve. We'll get dolled up, have a few glasses of wine, and let our hair down. I think you need it. Tom can look after the kids for a change. If he says no, you send him my way, got it?" Sally said, flashing perfect white teeth.

"Okay, I'll run it past him. Thanks, Sal," Clare said, squeezing Sally's hand before opening the car door.

Watching the Range Rover pull away, Clare felt tears readying to fall. Pausing in front of the holly wreath attached to the door—the whole family had made it together two Christmases ago—she entered the empty house.

•

Tom, slender, pale, unshaven, was sat at the end of the bar in O'Shea's with a pint of Guinness when Andre joined him, ordering a pint of Harp as he pulled up a stool. Andre, tall and burly with tidily cropped hair, glanced around at the feeble decorations. Tinsel girded the counter, but dismembered shreds littered the floor, giving it the appearance of a shimmering lake. The two men wore suits, though Andre's was noticeably neater and better fitting. It was Wednesday lunchtime, their regular catch-up day.

"You look exhausted, mate," Andre said, patting Tom on the back.

"I've been finishing late all week and probably will tonight and tomorrow too. Feel like I'm spending my life on commuter trains with strangers," Tom replied, not even looking up.

The usual Irish folk bands were playing through the speakers above the bar, performing covers of Christmas hits rather than the usual favourites like *Country Roads* and *Sweet Home Alabama*—a gruesome cover of *Last Christmas* was on. A few older men were sat alone at tables reading newspapers, the other patrons were office workers and businessmen enjoying a lazy midweek Christmas pint.

"The kids finished school yet?" Andre asked, sipping his drink.

"Next Tuesday. Couple of pointless days, if you ask me, stuck in school until damn near Christmas Eve," Tom grumbled. Downing the remainder of his Guinness, he ordered a second.

They both let their eyes wander to the television screen on

the adjacent wall showing a horse racing meet, though neither had any stake in it.

"How's the husband?" Tom asked, trying to break himself from the stupor into which he'd fallen.

"Call him Devon, will you?" Andre said, chuckling. "He's good. Actually, we got some good news. The adoption has been approved. We're having a baby!"

"Congratulations mate, I'm really happy for you," Tom said, shaking Andre's hand with vigour. "Make sure you enjoy it, they grow up fast." Shoulders slumped, Tom took a drink of his fresh pint before exhaling deeply and smiling again. "You're going to be great parents. Anyway, when they're older, stick them in front of the telly or the computer and you'll be okay."

The saloon-style doors opened, and a crisp breeze snaked through the bar.

"Thanks mate. Hallelujah, this black gay's getting a baby!" he cried jubilantly.

As Andre celebrated and Tom slapped him on the back, an invisible force glided indoors with the wind. Unseen by human eyes, the tall, powerful figure of Satan hovered above the two friends. He leant forwards, his lips near caressing Andre's ear, and whispered. Christmas was a time of year in which isolation and loneliness created vulnerability, vulnerability which Satan could exploit for his own fiendish purposes. It existed even in those who were outwardly fine.

"You know, you shouldn't do that, by the way," Andre said, the joy of his tone evaporating. "Stick them in front of a screen. It's bad parenting."

"What? It's not all the time, just gives us a break, you know? Not that Clare and I even speak that much these days, we're both so tired…" Tom began, but Andre interrupted.

"I know for sure that when Devon and I get our baby, we're going to be a happy family, that's all," Andre said, rolling his eyes.

Tom stood up and grabbed his jacket from the coat stand. "We're doing just fine, thanks," he said, and marched out of the bar, shoving through the saloon doors.

Hovering above the street corner, Satan watched as Tom pulled his coat up around his chin and strode off up the street.

•

It was approaching 8pm that night when Tom cut through the park by the side of their house and finally walked up the garden path. The lone holly wreath on the door appeared feeble in the dark. Tom heard shouting from inside. Rushing to get his key out, he unlocked the door and burst in. Stumbling into the lounge, he surveyed the peculiar scene before him. The Christmas tree lay on the floor, fir spindles and glitzy baubles of red, purple, and gold littered the carpet. Beside it stood Michael, his ten-year-old son. Except he was almost unrecognisable, his face red and contorted and ready to burst. Clare stood by the mantelpiece in front of a seething gas fire, crying.

"What the hell is going on?" said Tom, forcing his voice down a notch, "we've got bloody neighbours, you know?"

Melissa was a year younger than Michael. She'd been sat on the sofa, but stood up to address her father, her head tilted like a china doll. "Mummy won't let Michael have a new PlayStation," she said in a firm voice, "and I want a new phone because mine isn't new anymore." Melissa folded her arms and stared at her father with the intensity of an anaconda locking sights on its prey.

Clare stifled a cry and cleared her throat. "I tried to point out to both Michael and Melissa… that they both have perfectly good examples of those things already. Michael only got his games console last year and Melissa too. They don't need new ones. But Michael… Michael pulled the tree down and, something, oh god…" Clare quieted to a whisper, her face in her hands.

"Go to your bedrooms, please kids. Both of you," Tom said, stepping towards Clare. He placed a hand on her shoulder, but she winced at the touch.

"I don't want to go to my room. I want to know if I'm getting what I want! Why can't we afford nice things?" Michael said stubbornly from the door. Tom glared at him and shot a further glance at Melissa.

"I said go to your room now," Tom repeated. Relenting, Michael turned and stormed up the stairs. Melissa followed.

Tom hesitated, then placed his arms around Clare. Raising her head from Tom's chest, Clare spoke.

"Something is wrong. Ever since I picked them up from school, they've been different. Especially Michael. He kept talking about being poor. Having nice things. I don't even know what brought that on. But when I said he didn't need a new PlayStation, and the same to Melly… I've just never seen such anger in a child. Not our little angels."

"I'm sorry, Clare. I wish I'd been here to help. They've had a stern word now, hopefully that'll be the end of it. I'll talk to

Michael," Tom said, rubbing Clare's back. But then she stepped away from him and looked into his eyes.

"I'm serious, Tom, this was weird. I was scared of him. Our poor boy's face was… God, I don't know what was wrong with it, but it was *wrong*."

"I know it can be horrible when you argue with your kids, but ours are just getting to that age. They'll be teenagers before you know it. That's when it'll get really tough," Tom added, squeezing Clare's shoulder in reassurance.

Clare shrugged it off, walked over to the Christmas tree. "You aren't listening to me, Tom. You never do anymore."

"Now that's not fair, Clare," Tom began, before something flashed past the window. Then came an ugly crashing sound. The outdoor light turned on to illuminate the garden. Tom and Clare swapped a fearful glance and rushed to the back window. On the garden patio were the mangled remains of a PlayStation.

•

The following morning, Sally joined Clare in the school playground. The two of them huddled by the black railings around the edge. Sally's blonde hair was unusually unkempt and her face almost clear of make-up. She wore a big duffel coat and had her hands stuffed in the pockets. Clare was confused. Sally was *always* immaculately presented.

"Are you okay?" Clare said, her eyes still following her two children as they crossed the playground. Scanning the area, all the children seemed to be moving in slow motion. Parents were rushing off with the haste of a school of tuna sensing an approaching shark. Usually, most stayed to watch their kids enter the building, as Clare and Sally were, but today they couldn't get away soon enough.

"Not really," Sally said. "You look like death too. What's up?"

"Yesterday, the kids were acting… strange. Ever since I picked them up. Michael talking about being poor, as if we were on the breadline, you know? We had a horrible argument. Tom walked in and broke it up. But I'd told Michael he couldn't have a new PlayStation because he already had one. So Michael went up to his room and threw his old one out of the window. I felt sick. Tom went up and yelled at him, but Michael just yelled back. And then Melissa came downstairs, as if nothing were happening, and asked me if she could please, please, please have a new phone. They've never been like this before," Clare finished, staring at the concrete beneath her feet.

Beside her, Sally laughed. It was a sad laugh.

"I guess we've both had a night of it."

"What happened?"

"Charlie was acting strangely too. He kept talking about how he's always loved dogs. Now this kid has never expressed an interest in dogs in his life. Of course, we've got the rabbits."

"Jerry and Bumper," Clare said, nodding.

"Exactly," Sally said. "And Charlie loved those rabbits. Well, I said to him we can't get a dog at the moment because they need too much looking after. I told him we've got the rabbits and they take up quite a bit of our time. Anyway, there was some talking back, but Dan put Charlie in his place and that seemed to be the end of it."

She stopped and took a deep breath. Cars passed behind them in the street. Gulls chirped as they congregated in a corner of the playground.

"We got up this morning as normal. I went outside to check the rabbits' water and, oh my god, they were both dead," Sally gasped, tears in her eyes.

"Oh gosh, Sal, I'm so sorry. What was it, foxes?" Clare said, slipping her arm through Sally's.

"I don't think so."

They stood in silence as the children filed into the school. To their left, the empty church loomed. The last child to enter the school was a blonde-haired young boy. As he grabbed the door handle, he turned, and stared across the schoolyard at the two mothers. Charlie, Sally's son, gently pulled the door shut, and disappeared from view.

•

Clare and Tom lay asleep in bed on Saturday morning, desperate for some rest. Friday morning, the children had pestered them about Christmas presents. On the journey home from school, despite it starting to snow and a Christmassy glaze falling upon the town, Clare had been inundated with complaints. Michael fixated on their poorness, Melissa on the need to have what her friends had. By the evening, Michael was angry. Tom had to send him to bed early.

It was around 10am and Clare finally stirred, slowly opening her eyes, massaging them awake. Her vision focused.

Michael stood at the end of the bed, staring at her.

Gasping, she automatically grabbed Tom's arm.

"Hey, what's up?" Tom asked. He turned over and winced upon seeing his son. Michael looked pale, dark circles beneath his eyes, as if he hadn't slept at all. "Michael, son, are you okay?" Tom asked, sitting upright, glancing at Clare.

"I just wanted to know what I'm getting for Christmas. Obviously, I need a new PlayStation after my last one broke. So I guess that's what I should get," he said, his voice low, barely a mutter.

Clare's grip on Tom's forearm tightened. Her eyes remained on her son.

"Son, you broke your PlayStation deliberately. That's not the way we get new things. I think you know that, right?" said Tom.

Michael glared at his parents and his little fists bunched. With his chest heaving, he turned in silence and walked out of the room.

"What is happening to him?" Clare said, before burying her head in Tom's chest.

Wrapping his arm around his wife, Tom replied: "kids and their toys, Clare. This generation are spoiled. We've got to stand firm with him, that's all."

Clare unwound from Tom's embrace, pulled herself upright to sit on the edge of the bed, and placed her head in her hands.

•

Tom collapsed onto the sofa and stared at the Christmas tree. It was on the floor, baubles scattered about once more. Shreds of tinsel were lay beside fir tree spindles, resembling fallen soldiers lined up along a street. Michael had kicked and screamed, Melissa had kicked and screamed. They'd put the children to bed two hours ago, but he only now felt like he'd recovered. He didn't know where his wife had gone.

"Just a phase," Tom muttered, closing his eyes.

Outside, pure white snow fell.

Upstairs, Clare inched open the door to Michael's bedroom. The curtains were open, and moonlight offered the blue wallpaper an oceanic glow. It also offered her enough light to see Michael asleep in his bed. Eyes closed, breathing steady, there was a pale glow bouncing off the right side of his face. He looked angelic.

Shaking her head, Clare shut the door behind her and leant against it. She closed her eyes.

•

All I Want for Christmas Is You played on the car radio as Tom drove the family home from the last Sunday Service before Christmas. They had worn their Sunday best, smiled hard, and sang hymns with fervour. It had been cold in the church. Clare, her brown hair pinned back, stared absently out of the window. The weather had thoroughly turned over the past two days. A thick layer of snow adorned the ground.

"I can't wait to play my new PlayStation," said Michael, beginning to kick the back of his mother's seat. He nudged Melissa, who giggled.

"I'm going to get new games on my new phone," she said, and they both laughed.

"You aren't having those things for Christmas. You're lucky

you're still getting a Christmas after the last few days," said Tom, indicating and then turning left.

Melissa screamed. A prolonged, piercing noise. And Michael yelled as loudly as he could. But not words, just a seemingly endless noise, like a dark tunnel with no light at the end.

Clare cried silently.

"Enough!" Tom yelled. He slammed the brakes on, and the car screeched to a halt. Clare gasped, but continued to cry. The children, however, stopped.

"Fine. Are those things so important? Fine. Get out. Clare, please walk the children the rest of the way home. I'm going to the shops. Please, get out, now," Tom said, not looking at anyone, his eyes set upon the road before him.

Without a word of protest, Clare and the two children got out of the car. Skidding on the snow slightly, the car sped off, leaving the mother and her two children stood on the pavement. Exhaust fumes remained on the air. As if snapping out of a stupor, Clare took both children by the hand and pulled them across the road.

•

Tom stomped into the 24-hour Tesco and made his way towards the electronics section. As he turned down one aisle, he stopped abruptly. There was a dedicated counter for these items set up, and there was a hefty queue. A long stream of people ran back down the seasonal aisle, flanked by gift items, decorations, chocolates, Christmas themed lamps, and so forth. Sidling up to the end of the line, Tom stood and waited.

Christmas songs played through the speaker system. One of the Band Aid singles was on. But it made little sense because a brass band were playing in the foyer and could be heard clearly around the store. Hymns clashed violently with pop music.

The queue didn't seem to be moving and voices were already grumbling. People had joined the queue behind Tom, too.

"Well fuck you," shouted one voice.

"Fuck off," yelled another. Halfway along the queue, two men had hold of each other by the scruffs of their necks. One was sturdy and tall, the other slender, wearing glasses and a Christmas jumper. Grappling, they crashed into a wall of Christmas decorations. Baubles broke from a pack and scattered along the ground. As the two men struggled, they flew into others stood in the queue. Some people backed away, but others shoved back. And then the first punch was thrown.

Tom ran forward to break up the fight. But he was blind-sided by two women, one red-haired and the other brunette, grabbing at each other, and they knocked him into the display of Christmas lamps. Glass shards burst everywhere when the lamps hit the ground.

"That's my wife," a voice cried. A balding man with neck tattoos lunged at Tom, tackling him to the floor.

A flustered voice cried out over the store speaker system for security to head for the electronics desk. But it was already too late. A brawl had broken out. A mass of ordinary people were committing strange festive violence upon each other. Tom lay on his back, holding the man attacking him off, one hand on his throat, the other on his arm. Out of the corner of his eye, he saw the two men who had started the fighting. The man in glasses and a Christmas jumper lay on his back, similar to Tom, but his head was bleeding badly. The sturdier man held fistfuls of hair and was repeatedly bashing the skull against the floor. Tom saw fingers twitching.

And the man attacking Tom was yelling again, swearing. Tom couldn't shake him off, and then his arm was loose, and the man was punching Tom in the face. Without knowing what to do, he grabbed something nearby and swung his arm at his assailant. Tom felt something warm drip down onto his face, and a weight fell away.

Tom sat up and looked at his attacker. A large shard of glass jutted out of his tattooed neck. The artery may have been severed because blood was spurting out of the wound with the joyous glory of a baroque fountain. *O Come All Ye Faithful* blared out from the direction of the foyer. Screams danced about on the air. Tom remained sat on the floor. He watched a security guard run into the melee and, as if being identified as an enemy, was set upon by three men and two women. Seconds later the guard was prostrate on the floor. A kitchen knife was drawn, retrieved from a desolate basket, and the red-haired woman stabbed the guard with a violence borne of Satanic fury. As if struck by an ecstatic calling, the woman then stood and plunged the knife into the chest of the nearest man.

Tom again turned his attention to the two men who had started the fighting. Still clinging onto his opponent's hair, still hitting the head against the floor, the victor splashed blood and pulpy red mush about with every tired smash of the ruined head.

Tom picked himself up but slipped in blood, his legs struggling to carry him away. The aisle was no more. In its place a blood river flowed. Dragging himself away, Tom ran. Straight out of the store, straight past the brass band, still playing bravely. He jumped into his car and drove home.

•

Tom's face was spattered with blood. It shimmered under the moonlight as he stood outside of their house, their home, their family home. A thin film of snow covered the park. An inescapable taste of iron was making Tom nauseous. The chain links of the swing sets rattled as a cold wind blew.

Unbeknownst to Tom, a muscular humanoid figure hovered above the park. Giant black wings flapping, Satan's red eyes gazed through Tom and into the house. Satisfied this house had succumbed to evil, he smiled and flew away.

Tom stared at the lonely wreath on the front door, the one they'd made as a family just two Christmases past. The house was silent, a far cry from the tumult he had walked in on just two nights prior.

He pushed open the door.

Lay at the bottom of the stairs, head snapped back, open eyes facing the doorway, was Clare. Slowly, Tom walked over to her. Clare resembled Christ on the cross or an angel atop a Christmas tree, her arms spread to the sides, feet and knees together. Tom knelt down and whispered a prayer. He didn't want to look up because he knew what he would see. Finally, he conceded, and faced what he knew he must.

At the top of the stairs stood Michael and Melissa, their cherubic faces gazing down at their parents. Michael took one step forward, then spoke.

"Did you get our presents, daddy?"

A Study in Red and White

David Tallerman

Poised on snow-slicked roof tiles, the Santa Thing scents the wind.

The air reeks of snow. It licks across raw, red muscle and sinew, testing cavities and meaty crevices. The cold reminds the Santa Thing of home—and for a moment, it recalls older winters, deeper frosts, the uncluttered, frozen eons before shape and form and roiling, sickly life. An age when it seemed nothing would ever claw its way from the utter chill to crawl and mewl. An age when there was no need for subterfuge.

No time, no time for memory. Not tonight, most special and rich.

Here there's a simple way down—a jut of hollow masonry beckoning. Once, they burned fires in those depths. That recollection brings no comfort. But this is a different age and the blackness welcomes. Too narrow, though, for this current shape. No space for the Santa Thing's ebon hooves, no room for the curlicues of bone that splinter its face and cluster round its head. Change is needed, as it has changed so many times before.

It's a matter of a thought—for the Santa Thing is thought as much as matter, idea more than either. Flesh softens to jelly, to dripping wax. Muscle expands, contracts. A hundred bones click free. As they relocate, their note is faintly like the ring of bells.

A Study in Red and White

Quick as light, quick as sorrow, the Santa Thing spills into darkness. It flows through gloom, where ancient ash still clings—slops into multicoloured light. A tree, strung and adorned. One of their Signs. Once the decorations were mistletoe sprigs, once the lights were candles and a ward. But humans don't remember as the Santa Thing remembers. Now those flames are pretty and pointless. Though they sting the running jelly of its eyes, they can't keep the Santa Thing from entering.

Shuddering like an oil-slicked bird, the Santa Thing takes back its form. Already its helpers chitter from the shadows at its presence. Their half-life goes hard on them. They exist only for this moment. Now that it's come once more, they scud and shudder round the walls—flicker across cheap furniture, hung stockings, clumsily wrapped parcels.

The Santa Thing lets the moment drag, lets them drive themselves to the brink of frenzy with anticipation. Only when they seem about to tear themselves apart does it speak, its voice rich and foul with the pressure of ages.

"Gud ur Bad?" asks the Santa Thing. "Gud ur Bad?"

In unison, they shriek their answer.

The Santa Thing shakes its flayed head in mock censure. How they struggle, these humans—these bags of unshifting meat and forgetting. How they neglect the old rules, the forms laid down millennia before they skulked into the world.

Bad? Bad it is.

Its helpers quieten now, stilled by awe and all they understand of fear. So much waiting, just for this moment. Their dust-mote eyes stare from every patch and stripe of murk. The

Santa Thing gathers itself, reaches deep into the roiling galaxies within its form. Time stands on edge. Bladders swell, organs secrete, and arteries aslant from space drip piceous fluids.

Upon the brink of two realities, the Santa Thing releases.

To its own eyes, impulse and sensation spew and spray across the walls: A word of anger here, a casual blow there, an urge to hate drying in a filthy birthmark. To its eyes, a map in space and time charts pain across the patterned wallpaper. The colours are rich, delightful. Yet, for those who'll live out this portrait, nothing they'll ever see. If only they could register its beauty, perhaps they could resist its lure.

A sound. A stutter of shock. The Santa Thing has let itself be distracted. Something has sneaked up, noiseless until the very last moment. Even as it spins, the Santa Thing twists, reforms, tries to become what they have made of it.

Still, the small creature framed in the empty doorway looks afraid. It shouldn't be here, it knows. Fear strikes it dumb. Its lips tremble... a name hangs there. Not the Santa Thing's, but familiar. The name is a prayer. The prayer remains unspoken.

The Santa Thing hears nonetheless.

Forgive me, Father Christmas.

But the Santa Thing is father to nothing. Knowing what awaits this small creature, knowing what the new year will bring, it smiles its mouth round moist, shivering words.

"HaPee KrisMus. HaPree KrisMus, Litul One."

The Santa Thing doesn't wait for a response. Even for a being that lives between the cracks of time, there's much to be done this sacred night. It melts instead back into the darkness, a memory already fading and mixing with illusion in an infant mind that will never be quite sane again. Embracing the chill night wind, the Santa Thing flees for a star-slick sky, smears its long silhouette across a bulbous moon.

And in its wake, fluid with echo, trails a sound that might be laughter.

(Everybody's Waitin' For) The Man With The Bag
Jude Reid

"Just once, I wanted it to be perfect."

Marcie looked down at the tiny jewellery box in her hands, the ugly antique earrings with their blood-red garnets. "One perfect Christmas. Sitting by the fire, engaged to the man of my dreams with gifts under the tree. I don't get why that's too much to ask." Tears of self-pity prickled behind her eyes. "He said this year he'd come to Rusty Hollow for Christmas and meet my family."

"And?" Naomi, her roommate, was already pouring the wine.

"Work came up. Some big client died, so Nicholas needs to be in town to sort out the will and oversee the estate sale. But he made this big deal about my Christmas gift, said it'd be waiting for me when I got home, that it was something really special." She snapped the little box shut. "And I thought — I really thought this time it would be an engagement ring —" The last word came out as a sob.

"And what about his divorce?"

"Still not the right time. He'll make it up to me, he said. We'll go skiing in February, somewhere in Europe. Except before then I have to explain to my entire family that no, my boyfriend who everyone's so desperate to meet won't be coming for Christmas after all, because he hasn't left his wife yet." She wiped her eyes, smudging uneven trails of mascara across her cheeks.

"Face it, Marcie. He's never going to leave her." Naomi took Marcie's glass and refilled it. "Ditch him. Go back home to Rosy Hollow—"

"Rusty Hollow."

"Whatever. Go back and tell them all that you're forty years old, you're single and loving it and if they don't like it they can all fuck themselves a merry little Christmas."

Marcie managed half a laugh. "You don't know what they're like in that town. Ten minutes after I arrive everyone will know I got stood up. I'll never live it down."

"All right, then — here's an idea." Naomi rose to her feet, waving her glass with a raconteur's flair. Marcie suspected that the wine might not be Naomi's first that afternoon. "I've just taken on a new guy at the casting agency. Tall, dark, handsome, queer as Oscar Wilde and hungry for work. He'd be perfect."

"Perfect for what?"

"Perfect to take home for Christmas. I'll pay his fees, and he can guest star as your boyfriend. Everybody wins. My actor gets paid and you get to play at happy families one more time."

"It's a terrible plan."

"Isn't it just?" Naomi waved her wine glass again, slopping its contents onto her white angora sweater. "So what do you say?"

Marcie opened the little jewellery box and rotated one of the earrings idly on its post. A sharp pain shot through her index finger, and she jerked her hand back, a garnet-coloured bead of blood welling underneath her nail.

"Damn it, that's sharp. Stupid piece of junk. I bet he got them from some creepy old estate sale." She sucked the blood away, the salt-copper taste mingling with the tannins of the wine, and felt a rare flash of anger. This was all Nicholas's fault.

"So you'll do it?"

"I'll do it." Marcie raised her glass and touched it lightly to her friend's. The ugly garnet earrings caught a flash of light, almost seeming to glow—not a merry Christmas twinkle, something more like the smoky blaze of a dying fire. "To Hell with Nicholas, my family, and Rusty Hollow. The whole damned lot of them."

•

Snow was falling as the steam train pulled into the station on Christmas Eve, its plume drifting artfully through the freezing air. A string of brightly coloured baubles decorated the platform, tinsel draped around the station's sign in a gaudy halo. A year had passed since Marcie had last visited, but Rusty Hollow looked exactly the same, fossilised in a perpetual state of Christmas.

She checked her phone again. Nicholas's silence came as no surprise, but there was nothing from Naomi's actor either. He'd sent an initial email and had seemed keen enough, but after that had failed to reply to any of her messages. The thought of explaining Nicholas's absence to her family sat like a leaden weight in her stomach.

"Aunt Marcie!"

The shrill little voice cut through the cacophony of the crowd. Marcie stepped onto the platform to see her seven-year-old niece ducking under the barrier and sprinting towards her. She hurtled into Marcie so hard that they stumbled and almost fell.

"I missed you, big girl!" Marcie hugged the little girl to her chest and lifted her up so that the purple snow boots kicked delightedly in the air.

"I missed you too! Did you bring me a present?"

"I did. You can have it when we get to the house." Her niece's shriek of excitement was severed by a harsh-edged bray from the far end of the platform.

"Mind your manners, Olivia Annabelle Jackson! We don't go begging for presents like that."

Marcie's half-sister Jessica—younger, taller, and infinitely blonder—tapped forward on three inch heels, the fur trim of her hood framing her face and her baby blonde curls. Her husband loomed into view at her side, cartoonishly broad in his lumberjack shirt and Denver Beavers baseball cap, their new baby dangling from his chest in a tacticool camo-pattern sling. Jessica air-kissed Marcie's cheeks, wafting through a cloud of expensive perfume and setting lotion. Already her cornflower blue eyes were scanning the station for the long-awaited Nicholas. "How was your trip?"

"Fine. It was fine." Marcie's gut twisted.

"And when do we get to meet the man in your life?" Jessica's lips curved into a triumphant sneer, her eyes glinting like a shark smelling blood.

Time to get it over with. "He couldn't—"

"—find our bag at first." A man's voice came from directly behind her. "Someone must have moved it into first class. Sorry, sweetheart."

Marcie looked up into a pair of warm brown eyes, inches from her own. The stranger they belonged to was tall and dark, with high cheekbones and elegantly sculpted features. He smelled of amber, vanilla, and a light, unfamiliar musk.

"Where are my manners?" The handsome face broke into a smile as the stranger extended a hand to shake. "I'm Nick. And you must all be Marcie's family—Jessica and Mason, isn't it? And this must be Olivia. It's wonderful to finally meet you all."

Jessica's mouth flapped open like a landed fish, then shut with an audible pop. Mason tried to cover her embarrassment, and only partially succeeded. "We were starting to think you didn't exist at all."

Nick—or whatever his name really was—draped his arm around Marcie's shoulders and squeezed her gently. "Live and in the flesh," he said. "Aren't I, Marcie?"

Blood rushed to her face, her pulse pounding in her ears. It would only take a few words to pass the whole thing off as a joke, to confess the ruse to her family and move on, but the admiration in Olivia's eyes and the downright astonishment in Jessica's was too sweet to give up just yet.

"Absolutely," Marcie said, and kissed the stranger on the cheek to prove the point.

•

Naomi had been right—the actor was excellent. Squeezed in the back of Mason's station wagon with Olivia on her lap and the baby seat wedged between them, he managed Jessica's probing questions and Olivia's chatter with equal ease.

"We've been hearing about you for years," Jessica was saying. "So when are you going to make an honest woman out of our Marcie, Nick?"

Marcie felt her cheeks flush, but Nick seemed unconcerned. "I guess we'll know when the time's right." He leaned across the two children, and took Marcie's hand in his.

"Because Marcie isn't getting any younger, that's all I'm saying. Tick-tock, tick-tock."

"I've known plenty of folks get married young and regret it later." Nick's expression stayed guileless, his tone light. "How old were *you* two when you got hitched?"

Marcie couldn't see her sister's face, but she could imagine the scowl spreading across it. "You were eighteen, weren't you, Jess?" Like the real Nicholas, her sister despised the shortened form of her name. "And Mason was... what, twenty five? Twenty six?" He'd been thirty.

There was no answer from the front of the car. Mason tuned the radio to a baseball game. Marcie flashed a grin across the back seat; Nick caught her eye and smiled back.

It looked like Christmas might not be so bad after all.

•

Marcie's father's home was the last on the street at the top of the hill, backing onto open fields. Two miles further on a sign marked the town limit, the population painted on one side and a kitschy "Haste Ye Back" on the other. It wasn't the house she'd called home for the first decade of her life, before her mother's death and Pops's remarriage had changed everything. From time to time Marcie still dreamed of the cramped little row house off Main Street, long since demolished to make way for a development of half-timbered gift-shops.

Two yipping balls of rage slammed into the gate as the

station wagon pulled up, growling and barking in a vigorous—albeit laughable—threat display. Marcie's stepmother Caroline, elegant as always in white from her peroxide hair to the tips of her calf-leather boots, stood in the house's doorway, a holly wreath on the open red door behind her. "Snowy! Frosty! You stop that this minute!" One of the chihuahuas tried to hurl its tiny body over the gate to reach them, while the other one stayed hunched low, growling at some imagined enemy. Caroline grabbed the more active dog by the collar and hoisted it thrashing and wheezing into the air.

Olivia shot her aunt a worried look. Marcie took the tiny, cold hand in hers. "Can you maybe shut them in the house, Caroline?"

"They're usually so friendly!" Caroline lifted the second dog by the scruff. "What's got into you babies?" Both animals were snarling frenziedly, bug-eyes rolling in paroxysms of rage.

"Dogs don't tend to like me." Nick offered Marcie an apologetic smile. "I think it's the way I smell."

"You smell just fine to me."

He laughed, a rich, musical sound that sent a tingle down her spine.

Once the angry chihuahuas were secured in the rear wing of the house, Caroline shepherded the family to the living room, where Marcie's father was already sitting by the fire, face enfolded by his newspaper. Jessica vanished to put the baby down for a nap and to banish Olivia for what she cloyingly referred to as "Mommy's grown-up time", while Mason prodded the fire inexpertly with a wrought-iron poker.

"Now then, who's for sherry?"

(Everybody's Waitin' For) The Man With The Bag

Caroline poured six glasses of the golden liquid, filling the room with its sickly-sweet aroma. Marcie knocked hers back without thinking, and her stepmother refilled it with a knowing smile. "You always did like your drink, Marcie. I suppose it's a city thing for you now, isn't it? Still, you'd better be careful not to pile on too many more pounds. I'm sure Nick here wouldn't like that." She giggled, a silvery, girlish tinkle.

Marcie plastered on a smile and ground her teeth.

Nick gave a soft laugh. "Marcie's perfect. I don't care about her dress size."

"Such a charmer!" Jessica's voice dripped with syrup. "Tell me, how did you two lovebirds meet?"

Panic rose in Marcie's chest, but Nick was already answering with easy conviction. "Four years ago, at the open air ice-rink. There I was, trying to stay on my feet, when this stunning vision in a ski-jacket knocked me head over heels and took my breath away. By the time we stood up again, I was in love."

How could the actor know that? Marcie's astonishment faded as she realised that Naomi must have briefed him in advance. His description was perfect, except it hadn't been this Nick, it had been the real Nicholas who had helped her to her feet and shyly passed her his number. Months later, she found out that his wife and daughter had been in the Ice Palace Cafe at the time, but by then the damage was done.

"Marcie works so hard." Jessica batted her eyelids, her voice so sweet Marcie's teeth hurt. "That newspaper hardly appreciates her at all. I've always said she should be the editor by now, not writing that little opinion column that no one reads."

Jude Reid

Reproachful tutting came from behind her father's newspaper. "Now, Jessica. Marcie's entitled to play at having her little job."

Marcie got to her feet, frustration bubbling under her skin. "You know, I think I might be ready for bed."

"You must be *so* tired after your journey," Caroline said, all mock solicitude. "You can have your old bedroom, of course. And I've made up the second guest-room for Nicholas. I'm sure you young folk get up to all manner of hijinks in the city, but under this roof we keep to God's laws."

"It's none of your business what we get up to in the city." Marcie gulped another glass of sherry, then glanced over at Nick, knowing she'd gone too far. They weren't a real couple. There was no reason they should share a room beyond the fact that her stepmother didn't want them to.

"Don't go to any extra trouble on my account," Nick said. "Marcie and I would prefer to share anyway."

Caroline's smile broadened, bright and brittle as a Christmas bauble. "Well, when you're good and married, you can share a bed. 'Till then, when you're under my roof you'll sleep in separate rooms."

"That's pretty rich coming from a woman who fucked a man while his first wife was on her deathbed," Nick said.

The room fell silent. Nick's beautiful mouth quirked in a smile, his gaze absolutely level. Caroline drew a sharp breath, but her husband placed a hand on hers to forestall any outburst. Both of their faces had gone corpse-grey.

"And before either of these two join in," Nick pointed first at Mason, then Jessica, "*he's* banging his tennis instructor, and *she* pays for anal at the Rusty Hollow truck-stop."

An unexpected bubble of laughter rose in Marcie's throat. Jessica's face had gone scarlet, Mason sputtering in indignation, Caroline glaring at her husband with barely concealed hatred.

"And on that note," Marcie said, rising to her feet with a bright smile, "We're going to bed."

At the top of the stairs, Marcie dissolved into laughter. "You were amazing! Where did all that come from?"

"I did my research. There's no secrets in a town like Rusty Hollow."

"Is it all true? Mason and the tennis instructor? Jessica—the truck stop?" She stopped, the memory of her mother dying more than thirty years ago flashing into her mind. The wasted grey hand on the bedclothes, the face that looked less like Mom and more like a skull every day, but that still lit up in delight when she walked into the room. "Pops and Caroline, too? I guess I should have known."

She looked up and found his soft, dark eyes gazing down at her. The sherry had gone to her head, and the smell of him was intoxicating. On impulse, she kissed his lips. They were soft and almost unnaturally warm, sweet with sherry.

"Naomi said you wouldn't be interested. In girls. In me." Her face burned, her breath coming high and quick.

"Did she?" He was so close she could feel the heat of his skin on hers. "And what do you think, Marcie Halloway?"

"I think we should sleep in the same room," she whispered, and he kissed her again.

•

She woke, still tangled in his arms, moonlight painting his skin the same silver as the faded posters of nineties heartthrobs on her bedroom walls. She reached for her phone to check the time, but her hand encountered only the square electric alarm clock on the bedside table. Ten forty-five.

What had she been thinking? She had slept with a virtual stranger, cheated on Nicholas—though admittedly fidelity was a dubious concept when one partner in the relationship went home to a wife and child after every date—and humiliated her family, but the thrill in the pit of her stomach refused to subside. Nick was intoxicating, tender, passionate, as invested in her pleasure as he was in his own—a far cry from the usual cursory fuck with Nicholas, squeezed into a lunch hour or a few stolen minutes after work.

Everything was confusing. A cool glass of water would help the headache gathering like a storm behind her eyes. It might even help her make sense of what had just happened.

Her parents' bedroom light was still on, the rest of the house lit only by the glow of the Christmas lights, the fridge overflowing with food and drink for the next day. She found a bottle of Florida Orange Juice and swigged it, not bothering with a glass.

"Missing something, Marcia-Anne?"

Marcie jumped, juice spraying down her T-shirt. She turned to see Jessica standing behind her, her features cast in the refrigerator's eerie white glow. A bottle of gin dangled from one hand, a mobile phone from the other.

(Everybody's Waitin' For) The Man With The Bag

The phone's screen lit up as Jessica waggled it from side to side, displaying a photograph of Marcie and Naomi, half covered by the notification bar. "In fact, you've missed—" she gave the screen a theatrical glance, "—six somethings. Missed calls from someone called Nicholas. Which is kind of strange, wouldn't you say, given the dirty things you two have been doing upstairs?" Her slurred voice dripped with venom.

Marcie lunged for the phone, but Jessica jerked it out of reach.

"Your boyfriend's a fake, and you're a liar, Marcie Halloway. A pathetic, lonely liar who couldn't find a real date for Christmas—"

Marcie's fist lashed out. It struck her sister on the perfectly rouged cheek and sent her head slamming into the wall. Jessica slid down to the terracotta floor, the phone slipping from her hand as she stared with glazed astonishment. Marcie snatched up the phone, her knuckles throbbing and her chest swelling with a dark, jubilant satisfaction. That punch had been thirty years coming, and had been worth every minute of the wait.

"Shut your mouth, trucker fucker," she said, and spat in her sister's upturned face.

Outside in the hall, her heart pounded as she scrolled through the missed calls. Jessica had been telling the truth. Six of them, all in the last two hours, all from Nicholas. She listened to the only voicemail, his familiar tones as shocking as a faceful of cold water.

"Marcie—it's Nicholas. I'm sorry. I've been a fool. I've left Elaine, I'm coming to Rusty Hollow and I'm bringing you something better than those hideous old earrings. I don't know what I was thinking—the old lady who owned them last had a bad reputation, we found all kinds of crazy Satanic stuff in her bureau. They're not something I should have given to the woman I love. My train gets in just before eleven thirty." Marcie's mouth dropped open. The grandfather clock read eleven-ten already. "I love you, Marcie, and I want to spend my life with you."

Before the message ended she was at the front door, shoving her feet into her boots and grabbing a coat from the rack. This moment should have been full of joy and triumph—Nicholas, finally coming home with her for Christmas—but with the other Nick sleeping in her bed, his musk still clinging to her skin, everything had become infinitely more complicated. One thing was certain: Nicholas couldn't come to the house, couldn't see who she had brought in his stead. She sprinted for the station, almost dropping her phone as she realised it was vibrating in her hand.

"Nicholas?"

"Hey, Marcie!" Naomi. More than a little merry, judging by the sound of her voice. "How's Rosy Hollow treating you?"

"Rusty Hollow. And it's—complicated." Marcie struggled to catch her breath as she ran. "Nick came with me, he's great but now Nicholas has decided he's coming after all and his train gets in in a couple of minutes—"

"Marcie, wait. I don't understand. Who's with you?"

"Nick—fake Nick, that is. And you were wrong about him being gay, by the way—"

"Marcie!" The edge in Naomi's voice was enough to stop Marcie in her tracks. "Stephen, the actor—he broke his leg last week, skiing with his boyfriend in Vermont. I've only just heard."

"No. That can't be right—he'd been briefed, he knew everything about me and my family."

Snowflakes flurried along Main Street. In the distance, the golden glow of the train's headlamps glinted through the snowy darkness as it made its way towards Rusty Hollow. A chill crept down Marcie's back.

"I swear to God, Marcie—whoever you've brought home with you for Christmas, he's got nothing to do with me."

The train drew closer, smoke pluming from the funnel like the breath of an angry dragon. She could feel its vibrations through the ground underfoot, the clatter of its wheels, the insistent roar of the engine as it turned the last corner to the station at breakneck speed

Laughter drifted up the hill with the scent of mulled cider. The town's lights twinkled like a thousand tiny stars. Someone screamed.

A hundred tons of locomotive hurtled onto the platform, slamming into the buffers with a thunderclap, scattering pedestrians like pigeons. Metal shrieking in agony, the train jack-knifed off the tracks, the last carriage lashing into the air like the tip of a showman's whip. The boiler erupted in an enormous orange fireball that obliterated the train, the platform and everything around it.

"Nicholas!" Marcie screamed, her voice lost in the uproar. The station was ablaze, fire spreading from roof to roof, Christmas lights exploding one after another. Car alarms howled in hellish cacophony. Someone shouted "fire!" and suddenly the hill was alive, residents running, gawping, into the street from every house.

No, that wasn't right.

From every house except one.

At the very top of the hill, Marcie's family home sat in darkness, lit only by the faint glow of the Christmas lights through the broad bay windows.

"Marcie?" Naomi's tinny voice said. Marcie disconnected the call, her breath steaming in the icy air as she tapped Nicholas's name and waited for the phone to ring, nursing the dying hope that he had missed his train or got off a stop early, anything but the awful, inevitable truth.

To her astonishment, the call connected. "Nicholas! Oh, thank God, you're all right!"

"Of course I am." The voice was low and soft, almost a whisper. It took Marcie's mind a second to catch up with her ears.

"Nicholas?"

"Depends which one you mean." Nick—the one in the house, not the one whose body was twisting and blackening in the blazing wreckage below—laughed. "Hurry home, sweetheart. All you want for Christmas is waiting for you right here."

Lights flashed through the air as she climbed to the top of the hill. A tide of shouting bodies were making their way down to the station, some shouting into mobile phones, others carrying buckets of water in a futile attempt to slow the blaze that was consuming Rusty Hollow one chocolate box house at a time.

A growl came from ankle-height as she opened the gate. One of Caroline's chihuahuas glared up at her, its muzzle scarlet, teeth bared in a snarl. It held her gaze as it lowered its miniature jaws to rip another mouthful from the body slumped by the fence.

The other dog, a pair of novelty reindeer antlers hanging from its collar, was gnawing on the corpse's exposed throat with single-minded dedication. Jessica's face was turned up to the sky, her mouth frozen in an eternal scream, open eyes unblinking beneath the falling snow. From the look of the bare footprints on the path, she had been running hard when they finally brought her down.

A snowman sat on the lawn, a faded Portland Beavers cap perched jauntily on its head. Instead of arms, two iron pokers jutted from its chest at right angles, blood-red trails dribbling into slush at its base. Marcie kept her eyes on the red door, mind racing at the thought of what might be beyond it.

Music drifted from the hall: a scratchy gramophone crooning out old Christmas songs. She tried the front door. The handle turned, but instantly met resistance. A whimper came from inside. Panic tightened its grip around her chest.

"Olivia?" she whispered.

No answer. Marcie shoved the door and the obstruction moved, taking the doormat's *Christmas Blessings* with it. She crept forward, breath catching in her throat, and the door swung shut behind her, muffling the snarls and growls and tearing from outside.

Marcie had known what she would find inside. Two more bodies, wrapped in a terminal embrace. Her father's hands were locked around her stepmother's sagging throat, her eyes bulging from their sockets, tongue lolling down her chin like a bloated slug. A pair of silver-handled embroidery scissors were embedded in her father's left eye socket, blood and jelly running down his cheekbone in a glistening rivulet. Both faces were contorted, the

107

three remaining eyes glaring with undying hatred. She wondered when the grief would hit, but felt nothing except a faint, queasy revulsion.

Something rustled in the corner of the room. Marcie's head snapped round, her nerves jangling, and it moved again, shrinking deeper into the corner behind the widescreen TV—a spindly shape, too small to be an adult, large enough for a child.

"Olivia!" Marcie stepped over the corpses and shoved the cabinet out of the way. Her niece's skinny body was curled protectively around a small bundle of blankets. "Olivia, get up— we have to get out of here, okay?"

Olivia's eyes were pools of darkness, wide and empty. "They were fighting," she said. "Everyone was fighting. Even Frosty and Snowy. They bit Mommy."

"But you're okay, aren't you? You're fine. And baby Lucy." Marcie struggled to get a grip on her niece's arms, trying not to notice that the bundle clutched to Olivia's chest wasn't moving. Marcie forced her hand to the blankets, not wanting to see what lay inside them, but desperate to know. She pulled back the blanket, and a soft gust met her hand. She let out a breath she hadn't known she was holding. The baby was alive, sleeping perfect and serene amidst a nativity-play of blood. "We need to go now."

"He's in the living room." Olivia's eyes were wide. "He said I can't go until you get here. He said he's waiting for you."

Marcie closed her eyes as a giddying nausea swept over her. She thought back to how it had all begun: the earrings, the blood and a heartfelt Christmas wish.

To Hell with Nicholas, my family and Rusty Hollow.

(Everybody's Waitin' For) The Man With The Bag

"Big girl—can you work one of these?" Marcie's voice shook as she fumbled her phone from her pocket and pressed it into the girl's hand. Even as she spoke she knew it was a stupid question. Every kid can work a phone. "The code's twelve-twenty-five. Like Christmas Day. You take your sister and you head north out of Rusty Hollow as fast as you can. And when you're past the sign, you call 911, then you call Naomi Saperstein and tell her—" Marcie swallowed down the hard lump that had risen in her throat. "You tell her your Aunt Marcie needs her to come get you. Okay?"

The little girl nodded, and the baby stirred in her arms. Marcie kissed both small faces. "And whatever you see out there, don't stop."

She watched until they had passed through the garden gate and turned away from the burning town, the air full of woodsmoke and the sweet tang of roasting pork.

The door to the living room lay ajar. Firelight spilled into the darkened hallway. Two chairs had been moved to sit one on either side of the fireplace. The tree's tiny golden lights glittered on the exquisitely wrapped gifts beneath it. Nick rose as she approached, his elegant features lit by the soft, amber glow. He held out his hands to her. One was empty. The other held a tiny jewellery box.

"What have you done?" she whispered.

"All you wanted."

He stepped close to her and opened the box. Firelight caught on a diamond solitaire set in a blackened silver band. Nick slipped the ring onto her finger, where it sat cool and heavy as lead. He touched his burning lips to hers, and led her unresisting to the fire.

The Twelfth Day of Christmas

Karen Walker

By the twelfth day of Christmas, Doug and Mimi had had enough of the festive season, of this endless holiday song.

"Here they come." Doug groaned as he stirred white powder into the last guests' final cranberry punch.

Discordant drumming—a dozen musicians each playing a different tune and badly—grew louder. The cacophony marched up the couple's front walk, stumbled onto their porch. There was giggling, someone slurring that he couldn't wait, the sound of a stream flowing into the bushes. Then the doorbell rang.

"Christ, they're already sauced!" Doug shouted to his wife.

Mimi was busy in the kitchen. Irritable. "It'll make it easier. Took a lot to subdue those pipers yesterday."

The hostess hurriedly laid sprigs of parsley on trays of turtle dove rolls and nestled dishes of cucumber dip among partridge appetizers.

She glanced at the oven timer: fifteen minutes more for the sizzling legs of lordly meat. Served with roast potatoes, carrots, and a hearty pan gravy, the big beefy boys would be a delightful break from fussy glazed goose and stuffed swan entrees.

Mimi wiped her brow. At least dessert was ready. There had been tears and cries for help but, in the end, success. An abundance of dainty ladyfingers and sweet little milkmaid tarts were chilling in the fridge.

"Ready?" Doug's hand tightened on the doorknob.

Mimi threw aside her bloody apron. Smoothed her party black dress, slipped on the shiniest of the five gold rings laying on the kitchen counter.

Swatting aside the dying pear tree in the hallway, Mimi joined Doug at the front door. "Nearly done for another year. One more verse to go."

"I wouldn't mind if a few got away this time," Doug said. He twisted a grimace into a last holiday smile. "The freezer's full."

Have a Holly, Jolly Nuclear Winter
Olin Wish

The process for solving spooky physics is fairly simple. It involves a full-length mirror, preferably ovular, and a handful of fast acting pills.

"What if there is no air on the other side?" she asked, "What if there is no gravity?"

Her concern was well placed. Even I must admit I had my doubts.

"Honey," I said, "Our particles exist simultaneously in various places in the universe. It's called quantum entanglement. The physics will be there regardless of where we end up, so there is nothing to fear."

Nothing to fear. How profane those words seem now in retrospect.

"What about oxygen? What about slipping over the edge of an event horizon? Did you consider that? What if we spontaneously emerge at the bottom of a methane ocean or in the heart of a red dwarf?"

"*Methane ocean?*" I asked, somewhat smugly, somewhat reproachfully. She had been watching her programs again. "*Event horizon?* No, my dear. Nothing like that. You will be perfectly safe. I give you my word."

I said this while proffering to her a handful of the drugs I had engineered. Their application would soften her life's hold on reality. Make the essence pliable. If one were given to religious metaphors, these pills were the yeast that would make the soul sizzle and rise. With fall-off-the-bone tenderness she would then be able to experience instantaneous coupling, an element of quantum weirdness that Einstein proclaimed was too radical to be a part of any sort of sane reality he cared to do business with.

A photon of light, communicating faster than the speed of light. *Incredible*, I thought. *Just incredible.* In any sane universe the math for instant coupling would not exist. Maybe God is crazy? I postulated. For our purposes I acquired a Victorian full-length mirror with an ornate pewter frame from a local antique shop. It stood on claw-footed bracings, filthy from generations of skin oil and settled dust. I considered all the heiresses who had stared longingly into the mirror surface, searching idly for absolution.

"Are you ready?" I asked, solemnly.

"One more thing," she said, much calmer now. "How do we get back?"

"Easy," I said, shaking a plastic cylinder with a childproof lid in her direction, "We just catch the nearest pill home."

My words successfully lightened the mood. She held out her hand and I poured the drug, brightly colored according to purpose, slightly bigger than a rice grain, into her palm. *A collection of cosmic confetti*, I thought wistfully. Out of the bowels of Hell we had emerged to make beautiful music. Now we were going back down to play. And if the tune attracted flies? Well, then all for the better.

Olin Wish

"Down the hatch," I said, offering a stainless steel flask filled with passable single malt. I watched while it slid down her throat in two dainty gulps. Her coughing fit was brief, and the space that followed, when the icy blue pigment of her irises vanished beneath a spreading pool of inky pupil, even briefer. When we stepped through the full-length Victorian I wondered, not for the first time, if Lewis Carroll had been privy to some insider information about how the future of interstellar space travel might be achieved before he wrote his famous book.

Of course, for us, the experience was much different. We were not tumbling into a void with improbable characters or suffering from a lurid fever dream. That's not how physics works, I would tell myself, much later, even as the walls of sanity began to rattle. Going post corporeal at the speed of thought makes the membrane separating life and death transparently thin like rolled rice pasta while simultaneously honing the senses razor sharp. *This is what all those newly dead felt*, I thought in wonderment as the things they were feeling began shutting down, one after the other. Mercury mist, tip-toeing lightly like dainty angels on my cheeks and at my temples. A blooming hematoma of purple lightning rimmed with fragrant orange. Smells that were tastes. Sounds that were color. This is what slipping through the bony fingers of God feels like, I thought, relishing the once-in-a-lifetime tingle of burst capillaries reknitting just below the surface of the skin.

"Roland?" she asked when our feet were firmly planted on the other side. "Did it work?"

The room was roughly the size and shape of our sitting room, but with noticeable differences. The hardwood floor was slotted with rickety timber, as was the ceiling. Knotty pine rubbed smooth by shoes and bare feet. Windows too were boarded over with cheap pine bars that let in moonlight through the inch of space between them. The effect on the floor, the walls, and the scant furniture preserved underneath stark white sheets, was that of prison bars. It was night, I realized. *Night!* Where we had been previously was early afternoon.

Suddenly, a wave of vertigo slammed into the side of my head. Were we really on the opposite side of the universe, joined instantaneously to particles that had not shared real estate with our own since the seconds leading up to the big bang?

"Roland? Roland!"

I looked up sharply. Perhaps a full minute had passed.

"What do we do now?" she asked.

In my right front pocket was the weight of the pills in their plastic tube, heavy as a lead ingot. How easy it would be to take them with what remained of the whiskey and return home where it was safe.

"Let's have a look," I offered, striding to the window, whisper quiet. Despite caution, each step stirred up airborne dust. Motes passing through unusually intense moonbeams like fish scales in brackish water. Behind me, I heard my wife suppress a cough. *Good girl*, I thought. Better to be cautious. For all we knew, this house might be inhabited. With rats, most likely, the cynical half suggested. Or a rat-like substitute. Peering out between pine bars, I barely suppressed a gasp.

"What is it?" She asked, her worry as evident in her voice as the silence I replied with.

"Damnit, Roland! What do you see?"

What I saw was a quaint European village. Cobbled roads with oil burning street lamps regularly spaced. At the center of two intersecting streets, I could see smoldering bonfires from our second story vantage point. Elsewhere, the glow from similar street fires illuminated neighboring residences, casting each in ethereal shadow which crawled up the brick and mortar on gossamer legs. The street was empty except for a horse drawn carriage pulling a coffin. My thoughts shifted to the transition leading up to the age of enlightenment. A plague, perhaps? Had we inadvertently killed ourselves in the first five seconds of crossing over and not realized it?

No, I thought, watching the driver slow the hearse to a stop in front of the fire. Two men emerged from inside the carriage, heads shrouded in black, shoulders slumped. Together they dragged the thin sarcophagus down off its moorings, then unceremoniously laid it beside the creeping flames. *An inquisition, then?* I wondered, stepping away from the window with cat-like slowness. I didn't watch them drag the body from the casket and fireman carry it to be pitched into the flames. A swinging count of three and then lobbed like a rolled-up carpet. By then I had seen enough of this world.

"It's time to go," I told her, reaching into my pocket. Moonlight in the mirror showed me an old man prematurely aged in just the last couple of moments. *I made a mistake*, a voice inside answered. *A horrible mistake*. But there was still time.

"You're joking," she said, marching towards the boarded-up window. Her creaking footfalls sent an electric current through me. I was suddenly hyper aware of just how vulnerable we were. Here in this polarized vision of Hell, shrouded in perpetual night, the truth of our presence might be discovered at any moment. Just the thought of encountering people or things from this world, those responsible for the scene in the street, filled me with dread. In this room with only one directional viewing, we were like babes at the mercy of hidden dangers. Who else lived here? My thoughts raged. It was presumably abandoned, but by what and for how long? Who had taken the time to shroud the furniture and barricade the windows with flimsy floorboards?

"Stop!" I hissed in full panic before she reached the spot where I had glimpsed Hell.

"Really Roland, you're being ridiculous! You bring me here, tell me all about this marvelous invention. Then you say we have to go. What could possibly be so awful?"

She bowed her head slightly to put a gap between the boards at eye level. By then I had reached her. A thin smile spread across her lips.

"Roland!" She said, awe-inspired. "Look! It's snowing!"

Keep your voice down! the rodent of self-preservation implored.

"My dear," I began, placing my hands gently on her shoulders.

I watched as the smile faded, withering like some delicious, ripe fruit in an unseasonably early frost.

Now her eyes widened as the scene beyond the ashes came into focus like the church yard inside a stirred-up snow globe. Through a slot beside her, I gave into temptation and peered out once more, unsure exactly what I hoped to accomplish, but knowing what I would find. Confirmation, perhaps? Morbid curiosity, sated while risking death? There are any number of reasons why men do stupid things and die soon after because of it.

A flock of high officials glided purposefully down the cobbled street. The train of their virginal white robes cleared a path in the settled ashes of human debris. Heads lowered, hands threaded within drooping sleeves, as if in meditation, they paid no attention to the unearthly business of the mortician and his henchmen. They're above it—I knew at once. Why would a politician spare a glance for the toil of the common worker? In my own world there were similar phenomena.

On each of the men's heads they wore a crown-like pillar of piled white fabric. Coming to a point and ornamented with gold lacing accents and trim, they were, to my mind, the spitting image of "lesser Popes". *A world gone mad, ruled with an iron fist by men of God.* When presented with the unexplainable, the mind has a tendency to draw unreasonable parallels from the facts given, I reminded myself. Like seeing monsters in the grain of a closet door or a surprised expression in the man in the moon. These weren't men of the cloth in the strictest sense. Nor were they women to be judged. Their actions could not be compared to their sane counterparts an unfathomable distance away.

"Come on," I said, placing palms gently but insistently upon my wife's shoulders. "We've seen enough. It's time to go."

Down in the street the snowy stillness was broken intermittently by the crackle of bones exploding in the fire like damp cordwood. The sickeningly sweet odor of sizzling fat and hair rising up in a plume of acrid black smoke. *The whole world was a house fire*, I thought. *And none had survived.* Which wasn't strictly true. Some had, of course. Only some. There were always survivors in these circumstances. Which was somehow worse. If we had arrived to an empty world with the embers of corpses still glowing, that, I assumed, would have somehow been better. Instead, a flash of movement from below caught my wife's eye, just as she was on the brink of turning.

"Look!"

Through the shattered window of a house across the street materialized an unkempt Santa Claus, complete with stocking cap, fur lined boots, and a yellowish-gray wisp of a beard, made clumsy by the weight of the sack full of presents he dragged clear through the opening and hefted over one shoulder. We stared, transfixed, as the plump figure wiggled the rest of the way into the street. It was indeed a heavy sack—I could see by the way he staggered, leaning forward, nearly doubled over. Twice he had to set the bag down to catch his breath on his way to the pyre, brushing absently away at the flakes settling on his red velveteen coat.

Others, similarly dressed, began emerging from nearby houses, seemingly oblivious to the briskly moving wraiths in untainted inquisitor cloaks, or to each other. They were men performing a job, their demeanor suggested. Like garbage collectors in the predawn hours, they were completely separate from the politics that had put the task in front of them. When one of the Santa's coughed into a closed fist, my wife started. It had been the only sound since the clatter of the mortician's cart. The steady reverberations of nighttime activities—cats fighting in an alley, a distant siren, wooden structures settling—were all but absent. Of the corpse fire in the intersection there were tittering, inconsequential noises. The pain of the bodies which fed it was now over. All that was left were the whispers of their innards as they sizzled.

To us, their secret language had been the only sound in quite some time. There and yet not, like the background radiation of the universe. The man's cough had awakened the truth about who he was. Not a creature, per se. But a man who coughed to clear his lungs of the saturated air.

For a blessed instant after all the color had drained from her face, I thought the sight of the man had swayed her. That her fear had actually overruled the prime directive being satisfied by voyeurism. We could go home to where it was safe without ever knowing what was inside the bag or what the man dressed in an absurd yet horrifying parody of Santa Claus intended to do with it. The same false sense of security which killed many wartime journalists now possessed us. We had become divorced from the danger, mere spectators, secure behind the broken-out window frame, with only pine boards between us and it.

The howling certainty of knowing exactly what was in the bag and what came next was worth the risk to both of our lives, that sick, self-destructive side which lived in every man suggested. *If you leave without knowing*, it said, *your imagination will drive you insane. Maybe not soon, but eventually.* The worst part was, I knew it was true. More men with dishwater grey beards emerged from neighboring houses carrying, sometimes dragging, bags filled with "presents" through ankle deep ash.

The bags that were hefted dribbled incessantly while the ones which were dragged painted wide streaks over the cobbles, displacing false snow even as it stained the street, cutting through it, creating little artificial drifts.

"Just one more minute," she said in a dreamy voice as I tried, evermore insistently, to pull her away from the window.

The first out-of-work mall Santa to reach the fire upended his sack into the flames where they flared excitedly. *Nothing a person couldn't live without*, I thought, feeling the repulsive weight of this place lean against my eyes. The first sign of corruption will be morbid humor, I realized, grinning. Noses, ears, lips, and a few eyeballs tumbled from the yawning sack. It was hard to tell how many precious eyes were among the other frankly cosmetic parts of a face. People could go on maimed, having contributed to these bags of tricks, and consider themselves fortunate.

While others...

As long as they still had their eyes. The eyes were the ultimate insult. Perhaps the ones who had been blinded for their troubles had put up a particularly good fight. The ones who were bravest had lost the most, evident among the rest by sheer amount. I tried not to visualize the struggle that had led to this. The filthy parody of a gift giving saint with the inhuman, fixed stare, lurching gait, and icy grasp of a seasoned executioner, holding his victims down with one grubby, lecherous claw while the other went to work with the gardening shears, dismantling.

A blast of hot fumes hit me square in the mouth and I choked, throwing a hand over my mouth to suppress the expulsion. My wife spun wildly, cupping both palms over my mouth as well. If it meant never breathing again, so be it. I tried, in a rising panic over the uncertainty for the next breath, to think of other things. Lesser details about the town. There was a castle high upon a rolling hill. Presumably where a potentate lived. Cascaded in moonlight, the leaves of the surrounding forest were a shimmering suit of armor. Silver indentations like chain mail links.

Two moons, I thought. *There were two moons.* And both of them full. Huge as dinner plates in the night sky. Bright enough to see by, even for the most delicate of work. They were 'harvest moons', I thought, believing the tickle in my throat would never dissipate. As tickles went, it was the knife tip of the inquisitor as opposed to the feather's touch. Just the thought of a grain of human cremation settling down in there, making itself at home— I shifted rapidly to other things. What were the odds of two harvest moons occurring in a regular lunar cycle? Once every ten years? Longer perhaps? This is a celebration, I realized. We happened upon some sort of festival. A grim sort where people 'harvest' pieces of their neighbors to feed a rapidly diminishing fire. These people who were giving up pieces of themselves did so by the light of twin full moons. Willingly or not-so-willingly. It didn't matter to the ones doing the snipping.

The gasp that filled my lungs as she slowly lowered her hands still tasted bad. There was a scratchy piece of corruption down there and it would sit, festering perhaps, and I would let it. If it were a seed I would let it grow into a Georgia hardwood if it meant not giving away our position. With watering eyes the world took on an aspect of unreality as I ever-so-gently removed the remaining tablets from my pocket.

"It's now or never," I whispered, hoping the finality would convince her. To my supreme joy, she gave a tiny nod of resignation. There was nothing either of us could do about the misery we had witnessed. Any good we might be persuaded to attempt in exchange for our lives would be quickly converted to steam and snowy grey flakes upon the altar of sacrifice.

As she took a step forward, carefully so as not to disturb the dust, a floorboard let out a ghastly moan like a gaseous corpse lamenting the state of its own decomposition. On the other side of the wall directly behind me, I heard the distinct noise of weight shifting. Someone, or something, had been roused from a sitting position to stand. *Another squatter?* My mind insisted, hopefully.

Frozen to the spot, I tapped a measure of the medication which would reunite our cells with their earth-based counterparts into my sweaty palm. The trouble with these, the one failure about the delivery system I learned from this trial run, was that the pills would take about five minutes to dissolve in our digestive tracts and enter our bloodstream. Five minutes. Already, the figure opposite the too-thin wall was moving again, having decided we weren't a stray cat to be ignored. Next time, if there was a next time, there would be syringes, I decided.

Somewhere on the first floor a window shattered. Hands she used to cover her mouth returned to suppress a scream. Heavy boots stomping rapidly up a rickety staircase. Again, from the room adjacent, more movement. It had given up all pretense of stealth. Looking for a way out, I decided, based on where and how it was moving. There was more than one, I realized. An entire family, crouching, cowering, none with the courage yet to voice apprehension into a scream that might draw others, even as boots which had delivered the pseudo-Santa to the hallway outside the room began issuing savage kicks to the door of the adjacent room.

With five powerful kicks, the door shivered inwards, then finally surrendered. On reluctant hinges, the shattered pine let in corruption it had been shielding the family against. Then the screams. Screams and appeals to a God I had never known in a language vaguely Hungarian. Guttural shouts accentuated by the dull, meaty thuds of blunt objects meeting bone.

"Take this!" I said, stabbing my outthrust palm towards her, all effort at quiet abandoned. She dutifully swallowed the pill and waited an inch from the mirror as I leaned my weight against the flimsy door. I prayed whole-heartedly to a God I had just recently decided to believe existed that the man or thing dismantling the family in the room next to ours was too preoccupied to check for more squatters in neighboring rooms. *Let him forget about us*, I implored. *Just this once, let him forget all about clearing the rest of the house.*

No such luck, I realized as the last scream faded to a gurgling rattle. The man dressed as Santa Claus stomped efficiently around the room, no doubt collecting trophies. Business as usual, I decided. And we were next.

"Try!" I hissed, reverting back to the instinctual quiet of an animal in the jungle being hunted.

She touched her fingertips to the mirror surface as if it were a still pool. When no resultant ripples preceded the delicate pianist's caress, I hurried to her side. Was something wrong with the medication? In answer to this, and in my haste to procure an answer in the empty, hollowed eyes of my own reflection, I sank my arm elbow deep into the Victorian standing mirror.

"Go!" she said, without hesitation.

I stole my arm back as if my hand had happened on a scalding surface. I would have much preferred to die screaming than leave her here alone to face what was coming. I heard it then, over whispers of our frantic argument, breathing heavily. If it wanted to, I knew the force which had killed the squatters could come straight through the wall, splintering through the sticks used as support as easily as a man parting the grass. Instead, it chose to march languidly back into the hallway.

I thought about the sack full of pieces it had slung over one bulky shoulder and how easily we would be incorporated in with the family of strangers. Like stew meat eager for beef broth.

When it came to the door outside our room, it had the audacity to knock, once, twice, three times. With the authority of someone who knows it will never be answered, it spoke a short blast of words in that awful guttural.

"Go!" she bleated, pushing me towards the mirror. I held firm, resolute, shaking out a few more tablets. Why hadn't it worked? These trial runs are always temperamental, even during ideal circumstances. But the thing standing outside the rickety door wasn't a side effect. The majority of pills scattered across the floor between our shoes while a few stuck stubbornly to the perspiration of my hand.

"Here!" I said, handing her what remained, "Take it!"

"There's no time!" she said, pushing my hand away.

A booming impact shivered the doorframe. Motes of

125

ancient dust dislodged from the rafters and clouded the air between us. We were seeing each other through a miasmic haze of stirred up cremation, perhaps for the first time. Her look of feral panic mixed with stern resolve. She was right, of course. Another kick like the one which preceded it and the door would crater inwards. Why hadn't it worked? Those words would echo into eternity long after we were both dead. The field tests I had performed with animals had gone off flawlessly. Dozens of stray cats had been shoved boldly through the relaxing plasma of their own reflections.

Blood type? Allergen? Or simply an unanticipated mutation which kept the photons streaming one direction easily enough while preventing their safe return? These were all possibilities, each as unlikely as the next, for why her cells stubbornly refused to coalesce with their estranged counterparts.

"Roland!" she shrieked in her high, unmistakable register of triumph. "Look!"

She had placed her palm flat against the Victorian. Excitedly, I leaned forward, anticipating the ripples resonating from her touch. Instead, I was shoved violently and, caught off balance this time, experienced the temporal slippage. Windmilling, frantically trying to counterbalance as the pendulum of my upper torso glided helplessly past the point of no return. In the distance, I heard the tell-tale crack of the door giving way, shattering under the force of the executioner's boot in a galaxy of raining wood pulp and splinters. There was a blessed moment of absolute silence beneath the surface as time and space set about knitting me back together.

Have a Holly, Jolly Nuclear Winter

The momentum of her shove followed me across untold lightyears. I arrived sprawling on polished hardwood. I sprang up, clamoring out from underneath my writing desk, experiencing the first wave of disorientation and accompanying nausea. It was well after midnight and dark except for a desk lamp. I stayed there till dawn, waiting, hoping she would emerge.

For the next six months I spent countless hours drinking alone in a high back chair beside the Victorian, my reflection a perfect image of regret, longing, and budding madness. But it wasn't she who emerged some time later, long after I had given up hope. It was during the Christmas season, appropriately enough, when I awoke one night to see a familiar figure standing in the doorway of my bedroom. The licking flames of the dying fire in the hearth cast a pale amber glow across sunken cheeks, wispy fragmentary beard, and brass buckles.

I was wrong about many things, but most of all the gardening shears. They had been an invention of my overexcited imagination. In his right hand, the inquisitor held a thin bladed hatchet. It twinkled merrily in the places not coated by a thin grime of filth. The residual mess dripped, tapping regular as a metronome. This was nice, I thought, pulling the top blanket defensively up to my chin. Appropriate even. He had come calling to claim the pieces I so rudely denied him the first time.

As muddy boots approached, I took solace in the somber notion that pieces of me would soon be in the same place where she had ended up. Mixing, converging, making merry in the sodden bag of tricks.

Boat on the Bay
Sarah Crabtree

I saw three ships come sailing in
On Christmas Day, on Christmas Day;
I saw three ships come sailing in
On Christmas Day in the morning.
Pray, wither sailed those ships all three,
On Christmas Day, on Christmas Day;
Pray, wither sailed those ships all three,
On Christmas Day in the morning.
O they sailed into Bethlehem,
On Christmas Day, on Christmas Day;
O they sailed into Bethlehem,
On Christmas Day in the morning.

The wind was terrifying. Over the horizon, across the bay, the town's lights sparkled like a toy kingdom of glass and stars. *Carol of the bells* would be playing: ding-ding-a-ling, ding-ding-a-ling, ding-ding-a-ling, on and on and on. That restless, inciting Christmas spirit flowing through the night, squeezing itself under every door like invisible smoke. Yuletide ectoplasm entering each family abode: a whisper of glad tidings to all.

Earlier in the year, we recalled Maude Onions's moving recollection of the first great silence of Armistice. Nothing happened at eleven o'clock. Nothing except a silence, a glance at the clock.

I pictured Colin's cottage with its Dickensian room, lined with books and littered with papers, where a fire blazed in the

129

hearth. A kettle steamed upon the hob, and in the midst of the wreck of papers shone a table, with plenty of wine upon it, and brandy, rum, sugar and lemons.

Did I say it was Dickensian? Well mostly, except for the nineteen-sixties big, red, bubble-blown glass ashtray he kept mainly on the floor behind the table. He only ever needed to set it up on the table when Alicia came to smoke and tell him all her tales of woe. On and on and on she would go. Smoke, smoke, smoke. Whine, whine, whine. And still he chose her over me. Perhaps I was too much of the grown up. Until I got left behind on this uninhabited isle.

I had missed the last ferry home before dawn because I got carried away taking too many photos on my smartphone. Nobody noticed, nobody did a headcount, and they sailed off without me.

Alicia. I warned him of her ambiguity and damaged personality.

I hunkered down in the storm hut, counting the minutes to the hours before human contact again. Thoughts spiralled on the mappa mundi of my brain. Outside the hut, little patterings grew into louder rappings: "Let us in! Let us in!"

I played the radio app on my smartphone until the battery died. A fourth dimensional sound came; a sound outside humanity.

They, whoever they were, had come for me. Someone or something tried the handle of the door.

"Go away! There's nothing for you here!"

The rapping paused for a couple of beats, and then the whole hut shook me from side to side. Spray blowing from the sea gathered in big drops and flung itself against the tiny window.

Again, it stopped. So I wrenched open the door to escape my earthquake prison. The sand gleamed faintly on the shore. I turned my back to the sea and saw the east reddening through gaps in the trees. Several hours had passed since I entered the storm hut.

The wind raged again, wearing me down with its boundless energy. Thunder cracked the sky, and a fine spray blew into my face when I turned towards the bay again. Calm, storm, calm, storm rocked me like an evil lullaby.

Whatever's the matter with you? said a voice inside my head. *For pity's sake, woman, pull yourself together.*

Why didn't Colin wait for me?

Because he never invited you in the first place. You tagged along, hoping he would tire of Alicia and choose you over her.

It backfired, and all the demons on this lonely little isle have come to taunt you.

I found a charger at the bottom of my rucksack. When enough had booted up my battery, a WhatsApp from Colin appeared: J, When you get back to town, please can we talk? Love C, heart heart.

In the distance, a boat was growing larger.

Red-copper paint on a wooden summerhouse. Leaves scratch the asphalt. I'm standing on wet sand as the surf drags itself back to the ocean. I'm sailing backwards, even though I'm not moving.

In the distance, a Lovecraftian apparition of a white ship, a vessel, fit for a noble prince, an aetheling, icy, and eager to sail across phosphorescent depths. The ship glides silently over wave

Sarah Crabtree

tips beneath a bridge of moonbeams. Soft songs of sirens drift out of a forgotten dream of beauty from the green lands of Zar. Closer it looms, and a wraith howls: Haaaaaappy Blooooooody Christmassssssssssssssssss.

And all the bells on earth shall ring,
On Christmas Day, on Christmas Day;
And all the bells on earth shall ring,
On Christmas Day in the morning.
And all the souls on earth shall sing,
On Christmas Day, on Christmas Day;
And all the souls on earth shall sing,
On Christmas Day in the morning.

All Alone on Christmas
Chris Campeau

Christmas came and Ed Crescent still hadn't visited his family. Family meant love, and love meant heartbreak. Steve and his wife had no doubt spent an exuberant day in their lofty new home, a four-bedroom ranch-style with plenty of space for Ed; Steve had been quick to assure him of it. Instead, he chose to spend the holidays doing what he did best since Aubrey left. Being alone.

Ed sunk into the hot tub, let the jets work his back. Squinting against the steam, he took in the snow-capped pines and the river beyond the road. It was the perfect getaway, though he didn't have much to get away from.

Paradise, he thought. *But why doesn't it feel like it?*

He knew the answer. Knew that he should stop shutting folks out. That he really should spend more time with his son, whether he had Aubrey's eyes or not. It was their Steve, after all, who sent him the listing.

"What is it?" Aubrey had said, noting a change in the air from her reading chair.

"That chalet near Wakefield Heights? They finished building it. It's a vacation property."

"We should go."

"We should," he'd said, not mentioning the nightly price tag, knowing his CPP wouldn't cover such a weekend.

That was August, before she'd had enough.

Ed sipped his scotch, the tumbler toasty and wet. He wished Aubrey could see him now, finally good at saving money, and soaking his bones in style.

"Hello?"

The man's voice launched Ed onto his elbows, but he slipped back down. "Who's there?" he said, sputtering out foam. He wiped his eyes and stopped the jets. As the steam thinned he scanned the towering pines, their trunks ghastly in the floodlight leaking from above the chalet's front door. "Must be losing my mind," he said. And then he said it again, louder, if only to scare off intruders.

But what intruders? He and Aubrey had driven Chestnut Road often. They always took the scenic route home from her sister's, and there weren't any residences on the road but this one. Hell, it was in the listing's title: *Remote Chalet Near the Lake—No Neighbours!*

Ed crouched in the water and looked around. Nothing but trees and darkness. A gentle drift of snow. He'd heard about paranoia, what the mind can conjure if isolated. He laughed and blamed it on the scotch, but that didn't stop him from grabbing his robe and hurrying inside, leaving the hot tub open to simmer beneath the trees.

Inside, Darlene Love sang "All Alone on Christmas," her voice flooding the main floor. Ed dashed into sweatpants, flicked on all the lights, and set a frozen Hungry-Man on the counter. It wasn't much, but it beat drinking on an empty stomach—a lesson he'd learned too late. He sighed and twisted his wedding ring.

Outside, the night was impermeable; anyone within it would see him. He felt like a lab rat behind floor-to-ceiling glass.

A figurine on display. He scoffed at his bulky reflection—then screamed.

There. A silhouette on the balcony. Barely visible in the darkness. He cursed as he dropped his phone, the screen bursting into a latticework of cracks.

He thought about calling Steve, but what would he say? *Hi, Son. I'm all alone out here. At least, I thought I was. There's someone outside. What's that? Yes, I know you'd like to see me. No, I haven't been drinking.*

The oven beeped and Ed jumped. It had preheated to 350. It was enough to untether him from the moment—all he needed to realize what he was looking at: not a person but a statue. *The* statue.

He laughed. How did he miss it when he arrived? More shocking, how did he forget about it? He'd had to pull over the car last winter and wave to make sure it wasn't alive.

The safety vest and hardhat.

The beard covered in ice.

The plump pink face.

The labourers had likely put it out there, dressed it up as one of the crew. The chalet was just a frame then, and there, perched on the unfinished veranda, was a frozen Kris Kringle—Aubrey was sure of it.

"Look at the cuffs on his boots! The red pants! Come on!"

If nothing else, the Santa-in-workers'-clothing was conversation fodder, though the discourse died when they returned to the car.

Ed's stomach crooned as he remembered the oven. He asked

Alexa to set a timer, popped his dinner in, and turned his back on Saint Nick. Statue or not, he'd still heard someone outside.

"Alexa," he said again, "how far to the nearest police station?"

"Okay, playing the Police on Spotify."

Christ.

The drumroll opening "Spirits in the Material World" cut Darlene Love short. Ed followed Sting's voice to the mantle above the fireplace, traced the cord from the mini-speaker to an outlet at his feet.

"Technology," he said, about to yank the plug from the wall, but then a knock came at the door. A single rap.

Ed froze. Looked around. The voice from earlier, it was real now. And while it comforted him to know he wasn't going crazy, he almost preferred to be. Who could be outside at this hour, and where did they come from? Fear fanned the booze burning in his stomach.

Hold it together, pal. Probably just the owner.

He moved to the stairs splitting the main level from the ground floor, where the entrance was. He glanced at his phone but didn't grab it; if it were the landlord, he didn't want to keep him waiting. In blue pajamas in the middle of the woods, Ed Crescent opened the door.

"Thought you'd never come, son," said the man who wasn't the owner.

His use of *son* was the first thing that caught Ed by surprise; the gentleman was likely his age. Older, maybe. The second was his smell; Ed recognized it from 32 years of marriage. Aubrey loved to bake, especially around the holidays.

"Hi, sorry, is there something I can—" Ed stopped, struck by a sudden longing for his ex-wife. For anyone. And then the man's smile silenced him further: sickly black teeth, twinkling like tinsel.

"Sleigh broke down a few miles back, almost landed in the river. Just hoping to warm up for a minute if you don't mind."

Ed was sure the grisly looking man was joking. Teeth and tattered army coat aside, he did *sort* of resemble Santa Claus.

"Car's been acting up for weeks. I should've figured she'd crap out."

"Car," said Ed, smirking. Had he really misheard? "Of course. Yes, no, of course. Come in." The words just tumbled out. "No sense in you freezing out here."

"Thanks, son. And don't let this belly deceive you. I'm chilled to the bone!"

The man blustered inside and led himself up the stairs. The audacity of the act was absurd; Ed had to wonder who the guest was in the situation.

At least he removed his boots.

Ed followed him in a boozy haze, a trail of gingerbread tickling his nose, and nearly rear-ended the man as he stopped on the top step.

"Just marvelous," he said.

"What's that?"

"Look at the woodwork," the man said, his head wheeling as he took in the great room. "I've only seen the place from outside. And that fireplace, golly! Reminds me of home."

"And where's home?" Ed asked, spotting his phone on the ground. The man seated himself on the sofa. The leather squealed.

"Far from here, son. Though lately too close."

Ed caught the man's oddly cheerful tone. He leaned against the island and kept his distance.

"Do me a favour? Could you stoke the fire?"

Ed's jaw tensed. The man was quivering, visibly cold and tired, but who did he think he was? At the same time, Ed couldn't help but feel warmed by him. He had the charm of an old friend. A nostalgic pull.

Flames lapped the fireplace doors like the angry tongues of snakes. Ed sat on the loveseat, fire poker in hand.

"Thanks, Ed. Nearly caught my death out there."

Ed's legs went numb. "Did I give you my name?"

The man laughed. A boom that jiggled the stomach spilling out from beneath his coat. "Good guess, huh?" He waited for a reaction, then waved a hand. "Lighten up, boy! I'm just rousing your snickers! Truth is, I know everyone's name, everywhere people exist." He leaned forward, narrowed his gaze.

Ed wanted to speak but couldn't find his words. And why bother? The man, as harmless as he seemed, was clearly deranged —drunker than Ed, maybe. He was grungy, too. Dust masked the colour of his pants. Ice dripped from his salt-white beard, tinged yellow around his mouth. And smudges of dirt lined his eyes like war paint.

Was he sleeping in a ditch? How the hell did he get here?

And that accent. It was subtle, but Ed couldn't place it. Not Quebecois. Not from the valley. It was unlike anything he'd heard. A cross-section of culture.

Northern, maybe. He sounds… northern.

"Cookie?" The man patted his breast pocket, dug inside, and pulled out a sugar bread rocking horse. He extended an arm, but Ed was looking at his hand—at the heart tattoo between his thumb and index finger. At the faded blue name inside.

Does that say 'Vixen'?

The man thrust the cookie closer.

"Uh, no, thanks," said Ed. "Listen, can I call someone for you? A tow, at least?" It was an empty promise; he knew he'd have better luck winning Aubrey back than getting a truck at midnight. And it'd been snowing for hours.

The man sighed and bit the head off the horse, sprinkles dotting his beard like ornaments. "'Course not," he said through crumby lips. "I've been enough trouble as it is. I'll be on my way."

"Wait a minute!" Ed said. Who was he to hurry an old man into the cold on Christmas night? Hadn't he promised himself he'd show some empathy? Hadn't *Aubrey* wanted some? "Don't rush. Stay and thaw out. Like you said, you'll catch your death out there." Ed forced a smile, but the man only cocked his wispy eyebrows. A strange fury stole his face.

"Well, now that I have your blessing," he said, and Ed couldn't help but detect a dash of sarcasm. "It's colder than St. Petersburg out there, and I've been dying to spend some time in this place."

"Sure thing. I'll fetch us a drink. You a scotch man?"

"It's Christmas, isn't it?"

Ed helped himself to another bottle in the cellar—the door was no match for a locksmith, retired or not—but he stopped on his way out the door. Just upstairs was a man he didn't know. A man whose knack for juggling pleasantries with arrogance was festering beneath his skin. And why was he so keen on the chalet?

He obviously knows the place. Is he a local, then?

He stopped again, this time at the foot of the stairs. The snow had melted on the mat, and, as dim as it was in the hallway, he couldn't mistake what he saw.

He blinked. Still there. Boots from a Christmas card, a Coke ad from the '50s. Two brass buckles, furry-white cuffs.

Boots that only go with one outfit.

That only fit *one* man.

Even the booze couldn't stifle the chill that tightened Ed's scalp. Buzzed or not, he knew what he'd find now if he looked out onto that balcony—footprints and nothing more. Just like he knew he'd never win Aubrey back; he could feel it, like he'd felt her drifting.

Can't take any chances, old man. Who knows what this guy— this thing—is capable of?

It was a ridiculous thought, and Ed couldn't help but hunch over, head swirling from the absurdity. He took a deep breath and dried his palms. Easing the closet door open to keep the hinges from screaming, he grabbed his coat and felt for the car keys inside. He was almost out the door when he remembered his phone.

Shit.

He looked to the door, heard the hail smash the walls.

Get stuck in a bank and then you're really screwed. No choice.

Inching up the stairs, Ed was grateful the chalet was new; the wood didn't creak. He poked his head around the railing and nearly dropped the scotch.

Ed crouched and held his breath as the stranger warmed his naked body before the crackling logs, humming a tune Ed knew but couldn't place.

Jesus, what's on his back?

What he mistook as shadows he now recognized as frostbite. Bad frostbite. Steve had it as a teenager, but nothing like this. From neck to heel, the man's skin was a mess of black moguls, blisters holding their shape in spots but oozing like eggnog in others. Ed's stomach churned, but not from the sight. How could a man needing such urgent medical attention be singing? How could he be so...

Jolly.

Ed spotted his phone on the floor, then the fire poker on the couch. It was one or the other, and he needed to be quick.

Heel to toe. Heel to toe.

Not a creature was stirring.

Heel to t—

BEEP!

Ed stopped, dropped down. He should've known from the smell: the pathetic steak and gravy, the bubbling potatoes.

Alexa.

The timer.

Bent over, hand on his phone, he looked toward the man, to his cracked heels, then his calves and veiny buttocks. Up and up to the eyes looking back at him. The lurid eyes, webbed red like snowflakes.

"Ed Crescent," the naked man said. "I see you don't have a Christmas tree."

Ed's heart pumped double-time as the man continued humming. Only this time, the lyrics stormed his mind like a nasty bout of sleet.

Listen to the fireplace roar…

"A shame to have no tree on Christmas, son. Even worse spending the day by yourself." He paused, frost-seared back glistening in the firelight. "Worse yet, spending it outside. But that's neither here nor there, is it? You've got this warm place all to yourself now, don'tcha?"

Never such a blizzard before…

"How sweet it must be."

Baby, it's cold outside.

Ed pocketed his phone, forced his legs to do their job. But he could only inch backward—toe to heel, toe to heel—before the man spun around fully. Ed didn't dare look below his chest and bloated gut, which were as burned as his backside. And he was bleeding, too. Dark beads of holly, dripping from neck to waist.

Ed didn't wait any longer. The man's grin was enough: lips lined black like coal, mouth lopsided like he'd suffered a stroke. Teeth like shattered taffy. His laughter echoed off the wooden beams, the glass windows, the marble countertops. It rattled the decorative antlers overhanging the stairs, thrust the front door open as Ed fled through the snow, pellets of hail shaving the flesh off his feet.

He hit the hot tub before he saw it. His stomach pummeled the misty-wet lip and he nearly toppled in. Pain erupted in his hip, a blaze even the scotch couldn't dowse. At a glacial pace, he half-crawled-half-slid to the Buick. The man's laughter had quieted.

142

In its place the wind carried a sound of its own. A hundred voices caroling. A menacing choir.

Ed didn't feel his skin fuse to the car door, nor the pain as the pads of his fingertips stayed behind on the icy metal. He let the Buick glide him down the laneway, but the windshield was too frosted. The road came up fast—and beyond it, the river.

Click.

The seatbelt locked as he pulled the e-brake, spun, and hit a bank across the road.

His bladder let out first. Then his tear ducts. Then his nails were on the windshield, scraping to get a glimpse. The chalet stood stoic up the hill, a wondrous structure at night. Through whirling snow an outline was visible in the orange-red glass. A figure. A man. But whether he was outside or in, Ed couldn't say.

With bleeding fingers he found the messaging app on his phone. It was muscle memory; the screen was too damaged. He wondered what Steve would read in the morning: a mashup of auto-corrected words, or the question he was aiming for, one hazy character at a time.

I'm sorry, son. Plans for New Years?

The Night Before X-Mas
Warren Brown

It was there in the presents
all sealed with care
a gift misdirected
that came from nowhere

A slick sheen of paper
nobody had seen
gleamed weirdly
in ocher, turned bilious green

From Daddy?
From Mommy?
From Gram?
or Aunt Roe?
How it had got there
nobody did know

Someone's a joker
Daddy then said
The cat, he said nothing
Then cried to be fed

The Night Before X-Mas

No tag on the gift
revealed the giver
To whom would the parcel
of joy be delivered?

"Who's it for?" asked Mom
for I've never seen it
It's a holiday puzzle
but tomorrow we'll glean it

Presents we'll open
and their contents reveal
for kid or for grownup?
The mystery unseal

Little Timmy convinced
that the gift was for him
vowed in silence to open
when the lights were turned dim

When the family
was sleeping
all warm they were bedded
no alarums to issue
when the wrapping
was shredded

Warren Brown

Timmy feigned sleep
for what seemed like hours
trusting his stealth
and tiptoeing powers

He crept to the tree
fiend-faced in the lights
and sifted through gifts
with rustlings slight

The gift it was heavy
and fuzzily warm
tingly and hummy
and prickly like thorns

It's better than PlayStation
or Xbox or drone
thought Timmy in
handling that thing
in his home

He tugged at the covering
turned purplish skin
to get out for his pleasure
that which had been in

The Night Before X-Mas

The best gift on Earth
a prize ranked first-rate

But it wasn't from Earth,
And Timmy,
it ate.

Harry and Samir Are Still Asleep

Matt Singleton

"'Twas the night before Christmas and all through the ship..."
Samir shouts, throwing his hands wide, smiling. A short barrage
of empty drinking bulbs cut off his poetic impulses. They bounce
off the wall behind him before floating lazily around the room.

It's going to be hard to fall asleep tonight, Jason thinks to
himself as he begins passing out another round of drinks, pressing
the bulbs into each hand. His shoulders ache from congratulatory
slaps. High spirits and a lack of gravity have the other four crew
members bouncing off the walls, both literally and figuratively.
They'll all be sticky in the morning from the globules of spilled
cocktails floating through the room, and a bit bruised from
collisions with walls and each other. It's a moment worth
celebrating, though.

Jason knows he should be as ecstatic as the rest of the crew,
but he can't muster it. He fakes it for their benefit, but this is one
time that "fake it 'til you make it" isn't working.

*I've been working towards this since I was a kid. If he could do
it, we all could, but what if I was wrong? What if we aren't meant to
be there? Should I destroy the engine?*

He'd been so sure of himself for so long. How could he even
let himself think that? But at the back of his mind worry echoes:
there should have been nothing.

He thinks again of the moment they blinked from where they had been, just beyond Mars on a trajectory that would take them through the asteroid belt, to their current position on the dark side of the Moon. All tests had shown no time passing during the jump. He shouldn't even be aware it happened. But the moment after he hit the button wasn't nothing; he saw white and a flash of red. He saw what he thought was a face, and eyes. When he locked his gaze on those eyes the face twisted in fury. Then the eyes, dark whorls of infinity that were on the verge of swallowing him, were replaced with the blank gray stare of a lunar crater. His crew interpreted the scream boiling from his throat as a triumphant shout.

Now, hours after shutting down engines that had just sliced a hole in reality, Jason looks around the room seeing the joy on the faces surrounding him. He doubts any of them saw what he saw, not with how happy they all are. How can he ask them, though, without creating justified concern for his sanity?

Scrubbing the palms of his hands against his eyes until he sees sparks, Jason thinks about when he first pitched his engine to investors.

"Years ago I saw a poster," he had lied from his position standing in front of a screen, trying not to tug at his too-tight tie as he spoke. "The poster said 'Find happiness in the journey, not the destination.'" The words are projected behind him, he knows, written in a curly script overlaid on stock imagery of a beach at sunset. The most cliched of imagery to accompany the equally cliched saying. "But honestly, when you're talking about travel between stars, it's more boredom than happiness found in a journey. My engine lets us skip the parts of a journey we don't want to deal with. We start the journey, we end the journey, we don't deal with anything in between." The pitch was well rehearsed, the engine was real, but the poster wasn't. This tiny lie hung over him each time he told the story.

"And it's safe?"

"Probably."

Jason cringed as he heard himself speak. He needed to pay more attention to what he was saying. This wasn't a casual chat at a bar. This was an investor presentation. He continued speaking, hoping his audience wouldn't notice any pause. "That is to say: based on all available information to date we are confident in the engine's safety. We are continuing testing, of course." He kept his face neutral and waited for follow-up questions.

The person who asked, midway down the table on Jason's right, frowned, but moved on, as if moving through a mental checklist of questions. "How do you skip the journey? Where do you go?"

"It's another dimension," Jason responded, in an offhand tone, hoping to avoid too many questions on this topic. "Time and space work differently. You travel vast distances in no time at all."

Seeing a few heads nod, Jason relaxed. He may as well have literally waved his hand and told them they didn't have to worry about that, but apparently that explanation was enough for them. Then he noticed the CEO, sitting at the foot of the table, frowning.

"How much do we know about this dimension? How do we know something else isn't already there?"

Another be-suited attendee chimed in, looking at the CEO while speaking, "That's a great point, Sir. I saw a movie where demons drove everyone on a spaceship that went faster than light insane." He looked at Jason, face so serious it was hard for Jason not to laugh. "Have you considered that possibility?"

"With all due respect, we are not in a horror movie. Nothing in that dimension is worth worrying about."

"And you can prove this? How?"

Jason wonders that himself. How did he sound so sure of himself in that boardroom so many years ago? The memory of that glaring face floating among the sparks that Jason's palms were summoning behind his eyelids made him question every decision that had brought him to this point.

Jason feels a hand clap on his shoulder, "Time for bed, maybe, Captain?" said Harry, mistaking Jason's soul-searing anxiety for fatigue. "You could use some of your authority to call an end to the festivities. We have that call with mission control in six hours. We probably shouldn't all still be drunk during it. Maybe if they think we're behaving they'll finally tell us how long they're going to have us quarantine out here." The muscles in Harry's neck tense into taut cords as he tries to hide a yawn. Clearly he isn't making the suggestion just for Jason's sake.

Jason forces a laugh that he hopes sounds natural, "Not a bad idea. My mom always told me that I was the first one to bed on Christmas Eve anyway, so why break with tradition?

Samir has drifted over and says, "I could never stay awake on Christmas Eve either. I wanted morning to come so bad that I'd be dead to the world until the sun came up. Besides, Santa wouldn't show up until we were all asleep."

"I think we all know how important it is to listen to our mothers, so why start ignoring their wisdom now?" Harry asks as he is zipping himself into his sleeping bag and tightening the strap that will keep his head from drifting in his sleep. He closes his eyes. "Good night. Sleep tight. Don't wake me up if you see Santa."

When he can't put it off any longer, when the rest of the crew have strapped into their sleeping bags, Jason finally goes to bed. The high spirits, and probably the normal spirits, briefly banish the angry face wreathed in red and white, from his thoughts, but it floods back before long.

Lying in bed, trying to distract himself, he recounts the reasons he should be happy: the test was complete, the mission was a success. In nine months and 29 days they had travelled to Mars, just skirting the edge of the asteroid belt. In one day they had travelled most of the way back home.

Jason tries to relax into sleep. He can't. He can feel his pulse pound in his ears and he can't slow his breathing. The rage-filled face keeps intruding in his thoughts. Instead of focusing on it, he summons memories of sitting on the living room floor in his childhood home, staring at the snow blowing along the street. A hint of the downtown towers were visible, dark teeth biting the edge of the sky. He wasn't looking at the skyscrapers in this memory, though. Jason-as-child was watching the slivers of sky between them. He was waiting for Santa, just like he would every year. He wanted to see this man who could travel the whole world in one night. Beg him for the secret of how he did it. Even just a hint that it was truly possible would be enough to help him on the path to figuring it out.

Still in his sleeping bag, zipped in tightly, Jason listens to the crew sleeping around him. The sounds of soft breathing, the rhythmic in-and-out that surrounds him is barely audible over the background susurration of a spaceship powered down to nighttime mode. Lights dimmed, systems placed on stand-by. Anything to quiet the ship. Anything to make an environment more conducive to sleep.

Jason doesn't notice when he finally drifts off, but it feels like bare moments after he closes his eyes a furious-faced monster has caught him in its crushing embrace. Flame boils deep in its throat as it screams in his face. The scream is dry, and airless. *Of course it's dry*, some part of his brain, the part trained to stay calm in emergencies, thinks. *This is a being from another universe. Why would it move air when it made noise? Why would it have saliva?*

A small part of Jason's mind might be analyzing an unthinkable situation rationally, but the rest of Jason is relying on animal reflexes. He jerks away, wanting to duck before the monster can eat or broil him. Trying to raise his arms, to shield his face from the gout of flame he can see rushing outwards from the shadowy gullet, he realizes he can't. The creature's monstrous paws hold him tight, pinning his arms tight to his sides. He can't move. Panic blooms in his throat, bitterness filling his mouth.

For a moment he is lost; sleep and panic shroud the world in confusion. He doesn't know where he is and he doesn't care. He just wants to survive. He wants to escape the claws digging into his arms, his legs, his chest, and, oh god, his head. Fingers wrap tightly around his forehead. One twist and this thing will pop his head off.

The adrenaline surge that his panic kicks off also clears away the fog of sleep. The monster's grasp becomes the straps holding Jason's sleeping bag snugly against the wall. The monster's screams still ring in his ears, though. Jason can't decide if they had existed and suddenly stopped, or if he had imagined them. The fire brewing deep in the hellish throat is the spinning red glow of warning lights on a console in the next room.

The quiet is made more disturbing by the noise it has replaced.

The only thing that punctuates the silence is a mysterious beeping. A mysterious beeping on a spaceship is never a good thing. It isn't something he can ignore, so still shaking from his waking nightmare, Jason launches himself towards it.

The red warning light casts a demonic strobing within the cramped hall Jason floats through. The new light casts shadows which shift and flow and only serve to make the familiar rooms and corridors of the ship alien. Each time the light blinks off shadows surge forward to eat Jason's entire world. He knows where the beeping is coming from; one short jaunt down a hallway and he'll be there. It's 20 feet at most. After almost a year out in space he knows instinctively where the best handholds are, but the red light bathing the ship recasts the familiar into the disorienting, the threatening. He doesn't know what might be lurking in these newly shadowed corners, so he creeps where he had once flown.

Entering the next room, he sees a green glow. A single green light in a sea of red like an oasis. He rushes to it.

Harry and Samir Are Still Asleep

The round screen of the radar lights Jason's face. A sweeping line turns like a clock-hand running too fast around the circumference, as the radar explores the unknowable void beyond these thin metal walls. Glancing up at a porthole Jason sees a distorted, green-skinned monster staring at him. His heart jumps and he sucks in a breath in the moment before he realizes he is only seeing himself. The portholes that he'd spent hours staring out of, getting lost in the depths just beyond the glass, suddenly seem sinister.

Anxieties play across the back of his mind, teasing at his thoughts. *Are we still in the other realm?* A worry that has no basis in reality tries to worm its way to the forefront. He pushes it down and studies the screen.

A cluster of dots, small and moving fast, arc towards the center of the radar's disc-shaped screen. Each rotation of the line brings them slightly further along their path. A slow countdown that will terminate at the center of the screen, at the ship.

"What?" Jason mutters to himself, brow knotting as he glares at the screen. *Did we pull some asteroids back from the belt with us when we jumped?*

Shaking his head, as if to dislodge that thought, Jason tells himself that isn't possible. The forces generated by the jump would have pulverized anything outside of the ship's shielding. Even if anything had survived, had followed along in the ship's nonexistent wake, it would have continued on the path it had been following before the jump. He counts: eight dots. Then one more appears after the next sweep of the green arm, larger than the others. Eight identical dots and one blob.

Matt Singleton

Jason looks away from the screen and the window again catches his eye. He forces his attention to skid past, willing himself not to imagine what might be out there.

He wants to push himself back through the ship, hurl himself, really, and huddle deep within his sleeping bag. He wants to pull the fabric up over his head and zip it tight, pretend he hasn't seen the screen. He wants to slap all the buttons he can reach until he has turned on all the lights in the ship. He wants to change his world from red-tinged night to a blazing yellow day and banish the fear and confusion back to the dark outside the ship. He doesn't want these fears roosting in the shadows that surround him to drag him into their depths.

Before he can decide what to do, before he lets panic free the frightened child from the corners of his mind, he hears another noise. The pinging from the radar has stopped. Now he hears something else. A scratching from outside the ship.

Seeking some familiarity, he tells himself that it sounds like the air circulation fans have kicked in and one is out of alignment. An easy fix. The knot in his stomach loosens.

Jason doesn't get to feel that relief for long, though. There is no blast of air to accompany the scratching. No draft stirred up by a fan kicking on. The still air feels increasingly heavy in his lungs.

The scratching is still there, and it is coming from more locations now. First it had been just over his left shoulder, just to the left of the porthole he had been trying not to look out of. Now it is above his head, and behind him. It is increasing in speed.

Images fill Jason's head, images of millions of tiny demons

crawling over the hull, talons picking little pock-marks of metal out of the ship's flesh. They are looking for a way in. And if they can't find one, they will just make one of their own.

The scratching stops suddenly. Jason relaxes, until a thud echoes through the ship. Another thud quickly follows, then another. *Is someone walking across the hull?*

He looks up at the metal above his head, peering at bare metal, squinting as if he could see through it. *What's up there?*

A noise cuts through the ship, metal scraping on metal and a deep thrumming that he feels coming up through the hand he's been gripping the wall with.

They're cutting through the hull! He screams in his head, not giving himself time to wonder who "they" are.

He looks around, whipping his head this way and that. He doesn't realize in his panicked thrashing that he's pulled himself away from the wall until the vibrations disappear from his arm.

Reaching back to the wall, straining his fingers as he stretches his hand as wide as he can, Jason grasps at the air, ignoring the voice in his head that had paid attention during training. The voice is drowned out by panicked images of demons, little red imps, flooding through a hole they claw in the hull. Air rushes out of the hole, carrying him into their tiny claws and gleaming grins. Before they set on him, teeth glinting like tiny slivers of glass, they stop and they laugh at his helplessness.

Squeezing his eyes shut, Jason forces his breathing to calm. When he opens his eyes again the imagined monsters are gone and he sees the wall above his head is close enough to reach. Pulling himself along, not sure where he's going but glad to be able to control his own motion, a new noise fills the air. He recognizes this one: the airlock is cycling. The vibrations—air pumps filling the chamber—and sounds of metal sliding past metal, familiar and at most times unnoticeable, are decidedly more sinister in the dark. Sounds he's heard daily for the past ten months are new. Context changes everything.

"Please just let this just be someone on a spacewalk," he mutters to himself. He pauses for a moment, trying to summon the courage to push himself around the corner. He hopes it's just a crew member breaking every rule for going outside the ship and not one of the demons crawling at the edge of his imagination.

Jason edges along the wall, then pauses as he peeks around it. The corridor is empty. *Okay, just breathe; stop reacting to fear and breathe,* he tells himself. He forces a few deep breaths as he squeezes his eyes shut, trying to block out the noises that shouldn't be happening. *I'll just take a look at the sleeping bags. That'll show me who went out there.*

Looking further along the corridor towards the crew compartment, too dark to be able to count the sleeping bodies from here, Jason wracks his memory. Who wasn't in their sleeping bag when he woke up?

He doesn't know. All he can remember is the monster that was trying to crush him.

Jason glances at a monitor; a splash of colour in an otherwise red world. It's the crew compartment, and he can see each sleeping bag as the camera pans across the room. Pulling himself close enough to the screen that individual pixels blur the image he looks at each sleeping bag as it slides into view. *Please let one be empty*. Moments later he gets his wish. A moment of elation lifts him, until he realizes that It's his bag. The loose straps flap in a breeze stirred by air vents he can't hear over the noise of the airlock that fills his world.

How are they still asleep? He's jealous of the calm he sees on Samir's face as the camera continues a slow sweep of the room. He shifts his focus, trying to will Harry's eyes to open. He wants someone else to confirm what he is hearing is happening, or preferably that it isn't happening, though it would raise other questions.

Harry keeps sleeping.

Without wanting to, Jason looks back towards the airlock and the warning light embedded in its control panel.

On and off, another red light in the crimson atmosphere that bathes the room, on and off.

Red, black, red, black, red, black.

Green.

The airlock is pressurized.

The air pumps stop humming.

The radar isn't pinging.

The asteroids have stopped plinking.

The ship is silent.

Jason is terrified.

Jason approaches the airlock slowly, aware it could open at any moment. He doesn't push himself along the corridor, bounding in the air between handholds. Instead he pulls himself, inch by inch, towards the window in the door.

When the airlock finished its cycle, the lights inside turned on automatically, a startling white shining through the circular port, spotlighting an insignificant piece of the wall opposite the hatch.

Holding his breath so he doesn't fog up the window, Jason peers over the lip of the porthole. His nose presses against the glass.

The airlock is empty.

Jason lets out his breath and a blast of white opaques the glass. In the moment it took the frost to spread, he could have sworn that he saw an indistinct dark shape float across the room.

He's frozen, his nose aches from the pressure as he pushes against the window, straining to see past the condensation.

Wiping his sleeve against the glass, feeling the cold of space, or telling himself that he does, through the cotton. He looks in again.

The airlock isn't empty anymore. A red mass, crouched in the center of the room is shaking and shifting. Jason stares, confused, at a tableau so out of place that it takes him time to process what he is seeing. Focus clicks in, and Jason realizes what he's looking at: a fat man in a red jumpsuit trimmed in white is rooting through a huge black bag. His beard puffs out past his cheeks, white tufts visible from behind.

Pausing for a second, the red man withdraws an arm and places something on the ground beside himself. Now there is a second sack. It is small, the size of Jason's fist. It looks like burlap and rests on the floor, as if glued there, almost seeming to dare the lack of gravity to try and move it.

Before he can stop himself Jason smiles and laughs, feeling the tension release its grip from his stomach. He shouts joyously, "Santa!"

Harry and Samir Are Still Asleep

The red suited man slowly stands up from his crouched position, still facing away from Jason, leaving the object on the floor. *How did he get through the airlock?* Jason wonders briefly to himself, before remembering his mother's reassurance that even though they didn't have a chimney, and even though the windows were barred, Santa would have no trouble getting through the three deadbolts on their doors.

As Jason considers the impossible sight through the small porthole, Santa pushes himself away from the sack towards the airlock. He smiles at Jason, putting out a gloved hand that silently presses against the hatch, absorbing his momentum. Jason smiles back, until their eyes lock. The smile slides off Jason's face as sees the same eyes from his moment in the other dimension.

Santa peels back his upper lip, turning his jovial smile into a snarl, baring fangs that look as if they evolved solely to tear Jason's flesh.

Still staring into the room, unable to drag his gaze away from the horror that is distorting his childhood memories, Jason gropes towards the control panel with his right hand. In his head he can see the transparent cover over the red plastic mushroom. He knows that he just has to push the button and the outer hatch will pop open. No air pumps will vibrate the ship as they slowly drain the room to allow for a calm walk outside into vacuum. This button will explosively eject all the air and anything in the room that isn't tied down.

He drags his fingers over the plastic until he finds an edge. Working his fingernail under it he flips open the cover and pulls his hand back, ready to slap it down.

Matt Singleton

Crack!

Santa punches the glass in the porthole. A spiderweb bursts outwards from the center of the window and Jason rears backwards, pushing away from the airlock door with all his strength. Sending himself flying backwards across the hall he collides with the opposite wall.

Heart racing, his fingers clench against the wall, scrabbling for purchase so that he doesn't rebound and float back towards the broken glass.

He stares at the airlock door. If he evacuates the chamber now the porthole might shatter. He'll die. So will Harry, and Samir, and everyone else aboard.

Crack!

The porthole breaks a little bit more and Jason sees the furious face float back into view, framed in the window. Nostrils flare, but no breath fogs the glass.

Crack!!

Frozen, fingers aching from clutching the wall, Jason stares at the man who has graced the atria of a thousand malls. His bright red nose pressed, almost comically, against the glass, reminds Jason of the red button off to the side. Pushing off from the wall he'd been cowering against Jason approaches the glass and the red nose is replaced by fangs, gaping as if ready to swallow him through the window.

Jason presses the button. He hears the hatch swing open and collide with the exterior skin of the ship. Santa disappears, a fleeting glimpse of red receding towards the gray rock of the moon that fills the view beyond the airlock.

Harry and Samir Are Still Asleep

After letting the airlock reseal and refill with air Jason opens the hatch. Even as he cracks the seal he thinks how awful an idea it is. He opens it anyway. A few wisps of snow curl out, fluttering around him before melting into tiny globules of water that drift towards the nearest air vent.

He throws the door wide, and waits. Nothing happens. The chamber is empty, save for the bag he saw earlier. Approaching it cautiously, he reaches down to pick it up. It comes off the floor easily. Jason pauses, a wave of dizziness passing through him. Did he feel gravity holding the bag against the floor, or did he imagine it?

Securing the bag shut is a string with a small piece of paper on the end. Neat curling lines on the paper say, "I've destroyed the engine. Don't rebuild it. Don't come back. I won't tell you twice."

The Yuleist
Jon Hansen

I paused amongst the birch trees, snowshoes caked with snow, listening. Waiting. I checked my weapons again—icicle in my left, sharpened peppermint stick in my right—making certain I had not cracked them without noticing. Satisfied, I moved on.

There was not enough belief in this weary world for us all, and soon we turned on each other, killing to increase our share a bit more. One by one the weaker or less wary fell. The Yule Lads, the Winter Goat, Star Man. In time, only a few remained. Now this season would see the final battle.

I tracked Grandfather Frost for miles before I caught him on the Baltic shore. Hours we fought, before I finally knocked him down and held his head under the surf until he grew still. When I let go, he melted away, leaving a faint scent of snow and gingerbread. Now us two remained.

That night I camped in the forest, burrowed under snowy boughs for camouflage. Still, I woke to jingling bells. I crept out to find a small present wrapped in silver and gold not far from my nest. I unwrapped it to find a lump of coal and a note: I SEE YOU.

I made a fire with the coal and burned the note. "Ho ho ho," I whispered in the flickering light. In the dark morning, sun still below the horizon, I traveled north above the tree line. I knew where to meet him: our contested seat of power. Our holiday kingdom.

Jon Hansen

The short day had faded into a long winter night when I reached our goal. A simple pole painted red. I ran a gloved finger across it in simple acknowledgment. As I waited, the twinkling stars came out to watch. Then, from across the white fields, I saw him approach. "Kris," he said with a wink, blue eyes blazing above red robes.

I nodded back. "Nicholas. I've got a present for you." Joy filled me, for I knew this was the end to uncertainty.

We raised our weapons and charged, laughter echoing across the snow.

Deer Santa
Y Len

Deer Santa
this is Penny i am almost 6
i dont want another Barbie or a dress or candies
little Billy cries all the time
mommy and daddy are busy all the time
billy has fever billy has a stomak ake billy has a week heart
always billy billy billy
always doctors and pills and bills
and mom and dad tired and sad
dad said it may take a long time and mom said god i dont know if
i can take it any more
it is all becoz of billy
take him away
i want everything like before when dad and mom and i were
happy
that is all i want for Krismas

i put my Shaggyteddy next to the milk and cookies tonite you can
have him too

•

Dear Santa,

Remember me? This is Penny again. Haven't written to you in a while. Thanks for my previous wish. They searched for a long time but found nothing. Mother has been like dumbfounded since then. Doesn't talk much, just asks "Have you seen Billy?" and stares at you. Creepy. Even Dad is like afraid of her, leaves early, comes home late, and disappears on weekends. Says for work, but doesn't look at you.

My graduation is this spring. I got this sick dress already and the Louboutins with red soles. But there is a jam. My BFF Becky's dying to get tight with Brandon. She thinks he's like mad chill, but I know he only wants 53X and then will curve her. And I'm worried about that love-struck fool. If Brandon takes someone else to prom, she might go crazy and like drink vinegar or swallow some pills or worse. Take that damned Brandon away, or Becky's going to the dogs.

My grandmother gave me these cool, old-fashioned earrings with red stones. I'll leave them next to the milk and cookies tonight.

•

Dear Santa,

Penelope here. It's been a while.

Well, all is fine with me. Little Kenny is already in second grade, doing OK. Not the brightest bulb on the Christmas tree, but he is patient and obedient. Some boys and girls tried to bully him once at school. Called him a retard and pissed into his lunchbox. I didn't bother you. Becky helped me track those kids down and I talked to them, one by one. She's Special Agent Rebecca Williams now. Still single, still looking for Brandon, still wants to believe the truth is out there.

My husband Jim works for a Fortune 500 company. A steady job and decent money. Not that we couldn't use more. Recently, they posted a supervisor position and Jim applied. Dwight Slick said by the water cooler that he'd also applied and bragged about a friend in HR who will "see to it." Jim has kept his nose to the grindstone for ten years. Dwight was only hired last year but got the corner cubicle with a window already. Jim is going crazy, lost weight over worries, can't sleep at night. But he is too well-mannered and too soft to do anything about it. I'm afraid his heart may not take much more of this. Take this Slick guy away, please.

I've got some savings. Wanted to get breast implants, but will manage without. I'll put the money next to the milk and cookies tonight.

•

Dear Santa,

It's me again.

The damn doctor won't tell me the truth. Never looks me in the eyes, just flips through the charts and tables on the computer all the time. How much time, I ask, do I have? She says, your situation is difficult, but there is hope, so we'll stick to the treatment plan. Yea, right, that means you've got no time left to speak of, but we will marinate you with the chemo, anyway.

Kenny doesn't understand. Says, get well soon, Mom, and

smiles. Jim understood everything. Calls almost every day and always asks what they can do to help. "They" means he and his new wife, Rebecca. Yea, right, my Becky was investigating the Dwight Slick disappearance several years ago. One thing led to another and now "they" also include their two-year-old son, Brandon. Well, at least I know that—if something were to happen to me—Kenny wouldn't have to live with my parents, whom he calls hillbillies and is afraid of. I can't blame him. Plus, he'd get the little brother he always wanted.

This brings me to the point. I can't take this anymore.

It hurts all the time. I can't sleep at night. There is this flickering light whenever I close my eyes and weird humming in my head. But the last night was different. I swooped through my mattress, through the floor and kept falling. Not fast like a rock, more like a bird soaring in the sky. Then I became a fish swimming in a lake. Then it got cold and the water froze around me. I saw dead fish with eyes full of blackness. It was no longer night, but the morning hadn't come yet. Under the dark, aloof sky, there was a black cliff on the shore with a cave lit from inside and full of yellowed bones and empty-eyed skulls. Large and small. A strange creature sat in the cave uttering "oh... oh... oh." It had antlers and hoofs and a man's body.

I thought it was you. And I thought you looked old and tired, like you might need some help. I'll help if you let me. You can keep your reindeers and ho-ho-hos and bring people junk they think they need. I'll take away what they don't want. You do nice, I'll take care of naughty. Together we can make this world a better place.

Deer Santa

Take me with you, please. That's all I want for Christmas. I know it's only September and there's no milk or cookies in the house, but I'll reheat some leftover pizza and I will never have another wish for you again.

Yours truly,
Penelope

The Holly King
Dexter McLeod

"You're not the usual police counselor," I said.

She shook her head. "Does that concern you, Officer Albright?"

It did, but I didn't want to admit it. "Rumors is all. They say you're from Galbreath Asylum."

"Do they now, Officer?" Her smile let my question hang unanswered. "May I call you Dacre?"

I'm good at sizing people up. Her expression was unreadable, but I could tell she liked keeping people unbalanced. Always redirecting questions. It was a good interrogation tactic. You must be comfortable with silence if you want someone to slip up and say something unintended. I returned the favor and didn't answer her. I stared out the window, allowing our stalemate to stretch on for a few moments.

"Now that we've established what *they* say about me, what do *they* say about you?" she asked.

I smiled. She'd blinked first. "I think we both know Dr. Satir, or else I wouldn't be here."

"I'm only here to help, Dacre. I do consultations at Galbreath Mental Hospital, but I don't work there." She fidgeted with her notebook and switched on a small digital recorder. "Let's go back to two weeks ago. The night of Sunday, December 21st."

"Night of the winter solstice," I said.

"Yes, I suppose it was. Just start from the beginning. Take your time."

•

I should have headed back to my patrol car when the cadaver dog refused her handler's commands. She's a fifty-pound Belgian Malinois, and well-trained. She wasn't being fussy when she refused to go further down into the frozen marshes of the Clarks River bottoms. She was scared.

I haven't been on the force all that long. I can only count on one hand the number of times I felt there was going to be bad news on a shift. That night was one of them. The wind had been rattling my patrol car in fits and starts and the downpour of sleet kept switching from vertical to horizontal. The thin whisper of the county road I'd been on had all but disappeared in my rear-view mirror, buried under a glassy slick of ice and snow.

After miles of creeping at a snail's pace through the blinding mess, I had mixed feelings when I could at last make out the glow of blue lights at the dead-end. I was glad I wouldn't have to white-knuckle it through the sleet storm any longer, but I dreaded arriving all the same.

If you could find Castleberry Lane on a map of Marshall County, you'd see the tiny road stopping abruptly at the southern edge of Burkholder Deadening, a sizeable bottomland forest that the Clarks River slithered through. When it overran its banks in the rainy season, the thousand-acre Deadening would turn into a swamp.

"They say it's almost like a body farm down there," Cheryl had whimpered over the dispatch, audibly shaken. "They've pulled four out so far."

"Four?" I repeated. "Are they finding them in the national refuge?"

"Yep. The folks at Fish and Wildlife are letting us take point. Between the storm and the swamp, the troopers are iced out till morning. Sheriff said the State Police Post 1 boys out of Mayfield are sliding around worse than us. Black ice everywhere."

"That storm is headed north to us. The county's about to get hammered."

"Yeah, and I'm sorry to say it Dacre, but you're going to be out in it tonight. The sheriff has asked us to keep the crime scene watched until the weather breaks and the Kentucky State Police can get here. You drew the short stick. I hope your thermos still has plenty of coffee. You're babysitting a field morgue tonight."

It had taken me nearly an hour since Cheryl dispatched me to crawl the four miles from Benton to Burkholder Deadening, and after hearing about all the bodies it made the pulsing blue lightbars parked ahead of me feel like an obscene imitation of Christmas lights.

•

"Bad business," Deputy Keith Sutton said as I walked up.

The wind was horrible. It would slice right through me for a few seconds straight and then fall eerily still. Then it was rinse and repeat.

"Any more?" I asked. I could see the vapor in my breath.

He nodded, pitching a cigarette into the snow. "They just pulled out number five. It's Carl Danby's brother Roger."

I hung my head. "Right before Christmas."

"Yep. Sheriff just left to tell Carl. Bet he's been at church all day today. Brother's been missing a week, but Carl put on a brave face to dress up as Santa for all them kids. Good people deserve better news. Some things just ain't right."

"It's a damn shame." I nodded out into the dusk. "Where am I headed?"

"The white coat has got a field tent down there at the edge of the bottoms. She and the sheriff got it all set up before Old Scratch turned on the blizzard. I couldn't stay in there though. That Barrows woman is one of them, well, you know."

"I think Wiccan is the word you're looking for."

"Well, I'm old fashioned. She unnerves me. Always seems to know what I'm thinking."

"That's easy—football and beer. But they say Siobhán Barrows is one of the best. Sounds like we could use ten of her tonight."

"Mayhap. Just wait till you're down there. It's creepy is all, right by the Deadening. When the wind whips around that damned tent something awful it sounds like a bobcat screaming. And all them bodies…"

"Who found them?" I asked.

"Hunters. Father and son out with their muzzleloaders looking for white tails around the edge of the bottoms. Imagine that. Looking for deer, and they run across two corpses frozen in the mud. The father was a wreck, but the kid will be high school famous this time tomorrow."

Keith squinted as the wind changed direction and swept sleet in his face. He nodded to the west. It was nearly five o'clock and the last glow of sunset was dying. Blackness began to swallow the Deadening.

"Dark's come. You best get down there. You're my relief, I'm happy to say."

"At least I won't be driving in it, Keith. Sorry you have to in this weather."

"It'll take me the better part of two hours to drive home to Calvert. But hey, the mother-in-law's in town for Christmas, so maybe it'll take me three."

He laughed to himself as he vanished back the way I'd come.

I switched on my flashlight, tightened my coat, and dodged the brambles as I worked my way down to the edge of the tree line. The blue lights from Keith's cruiser cast my shadow down into the bottoms in grotesque, oscillating patterns, like a hellish version of one of those spinning nightlights for children.

I had thought the drive was slow going, but walking through the half-frozen mud as it sloped down into the wetlands promised to be an ankle-breaker. With waves of sleet peppering my face, it didn't take long to start feeling the windburn. My beard kept the worst of it at bay, but my chapped cheeks stung.

When it's quiet out and everything has a thick coat of snow, the cold usually has a strangely clean smell. Unless the weather has you congested, a real deep winter can open your sinuses. No pollen. No flowers. No animals. Just that bitterly cold aroma that's more of an absence of smell than the presence of one.

But not that night. Underneath the clean scent of the snow there was a wet stink. It was that sudden burst of foulness you get when you throw back a long-forgotten tarp and the smell of wet mud, dead leaves, and mold rushes out. That was the odor wafting out of the wetlands that night. It wasn't just death, it was decay.

A small clearing opened as the slope flattened on its way into the swamp, and despite my watery eyes I could make out the fluorescent glow of the tent's lab lights. As I got to the door flap, the low hum of the generator began to sing above the whistling of the sleet.

"Siobhán," I said, announcing myself as I slipped inside the tent.

I wasn't prepared for what I saw. Siobhán had set up a series of tables with multiple levels. They looked like bunk beds. On each shelf rested a body, each in various stages of decomposition. She was hunched over a mobile autopsy table.

"Dacre," she said in a matter-of-fact greeting. Her hands explored the remains of Roger Danby.

I caught myself taking my hat off out of respect, though my shaved head quickly reminded me just how cold the interior of the tent was.

"How did you get here so fast? Your lab's out of Madisonville. The troopers are closer and can't get through the storm."

"I was already here," she said. "Got here last night to process a body from a meth lab outside of Murray. I was about to head back to Madisonville when I got the call."

Siobhán looked up at me for the first time, her green eyes magnified comically in her autopsy visor below her crown of black hair. A pentacle necklace peeked from her blouse.

Dexter McLeod

"I'll do the preliminary workups here until the weather breaks. Sheriff got my stuff down here by ATV, but there's no way we're getting all this out of the bottoms in an ice storm. I don't have half of what I need. It all must go to Madisonville. The State Medical Examiner has kept my phone hot all afternoon."

"Do you have enough body bags?" I asked.

"It's too early to tell. You just missed Deputy Driscoll. He took his dog Lucy out for another grid sweep. For all we know there are more bodies. The Clarks River concerns me. We may be searching these bottoms until spring to find out that more victims got washed downriver. I doubt they could make it downstream as far as Paducah. But when the water level drops in the summer months, we may find bodies tangled in roots beneath the water line, especially in the bends of the river."

Siobhán handed me two evidence bags. They reeked of spoiled mud. My nose had begun to warm up enough that the surrounding decay was getting stronger.

"Two of these bodies still had IDs. That teenage boy there is the one that went missing from Murray State University. That man over there is the long-haul driver whose eighteen-wheeler was found abandoned at that travel stop in Calvert. And the sheriff already knew Mr. Danby here."

"Yeah, we know Roger. He and his brother Carl do charity work around town. So, the wallets were still there? Not likely robbery, then."

"Nope," Siobhán said. She turned back to the body. "I daresay none of them were victims of robbery. It's super preliminary at this point, but I'd say you've got a serial on your

178

hands. And a vicious one at that."

"Five bodies, yeah that's vicious."

"It's not the number, it's the method." Siobhán jerked her head, drawing me over.

Roger's body was frozen into the contorted position he had come to rest out there in the swamp. Leaves and detritus were still iced to his hair. I tried not to look at his face. A quick glance revealed his nose and part of his ears were missing. His mouth was frozen agape, full of river trash. His eyes stared at me, milky and distant.

"Ah yes, the face has suffered some predation," she said, recognizing where my gaze had come to rest. "There are plenty of critters in the bottoms who would go for the soft bits. Then there's this."

Her gloved hands removed the plastic sheet.

Roger was shirtless, with puncture marks all over his chest. She touched a large piece of wood that was protruding from his chest.

"This took force," she said. "And lots of it. Someone pushed this through his breastbone."

"Couldn't his body have been caught up in river debris?" I asked. "Clarks River can get quite a current during the rainy season."

"He needs a full autopsy, but I think this was perimortem. It's what killed him. See what it is?"

The branch had been in the water and mud for several days, but I could see the sprigs of evergreen and clusters of faded-red berries. I shrugged, not understanding what she was trying to tell me.

"It's a branch from a holly tree," Siobhán explained. "American holly grows in Kentucky, but it doesn't grow in swamps. There's plenty of bald cypresses and tupelo gum trees and overcup oaks where we found him. Here on the edge of the bottoms you'll find hickories, maples, willow oaks—all sorts of flood resistant trees."

"Meaning?"

"Flooding would kill an American holly tree. They grow on higher ground than in the bottoms. They need well-drained soil and ample sun. The killer didn't just randomly pick up some fallen branch in a crime of passion. It's not a weapon of opportunity. Whoever killed Roger brought this holly stake with him. It was premeditated."

I didn't want to admit what I was thinking, but it needed to be asked. "Do you think it's like a vampire thing?"

She shrugged. "Anything's possible, but if this whack job thinks he's Van Helsing then he's got his folklore wrong. The legends call for dispatching vampires with an oak stake, not a holly one."

"You sure know a lot about trees for a medical examiner."

"In my faith plants are sacred."

"Why holly, then?"

"It's hard to know what gets these monsters off." She reached up and touched her pentacle necklace. "It's almost like…"

She hesitated, staring at the holly stake.

"Like what?"

"Like something much older. Never mind." She shrugged, offering a weak smile before pointing toward the occupied tables.

"Two have undergone a great deal more predation and decomp, so cause of death may be harder. But based on the entry wounds in the chests, I'm guessing the same for them."

"Weird."

"Oh, if it's weird you want, I'm just getting started. The victimology is awfully specific. Check out those IDs."

I looked at the open wallets in each of the evidence bags. "Wait, same birthday?"

"Yep. June 21st. I used the laptop over there to pull up Roger's driver's license. Same for him. Someone's killing men born on the summer solstice. Which is creepy considering their bodies are being found on the winter solstice."

The sleet outside picked up, peppering the canvas tent like a drumhead. A beep punctuated brief static as a walkie-talkie came to life.

"Siobhán, do you read?"

She popped her gloves off and took the walkie out of its cradle. "I'm here Blake. What do you have?"

"Is Albright there yet?"

"Yeah. We're both here. Go ahead."

"I think you guys need to come see this. I'm in grid 6E. Gonna need a few more bags."

I could hear Lucy barking her head off in the background. Blake's voice didn't sound much better.

Siobhán looked at me expectantly, and I nodded.

"Okay Blake. Be there in a few minutes."

•

The wind was an icy knife as we slipped out of the tent. I had dreaded descending into the bottoms, but at least the forest acted as a windbreak once we made it a few feet into the swamp.

Thank God for small favors, I thought, until my feet broke through some surface ice and sloshed through a shallow ditch. *The Lord giveth, and the Lord taketh away.* My boots were waterproof, but my feet were already numb.

I could hear trees snapping in the distance, buckling under the weight of all the ice. Then there would be a splash as a shattered branch would tumble down into the water.

"I hate that sound," I said. "Reminds me of that big ice storm we had back in 2009. I'd get half to sleep and hear limbs cracking out in the forest. Sounded like the trees were exploding. You'd drift off, and another one would pop like a gunshot. I'd go out onto the porch and listen. I remember it was a new moon, and with the power outages it was so dark outside. Might as well have been a hundred years ago. It would be deathly still, then another branch would crack. Sounded like some extinct animal was trudging through the trees, ripping them down as it came."

"Don't remind me," she said. "My power was out for a week. I've never eaten so many canned beans."

There was a large splash to our left. It was followed by a sucking sound, like when your foot gets stuck in the mud and you try to free yourself. I aimed my flashlight out into the darkness.

It was fleeting, but I thought I saw two bluish reflections of my light, like an animal's eyes. Something red lumbered in the shadows, just out of the reach of the flashlight. Then it was gone.

"You see that?"

Siobhán aimed hers as well. The only thing moving was the steady downpour of snow that made it past the dead canopy of the swamp.

"Deer?" she asked.

"Maybe."

We lingered a moment longer, listening to the wind before heading further into the wetlands.

•

The bog had dipped further, giving way to more ditches and tiny creeks that would eventually drain into the Clarks River. Fallen logs became more frequent as the rotting earth betrayed the weight of overly tall trees. What land remained was mostly fetid mud, punctuated by occasional strips of solid earth held together by thickets. The corpses of cattails watched us as we passed.

I heard Lucy barking before we saw her and Blake.

"Driscoll," I said as we joined him.

He nodded at us gravely and shot his flashlight out to the side. Through the snow I could see a dense copse of cypress trees blocking our path. There was a single gap in their midst, creating the illusion of a doorway made in the tree line. The ground dipped sharply just past the gap, and the trail led down into a ravine. On either side of the gap were two pairs of ice-covered bodies, staked like the others. They were leaned against the wall of trees like decorations, human gargoyles flanking a living doorway like a nightmarish swamp cathedral.

"Whatever we're looking for, I think we found it," Blake said.

Siobhán walked over to the men and shined her light on their wounds. "More holly stakes. Can't tell how long they've been here, but they're frozen solid."

"Something tells me we aren't going to like what's down in there," I said.

Lucy barked in agreement.

"No time like the present," Siobhán said, heading for the ravine.

We started after her, but Lucy refused to budge. She growled and barked at the gap like the Devil himself was at home. Blake encouraged her to go, but she popped her leash loose and bolted back in the swamp the way we'd come.

"Dammit, Lucy," Blake called. "Come back, girl. I gotta get her." He vanished after her.

Then Siobhán and I were alone by the gap. The four dead men watched me like those paintings whose eyes follow you. I wanted to go into the ravine just to escape their stares.

"Well," she said.

I nodded and led us through the gap.

•

The cypress trees bent together overhead, forming arboreal arches as we descended into a narrow clearing. It was bordered on all sides by thick stands of trees. Had it not been for the open sky overhead, I could have imagined being inside a building. The snow had turned to sleet again, and it drummed on the rim of my hat. I could hear the Clarks River nearby, rushing westward as it defied its banks.

Siobhán shined her flashlight into the center of the clearing and gasped.

"Dear God," I said.

Before us was a pile of dead logs and driftwood tangled together forming a rough altar. On it lay the remains of two intertwined bodies, one staked atop the other. They were rotated apart forty-five degrees, with arms and legs stretched out like the spokes of a wagon wheel. The men were encircled by a holly wreath. They reminded me of da Vinci's *Vitruvian Man*.

"It's a horrible version of the Wheel of the Year," Siobhán said.

"The what?"

"A circle with eight spokes. They represent the solstices, equinoxes, and the four midpoints between them."

She walked clockwise around the altar. "Imbolc in February, Ostara for spring, Beltane in May, Litha for the midsummer solstice, Lammas for August, Mabon for autumn, Samhain for the end of October—"

"Samhain. Like Halloween?"

She nodded. "And Yule, the winter solstice."

"Today."

Gunfire echoed in the swamp behind us.

"Blake," she said.

We turned and ran back up out of the ravine. Moving fast in the marshes was almost impossible without falling, but we huffed it as fast as we could manage back the way we came.

More shots broke the stillness. I could hear Blake screaming somewhere ahead of us.

"Blake!" I yelled. He didn't answer.

Siobhán grabbed my arm and stopped me. When I turned to pull away from her, she put her fingers against her pursed lips to shoosh me. She pointed.

I saw Blake's submerged flashlight bobbing in muddy water. Its muted light rocked upward into the downpour of sleet, glinting off the falling ice and amongst the tangle of tree limbs. I could just make out Blake's shape on the ground. As the flashlight swiveled, it came to rest on a red figure looming over him, muddy and dark in the pale glow.

I drew my Glock 17 and turned my flashlight toward Blake. His dead eyes stared back at me through the sleet, well beyond my help. As I moved my light, I saw the thing towering above him was dressed in a soiled Santa costume, a wreath of holly crowning its head. The shadows and sleet hid the thing's face, but its eyes glowed ice blue in Blake's upturned light.

The downpour paused and the swamp went quiet. I stepped forward, my flashlight piercing the thing's shadowed veil.

"Carl?"

It might have been Carl Danby that lumbered above Blake, but it was something else staring back at me. He was so still I thought he was dead too, frozen on his feet. The pause in the storm ended and the sleet whipped back through the swamp, swallowing Carl in darkness.

His shadow darted toward me with arms upraised. His torso barely recoiled as I shot time and again into his chest. Whatever blood he shed was lost in the filthy red Santa suit.

He tackled me to the ground, clawing at my face like a wild

animal. I became lost in his gleaming eyes. It wasn't a reflection. They were glowing blue, like smoldering coals of ice above a vulpine snarl. He choked me, slamming my head on the wet clay.

Lucy sprung from the underbrush, clamping down on Carl's right arm. He picked her up with ease and tossed her into a nearby bramble. He reached into his belt and drew out a sharpened holly stake. I had barely caught my breath when he slammed it down into the meat of my thigh.

I screamed, nearly passing out from the pain. I couldn't see how bad, but I knew he hit bone.

Siobhán appeared behind him. She swung a branch into the side of his head like a baseball bat. As it connected, a blue flame engulfed his face like foxfire. Carl wailed. He leapt off me and hissed as he bolted, vanishing into the swamp.

•

"You have to stay conscious," Siobhán said as she used my own belt as a tourniquet. "I can't take it out, Dacre. Looks like he hit an artery. Holly is poisonous, so I can't leave it in you long either. I need your help. Gotta get you to the tent."

"My radio." I clawed at my shoulder. "Dammit, he cracked my radio. Phone?"

She shook her head. "In the tent. And you're laying half-way in a ditch. If you have one, it's soaked."

She helped me up, and I got an arm around her. The pain was instant. I could feel the stake scraping across bone. She used her club as a walking stick.

"So that was Carl?" she said.

"Couldn't have been. It looked like Carl, but I shot him four times. Did you see its eyes? That blue fire when you hit it?"

"Yeah." She patted the branch.

"More holly?" I asked.

"White swamp oak."

"You know what's going on here, don't you?" I demanded.

"I think I'm beginning to."

"Well?"

"You won't believe me."

"A fucking zombie Santa Claus burst into blue flames. I'm all ears."

"Fine, but we have to keep moving."

We trudged through the muck, heading back to camp.

"Have you heard of the Holly King and the Oak King?"

I shook my head.

"European folklore. The Oak King reigns during the sunlit months, until he's defeated by the Holly King who rules through the darker days. They battle at the solstices. One kills the other, one is reborn, and the wheel turns again. Folklorists think the Holly King might be an inspiration for Santa Claus. He's usually described wearing red with holly, driving eight stags."

"Jesus, so Santa Claus is a serial killer?"

"No. The Holly King isn't bad. He's elemental. A force of nature. Perhaps that force has possessed Carl. He's killing people born on the Oak King's day of power, the summer solstice."

"But why?"

I could see the light from the tent in the distance.

"The Greeks supposed the Olympic rituals were so crucial to

the natural order that the gods themselves would perform them if men couldn't. The Aztecs thought their gods needed sacrificial human blood to keep the sun moving. The Sumerians believed mankind was made so the lesser gods wouldn't have to maintain the machinery of the universe."

"What's your point?"

"For all of them, without some human ritual the cogs of reality would begin to wear down. Maybe that's what's happening. The ancients used to act out these rights—winter overthrowing summer, and summer defeating winter. Cycle of the seasons. All that's gone now. We don't revere nature anymore. Instead, we have climate change and pollution. We've spent all this time trying to change nature. Should we be so surprised when we get what we asked for? It's like we've broken this whole metaphysical engine."

"So, what do we do?"

"I have a theory."

"I just bet."

We hobbled up the final slope and Siobhán helped me into the tent. I dreaded the pain of sitting down, but I had to elevate my leg.

She rushed to her laptop. After a moment, she spun it to face me. Carl's driver's license was on the screen.

"We knew Roger was born on the summer solstice. Looks like Carl's birthday is today. Two brothers, born on opposite solstices. It's like Nature chose them to play out this battle, but all these people got caught in the crossfire."

She checked her watch. "Dear Goddess."

"What now?"

"The solstice happens in five minutes."

Something rustled at the door. I drew my gun, fat lot of good it would do. After a moment, Lucy's head poked through the tent flaps. She stepped forward. Her hackles raised as she bared her teeth in a rumbling growl.

Siobhán took a tentative step forward. "What is it girl?"

Lucy's gaze was locked on the table where Roger was laid. She barked and stepped back, whimpering.

As I lowered my gun, the wall of the tent distended. Lucy vanished from the door as the heavy canvas ripped apart. The Holly King burst into the tent, flinging me backwards in my chair as he came. His glowing blue eyes leered down at me. He jerked the stake from my thigh, sending blood spurting.

Siobhán lunged for the oak branch, but he stepped in front of her. He picked her up and threw her into the tables. She spilled to the floor, and the corpses piled atop her.

I got to my feet, holding to the autopsy table for support. He turned for me. The oak branch was behind him. I knew I couldn't reach it.

"The Oak King," Siobhán screamed. "Roger!"

As Carl came for me, I looked down at Roger's body. I didn't know what else to do. I pulled the holly stake out of Roger.

In answer, the side of the tent came unmoored in the storm. Sleet blew horizontally through the gash Carl had made. The canvas flapped in the wind so hard it sounded like a boat propeller.

The Holly King knocked me to the floor, wrapping his frosted hands around my throat. My vision blurred as he tried crushing my windpipe, but I could see movement just behind him. At first, I thought Siobhán had gotten free. The sleet blew in my eyes and I struggled to focus, but at last I saw it was Roger's corpse trembling on the table. His movements were herky-jerky, a seizure accompanied by sickening sounds of frozen muscles and bones popping as they convulsed.

Each time I caught a breath, Carl's fingers slid tighter around my throat. Black spots clouded my vision. Just as I felt myself start to pass out, Roger sat up on the table and stared down at us. His eyes were glowing embers of yellow sunlight.

Roger spun off the table, his joints popping like the cracking of frozen trees in the Deadening. He vanished from my periphery, but Carl's hold was firm. I couldn't turn my head. A heartbeat later, I saw Roger thrust Siobhán's oak branch through the center of Carl's back, sending icy ichor over me like a waterfall pouring from Carl's chest.

Carl's face strained for a moment, almost smiling, and then the blue cinders in his eyes went dark like crushed fireflies. Roger's sunlit eyes died likewise, and they both collapsed to the ground together like felled trees.

•

Dr. Satir turned the recorder off, satisfied with herself.

"Well," I asked.

She took out a sheet of paper. "I see you've put in your notice."

"They think I cracked out there. Too green, some say."

She ripped up my resignation and threw it in the trash.

"Dacre, not many survive a night like you did. We need people like you on the force. I believe I can help. I specialize in PTSD for people in your... situation. Trauma can be tricky, even at the best of times. And these aren't the best of times."

"So, you believe me?"

"Ever read *Hamlet*?"

"Might have skimmed it in high school."

"There are more things in heaven and earth than are dreamt of in your philosophy, my dear Dacre. Let's just say you aren't the first officer here to see something he couldn't explain. I'm sure you've heard local ghost stories. There are other things near these rivers and lakes than the Holly King. We need more like you, keeping the bonfires lit."

She stood to go, patting me on the shoulder. "We'll be in touch. The watchtowers need watchmen, Dacre."

I nodded as she left. "They most certainly do."

A Night of Many Months
C.L. Holland

Editor's note: This story first appeared in
Every Day Fiction, 2017.

He'd wondered, when he started the job, why he needed a belt with so many holes. Now he knew—it fitted around him twice and felt like it needed tightening again. It took months to visit every home in one night and he'd lived every minute, surviving on what was left for him. In some houses it was mince pies and a glass of sherry. In others, milk and cookies and a carrot for the reindeer.

In most, it was nothing at all.

The residents of this house had put out a slice of Christmas cake and a bowl of nuts for visitors. He cracked open a walnut and ate the crinkly sweet flesh, then put a handful of hazelnuts in his pocket for later. More than that would abuse their hospitality, something he'd been warned against.

He ate the cake with one hand and filled stockings with the other. He'd learned early to take short cuts where he could. The cake was shop-bought, crumbly and too dry, with no brandy-tang to wake a mouth that was starting to feel like it was full of cotton wool. Still, he was grateful.

He ate another walnut before disappearing up the chimney.

A Night of Many Months

At the neighbours' the tree was huge and bushy, with the angel bowed beneath a ceiling festooned with red and gold. Every surface sparkled. At first glanced it appeared they'd left nothing, but then he saw a bottle of sherry with a label around the neck. Sure enough it was addressed to him.

Please take the whole bottle, or Gramma will drink it all and ruin Christmas. Love Johnny.

"Bless you, kid," he whispered.

On the roof, he tipped the sherry into the drainpipe. He'd had more than enough and the bottle was a more valuable gift. He dug in the footwell of the sled for a card left for him earlier on this endless night, and curled it into the neck of the bottle as a makeshift funnel. Behind him the reindeer snorted impatiently as he shoved in handfuls of snow—no one ever thought to leave out drinking water.

The reindeer had accepted a single carrot each, when offered, but left the rest for him. They didn't seem to need more, but then he supposed flying reindeer had their own rules.

Europe finished, they pulled the sleigh west out over the Atlantic. The advert had mentioned travel, but he'd thought it was touring malls. Then, at induction they'd told him travelling east to west made the most of the varying time zones, and to trust that the reindeer knew where they were going.

"You are not permitted," they'd said, "to bring anything with you. Only that which is left out can be taken. You are not permitted to eat the reindeer."

High over the ocean, the tears froze on his cheeks. He'd known there were others before him, but no one had been willing to talk about them, only mutter about changing times. As he huddled against the cold he looked down at the water, shining like ice in the moonlight. At this distance it would be like hitting concrete.

He just had to get to the end.

In South America it was summer, and he felt the welcome heat soak into his bones. He drank *sidra* and ate *pan de Pascua*—it seemed every nation had its version of fruit cake. As he went north it grew colder, and he nearly cried as he saw the bulk of the USA and Canada stretch out before him, each house waiting for a visit. His teeth loosed in his gums and he had to suck the sugar cookies left for him before he could eat them. His nails peeled away from their beds. Just before they crossed into Canada he gorged on snow until he was sick. He wondered how many Santas before him simply didn't survive the trip, and what happened then.

The reindeer flew on. The snowfields of Canada were so vast he didn't notice they'd crossed into Alaska until they came to the ocean and the reindeer banked to head towards the pole.

"That's it?" he croaked. "We're done?"

The reindeer didn't answer. He huddled in the sled's footwell to sleep and didn't care if he never woke up.

The next thing he knew it was warm. Hands pulled at him but he struggled away and slid to the ground.

"Well done, sir," a cheerful voice said. "Now you can rest. Eat, sleep, and prepare for next year."

"Next year? I thought this was a seasonal job!"

"Seasonal, yes. But it is a permanent position."

A Night of Many Months

The elves pulled him to his feet and shuffled him towards the snow-covered log cabin he'd stayed in before, with smoke coming out of the chimney and the roof edged with fairy lights.

As they ushered him in, he wondered why he hadn't noticed before there were candy cane bars at the windows.

Daddy and Mommy and Me
Stephen Oliver

I can hear Daddy and Mommy in the bathroom. He's washing her. He does it every day.

He told me to stay here and carry on with my drawings, but I can't. All I can do is listen to them in the bathroom.

He's talking to her again, too. I don't understand the words, but I'm sure he's crying. He's sobbing, in fact, even though he tries to hide it.

I know that Mommy's very ill because he has to carry her everywhere. To the bathroom, to the bedroom, to the table for meals. He even tries to feed her, although she doesn't eat anything much anymore.

Here they come. He's dressed her in her pretty summer dress, the one she was wearing when she fell ill six months ago.

Daddy looks at my drawing stuff and sees that I haven't done anything. He looks sad as he gazes into my eyes.

Once he's seated Mommy at the table, he gets the boxes of Christmas decorations out of the back bedroom. He starts stringing tinsel and stars and globes all around the room, trying to make it look joyous and festive, but he's not fooling me. He tells me he doesn't need my help, not even to unpack the boxes. He even drapes a bit of tinsel around my neck. It tickles but I can't be bothered to brush it away.

Daddy and Mommy and Me

He drags the Christmas tree in from outside, shedding pine needles all over the place. Once it's upright in the corner, he takes the rest of the decorations, including the electric lights, and strings them around and around until it's almost impossible to see the tree itself.

He plugs the vacuum cleaner in and hoovers the needles up again because he likes the place to look spick and span. It's how Mommy used to keep it before she got ill.

I don't help him as clears my drawing stuff away to lay the table for dinner, either.

I watch him put a saucepan on the stove and empty a can of tomato soup into it. As it warms up, he slices some bread and sticks it in the toaster. While everything's cooking, he brings cutlery and the butter to the table. I hear the whistle of the kettle as he drops tea bags into the pot.

Soon he has everything ready. While he tries to spoon some soup into Mommy's mouth, with little success, he watches me, waiting for me to eat.

I don't feel hungry. I rarely do these days, so I leave my soup and toast standing until they get cold.

After we've eaten all that we're going to, Daddy clears the table, does the washing up, then dries and puts everything away. He always insists on doing all the work. Mommy's too weak and sick, he says, and I'm too young.

Afterwards, he turns on the TV and carries Mommy over to sit next to him on the sofa. He knows I can watch from my chair here. Anyway, there isn't a seat for me over there. It's some silly game show that doesn't appeal to me, but I can't drum up the interest to do anything else. This is followed by some skiing from Switzerland, which Daddy loves to watch. Then, a carol service with the words at the bottom of the screen so that we can sing along. Daddy sings in a loud voice. Mommy and I don't join in. Afterwards, there's a sentimental romantic Christmas film from Hallmark. Daddy cries as he watches it. When the news has finished, he turns the TV off, picks Mommy up, and takes her to bed.

He tells me I should go to bed, too.

Once the lights are off, I stay and stare across the room for a while, watching the snow fall outside the windows opposite. The room gets colder because Daddy doesn't want to waste money on heating at night. He left the Christmas tree lights on, though, so I still see them, their patterns continually changing but repeating if you wait long enough.

In the morning, Daddy sees that I'm already up, but he knows that I don't sleep much. I don't think he does, either. There are dark rings under his eyes, and the lids are rimmed with red, like he's been crying again.

I don't know why he's so upset all the time, but he is.

I don't eat much at breakfast.

Daddy takes Mommy hers so that she can eat in bed. When he brings the tray back, he tells me she's going to rest some more. He looks at how little I've eaten, and he gets sad again.

When he's finished washing up, he picks up my drawing things and puts them in front of me, then he gets his tools out and places them on the other end of the table.

He's a taxidermist, and he's stuffing an otter someone

brought in last week, positioning it as if it's getting ready to dive into the water. It looks very good, almost lifelike.

I watch in fascination as he's working on the head, pulling the skin back on over the shape he's made, making sure that it fits snuggly, enhancing the feeling of reality. He sticks it down, matching the seams. He then puts in the whiskers to make it look as if it's gazing at something below it. There's even a sprinkle of white on the fur, suggesting that it's out in the snow.

After he finishes setting the glass eyes in place, he puts on his coat and wraps a scarf around his neck against the biting cold outside.

It's shopping time, but he doesn't offer to take me with him. He knows I don't like to go out of the house when it's chilly and wet like today. Instead, he tells me to listen out in case Mommy needs anything and call him if she does. I'm not to do anything on my own. He leaves his spare phone in front of me on the table.

Once he's gone, I sit and listen, waiting for Mommy to say something or call for me.

It's quiet, so I just sit and wait some more, gazing at the otter, which appears to stare back at me. The snow is still falling, big white flakes drifting past the windows and settling, piling up on the outside windowsill and beginning to cover the panes of glass.

Maybe an hour later, someone knocks on the door. They wait a moment and knock again. I hear them calling. It sounds like Mrs. Rivers, my schoolteacher. She probably wants me to come to the End of Term party at school. I don't like going to things like that. All the other children are noisy and boisterous, especially when they know that there are weeks of holidays ahead without any teachers.

There's another, louder, knock, then she tries the door handle, but Daddy made sure to lock it when he left.

I don't say anything. Daddy has told me to be quiet if anyone comes around, and to pretend that there's no one in.

I hear her moving around the house, and I catch a glimpse of her trying to peer in through the windows. Fortunately, the snow, the misting of the panes from the cold, and the darkness inside stop anyone from seeing in.

She tries knocking on the door a few more times, then gives up.

Sometime after that, Daddy comes back with the shopping, brushing fresh snow off his shoulders and stamping it off his boots.

He unpacks everything and puts it away.

He sits down to work some more on the otter. He combs the fur to cover the seams where he gutted it before making the shape and filling it up again. It would never do for the customer to see where he cut it open.

I sit and watch.

We're interrupted by hammering on the door and someone shouting.

"Open up in there! We know you're inside. We saw you go in."

Daddy looks at the door. He's frightened.

I can't move.

The banging gets a lot louder, and then the door flies open, admitting a gust of wind and a flurry of snow.

Men in dark blue uniforms burst in, followed by Mrs. Rivers and two men in white carrying medical bags. They spread out through the house, pushing aside the Christmas decorations.

"What's going on here?" Mrs. Rivers shouts. "Amanda hasn't been to school for over a month. You told the school secretary that she was visiting her aunt because her mother is ill, but I can see her sitting at the table."

Before she can continue, one of the policemen staggers out of the bedroom. He looks very white, like the snow blowing in through the open door and piling up around the Christmas tree.

"She's… she's been…" he begins before throwing up all over the rug. Once he has emptied his stomach, he starts again, "She's been stuffed, like an animal."

Mrs. Rivers turns and peers at me over her spectacles.

I stare back at her with the taxidermist's glass eyeballs in my head.

I Still Believe in Santa Claus

Martin Munks

It must've been three or four in the morning, back in 1996. I heard something on the roof: a *thunk*, the jangling of sleigh bells, then the slow plodding of footsteps.

Quickly I ran downstairs, careful not to wake my parents. Then I waited by the cookies and milk, hiding behind the couch. The jangling grew louder, echoing down the chimney. Thuds, scrapes. Wind whistled. Dark soot fell and clicked off the cold coals. I remember looking down and seeing how hard my little fingers gripped the top of the couch. The squeak of the leather, the whites of my knuckles. It's all stayed with me.

A black boot slipped out from the chimney and kicked up dust. The red of his suit was frayed, like the hem of a castaway's pants. Colour faded to a soft pink. Not like the mall Santa at all.

The other boot fell. This one had a manacle crimped around it, so tight it had eaten through the leather to bite the skin underneath. From there a length of heavy chain jangled in the hearth, leading back up the chimney. It wasn't sleigh bells after all.

He sat on his heels and stooped forward, joints popping in a cascading crackle. Then came his head, pushing through the hanging stockings, threadbare hat tilted low, with strings of white, matted hair clinging over his face. He limped into my living room, short, emaciated, dragging a red burlap sack blackened by soot.

"Santa?"

I Still Believe in Santa Claus

The man looked up and stumbled. The face. It just—I couldn't believe it. The deep wrinkles. The wiry beard, coated in sediment from infinite chimneys. The shape of it, too—not jolly and round, no—concave, with hanging, sallow skin. He cowered away from me like a dog used to being kicked, but I still caught his eyes. Small, impossibly black dots, darting away to look anywhere but back at me.

He dragged his chained leg to the tree and began dropping beautifully wrapped gifts beneath it, a facade to mask the horror. There came a sudden clinking as the chain lifted off the ground, tightening, reeling him in. He moaned in fear, quickening his pace. He stretched and took the cookies in his hand, shoving a whole fistful into his mouth, then chugging the milk so fast it streamed over the sides and onto his dirtied suit.

A fierce tug took his feet out from under him and he smacked his face onto the carpet. With those desperate black eyes, he finally stared up at me.

He stretched out his hand.

I remember the look he gave me. Pleading, begging. Tears running zig-zags down his trembling face. And I can hear it—the whimpering as he slid backwards into the fireplace, the frantic scraping of fingernails on the inside of the chimney, and then, from the rooftop, that jolly, merry laughter of whatever pulled him up. The laughter that keeps me up every Christmas Eve.

I still believe in Santa Claus.

I just wish I didn't.

Heart of Christmas
Brandon Ketchum

Frosty the Snow (News) Man
@Frosty1

Apr 1
Frosty News Network expose: Jack Frost and Kourtney Clause itemized? Savvy news snowman Frosty with the cool scoop. North Pole scandal—clubbing, party drugs, public sex. North Pole authorities investigating. Paparazzi on red alert. @BigRedClaus, @MrsBRC decline comment

May 13
Boss @BigRedClaus picks backwater Antarctica for new toy factory. Host of elf execs in the running to head the project. North Pole administration questions expansion south of equator. Division at North Pole? #FactoryGate

Jul 10
@BigRedClaus breaks snow for Antarctic factory. Great day for Christmas, North and South united #ChristmasinJuly

Sep 3
Breaking: Sheldon Shakes appointed head of new Antarctic factory, set to prove self in wilderness. @BigRedClaus gushed:

Brandon Ketchum

"Shakes is a remarkable elf and top-notch manager" #MakeChristmasGreatAgain

Sep 15
@ShakesIsGreat employs open office, non-conferences, other leading-edge concepts. Creates friction with old-school management, draws plaudits from young turks

Oct 9
Antarctic factory out produces Greenland and Alaska combined. @ShakesIsGreat credits local labor pool and low overhead. Head of North Pole production tips Shakes to be recalled for upper management role

Nov 23
Bizarre changes at Antarctic factory? Hiring freezes, leaves denied. @BigRedClaus, North Pole question Shakes management style, blame local influence

Nov 24
Shakes is shaky. Antarctic factory production grinds to halt. Exports stopped. Can Christmas quotas be filled this season? North Pole rep sent to investigate

Nov 25
Breaking: North Pole rep's sleigh disappears. Rep, Dasher, and sleigh team missing #ShelfTheElf

Nov 28

@BigRedClaus deploys Elven-Reindeer Task Force 2 to Antarctica to arrest Shakes and bring him to North Pole for questioning. Savvy news snowman embedded with expedition, will provide up to the minute coverage for Frosty News Network

Nov 29

Hooves on the Ground: Captains Comet and Blitzen question old-guard elf in abandoned outer station. Claims Shakes is a "transcendent elf" who has "gone beyond Christmas, beyond the spirit of the season." No solid intel

Nov 29

Eerie scene in Antarctic countryside. Flat, unbroken landscape. No boot or hoof prints anywhere, no sleigh or sled tracks. Snow, ice undisturbed. Factory truly isolated. Task Force 2 subdued

Nov 29

Gruesome discovery! Line of seal heads stuck into frozen ground on shards of whale bone, flanking approach to Antarctic factory. Rows of penguins flayed and staked to ice. Camped for the night, advancing into Shakes territory at dawn

Dec 1

Rabid penguins, feral elves with whale bone spears, rampaging seals, Blitzen slaughtered, Comet mortally wounded, hostiles all around god oh god why why WH

Brandon Ketchum

Frosty the Snow (News) Man @Frosty1
This account has been suspended. Learn more...

Dec 2
Comet and Blitzen recuperating after training accident. Task Force 2 healthy, morale high. Blizzard obscured landscape, @Frosty1 panicked, now embarrassed. No attack occurred #fakenews

Dec 3
All is well in Antarctic, @ShakesIsGreat assures. Business as usual, savvy news snowman tweets from factory floor. Factory cranking out toys at record volume to save Christmas, stockpile for 2022

Dec 4
@ShakesIsGreat warms hearts, buoys spirits in Antarctic factory. Shares visions for future with @Frosty1 over eggnog. Says Shakes: "Soon the world will know"

Dec 5
Slipped my security detail, on the run inside factory. Staying online as long as possible #resist

Dec 5
Shakes a charming monster, rules Antarctic with smiles and violence. Latter implemented when former fails. Seeks to overthrow @BigRedClaus #WarOnChristmas

Dec 5
Mayhem at doll assembly line, body parts everywhere, workers rioting, three dead. Asked who, if anyone, in charge, a walrus answered only "Yeah, buddy, yeah," before fading into shadows. All is chaos. Shakes has lost control

Dec 5
Shakes recruiting troops among locals, assembling ice sleds, seal teams, reindeer, sleighs. Invasion force or paranoid self-defense?

Dec 5
Capture imminent, hiding phone POW-style. Will continue tweeting as long as possible #CantStopTheSignal

Dec 6
Locked in furnace room, given only hot chocolate to drink. Beginning to melt. Lost 3 quarts already, waistline receding, phone in danger of water damage. Minions gleefully applied lighters, welding torches. Can barely type #AntarcticGitmo

Dec 8
Female elves laugh, take pictures, touch and tease me, mock size of my carrot. Force-feed me snowballs, laugh when I choke. Life is hell

Dec 10
Penguins heated metal sewing pins, drove them through my button nose, under charcoal eyes. Try to remind self I have no

optic nerves, sense of smell not in button. No permanent damage but pain unbearable. What have I done to deserve this?

Dec 12
No sleep. 24/7 full-volume Nat King Cole and Christmas carols, floodlights, heat lamps

Dec 13
Snow is our friend, death is the beginning, I long for sweet surcease. Tripping the light fantastic in the end times to the devil's accompaniment

Dec 15
@ShakesIsGreat berates tormentors. Apologizes for confusion, treatment, disavows knowledge. Moves me to freezer suite stocked with popsicles and ice cream, doesn't take phone away. Too exhausted and pained to think

Dec 18
Recovering strength. Gained 5 quarts of snow-weight in 3 days. @ShakesIsGreat visits daily, talks life, the universe, and everything with @Frosty1. Seemingly kind elf. Can he be trusted?

Dec 20
Worker rebellion blamed for factory disruption. Explains @ShakesIsGreat: "Bad communication with locals and lack of department-level leadership led to crisis." Vows to take more hands-on role #ManagementDoneRight

Dec 21

Watching @ShakesIsGreat putting out literal and figurative fires on factory CCTV. Shakes shows initiative, strong interpersonal skills. Led team that suppressed and cleared disaster at doll assembly line with bravery and valor

Dec 22

@ShakesIsGreat leads breakout session with department heads, guides corporation into the future with visionary solutions. All awed at His ingenuity, agree elf has surpassed master, @ShakesIsGreat stronger than @BigRedClaus #recognize

Dec 23

Benevolent leadership of @ShakesIsGreat telling, Antarctic factory runs as well-oiled machine. Humble elf seeks no glory, is willing to sacrifice self to save Christmas. Subsumes personal desires, risking pain/death for greater good of all elven/humankind #HeIsRisen

3h

@ShakesIsGreat shows @Frosty1 True Meaning of Christmas, appoints savvy news snowman Antarctic ambassador to the world. @ShakesIsGreat will defeat @BigRedClaus to win the War on Christmas and save us all

The Naughtiest
John Lance

"Another successful delivery," Mrs. Claus said as she watched the sparkling trail of Santa's sleigh disappear on the horizon, his final *Ho, Ho, Ho,* hanging in the air. Clouds of breath wreathed her wrinkled face like she was smoking one of Santa's pipes and she shivered despite her heavy red coat and thick white mittens.

Beside her, Bobkin the elf plucked an almost imperceptible thread from his red and green vest, brushed a bit of reindeer fur from his crimson tights, adjusted his cap, which caused its bells to jangle pleasantly, tucked a stray strand of his blue hair behind a pointed ear, and then started brushing at his tights again.

Mrs. Claus watched all of this from the corner of her eye. Her lips were pressed firmly together but the laugh lines around her mouth quivered. Finally, she chuckled, "Go on, say it, I know you want to."

"What? Oh, nothing. I have nothing to say," Bobkin replied.

"Really? I could have sworn that last year, and the year before that, and, well, the decades before that, you always did have something to say."

Bobkin couldn't contain himself. Drawing himself up to his full height, which put him level with Mrs. Claus's shoulder, he said, "I just think it's important to be accurate and to remind you that at this time no presents, goodies, or anything else has been delivered. It takes a full twelve hours for Santa to complete his deliveries. We aren't officially successful until his return."

214

Mrs. Claus laughed, her blue eyes twinkling merrily. "Feel better?"

"Yes, yes I do," Bobkin replied truthfully.

"Good," Mrs. Claus smiled. "I assume everything else is in order. You activated the beacon? When I checked the radar, it looked like a storm was headed our way."

Bobkin felt the tips of his ears quiver, as they always did when Margaret, no, Mrs. Claus, smiled at him. To cover his embarrassment, Bobkin needlessly double-checked the glowing face of the tablet computer he held.

Step eighteen of the preflight checklist was marked complete, just as it had been the last three times he looked. The beacon itself was hidden from view by the barn that housed the reindeer. He was tempted to walk over and quadruple check that the blue light was still pulsing its hypnotic beat, but even he felt that was overkill. Bobkin settled for patting his vest pocket one more time to be certain the key to the control box hadn't gone astray.

A jangling of bells announced the arrival of three more elves. Winky, Snaggle, and Grimdark were carrying mugs of cocoa and singing Holly Jolly Christmas at the top of their squeaky voices.

Winky offered mugs to Mrs. Claus and Bobkin.

"It's a little early for celebrating, don't you think?" Bobkin asked.

"Told you he wouldn't appreciate it," Grimdark muttered under her breath. Winky's eyes widened in panic and for a moment Bobkin thought he would snatch back the mug.

But Snaggle, her face wrinkled like a prune and pointed ears drooping in sympathy with her ancient, sagging shoulders, just waved her hand. "Pish posh, I think this was the smoothest launch we've had in twenty-five years."

"Except for the fiasco with Dancer's harness," Bobkin replied.

"Dancer's straps are always getting tangled. If she would hold still, harnessing her wouldn't be a problem. Of course, then we'd have to rename her…" Snaggle replied nonchalantly.

Mrs. Claus laughed. "I agree, Snaggle. I think what Bobkin is trying to say is that you all did an excellent job. Right Bobkin?"

Bobkin slowly nodded. "Mrs. Claus is right, of course, a fine job by everyone. Though, if the procedure for putting the harness on is followed…" A warning glance from Mrs. Claus made Bobkin fall silent.

The group sipped their hot chocolate and watched the last of the sleigh's glittering trail fade away.

Finally, Mrs. Claus shivered and stomped her feet. "I know elves don't feel the cold, but I have to get indoors. I'll make some cookies to celebrate."

Bobkin said, "Mrs. Claus is right, enough dilly dallying, we need to start tidying up so everything is spick-and-span when Santa returns. Where is Frostflower?"

"In the barn. She has an idea for a new harness for Dancer and wanted to start working on it. You know how she is," Winky replied.

Bobkin nodded. Once Frostflower set her mind to something, she was like a reindeer with a carrot—she wasn't going to give up. Still, there was a time for work and a time for play.

"Winky go collect her. The rest of us will start cleaning up the workshop."

•

The workshop was a mess. It always was right after loading. Hammers, screwdrivers, bottles of glue, half-finished bows, and mounds and mounds of wrapping paper cluttered the work tables and lay scattered on the floor. An occasional broken toy could also be spotted. Here, a doll with a cracked face, there, a race car missing a wheel. Casualties of the final rush to get everything aboard Santa's sleigh.

In the rear of the workshop were shelves of backup toys, just in case of catastrophe. No one wanted a repeat of the great Toy Topple of 1888.

"Hey, who didn't wipe their shoes?" Grimdark pointed to a set of muddy footprints. "Where's Frostflower? She's always tracking mud from in the barn."

"I don't know, those look more Santa size," Snaggle said.

Bobkin clapped his hands. "Focus people, focus. We have to get this place spick-and-span. Snaggle, why don't you start picking up the wrapping paper. Winky can sweep up the floor and Grimdark can take the leftover toys to the warehouse. Where are the RELFs?"

Bobkin spotted the two robotic elves, or RELFs, standing at attention in the rear of the workshop. Their glass eyes pulsed a faint orange, indicating they were in standby mode. They had boxy metal bodies, blocky heads, and wiry arms and legs. Each of their hands were vice-like clamps and their feet were blocks of iron.

For as awkward as their overall appearance was, however, each RELF had an exquisitely realistic set of pointed plastic ears attached to their heads.

Winky had built both RELFs, and while Bobkin never quite understood how the machines worked, he found them quite useful.

"RELF 1, RELF 2, help Grimdark," Bobkin ordered. The RELFs' eyes lit up bright yellow and they began clanking their way toward the shelves.

"Oh no, absolutely not!" Grimdark shouted.

"Grimdark please, it's just until we get this cleaned up."

Grimdark stomped her boots. "I told you before, I won't work with those abominations. They shouldn't even exist. They're going to replace us and we'll be doomed to wander the frozen wastes like our elf forebearers before Santa found us. The RELFs…"

"Okay, okay, you collect the broken toys for recycling. I'll work with the RELFs!" Bobkin cried, silently berating himself for his mistake. He had heard Grimdark's sermon a thousand times and knew better than to have her work with them.

"That's not the point!" Grimdark protested.

Her rant was cut short when Winky threw open the door and shouted, "Something terrible has happened to Frostflower!"

•

Frostflower was dead. Though she lay on her stomach, her neck was twisted around so far that she was looking straight up at the barn ceiling, like a snowy owl. Frostflower's thin eyebrows were arched and her lips pursed, as if nonplussed by her predicament.

"Grimdark, fetch Mrs. Claus," Bobkin said.

"There's no procedure to handle this, I bet," Grimdark muttered as she hurried away.

"Poor Frostflower," Winky sniffled as he twisted and wrung his hat between his hands.

Instinctively, Bobkin said, ""Hat on Winky. You know rule #24234."

Snaggle frowned, "Maybe now is not the best time for rules and procedures Bobkin,"

"It's the perfect time. We must maintain order if we're going to get to the bottom of this accident."

"You mean murder," Snaggle replied.

"Don't be ridiculous. Who would want to murder Frostflower? Who could have murdered Frostflower? There is no one for hundreds of miles," Bobkin scoffed.

"Frostflower broke her neck in the middle of the barn, where there is no ice to slip on, or ladder to fall from. How else could that happen?"

"She must have, um," Bobkin searched for an explanation. Before he could think of one, an out of breath Grimdark returned. "Mrs. Claus has been kidnapped!" She cried.

•

Grimdark cautiously swung the kitchen door open, wincing at the squeaking hinges. Placing her finger to her lips, she ushered the others inside.

Everything looked normal. Pots and pans hung undisturbed on overhead racks. The counters were clean and clear, dotted with jars of sugar and salt and a rack that contained every spice in the world. Fresh apples and oranges from the greenhouse rested in a basket.

Bobkin caught the scent of burning cookies and spotted grey wisps of smoke spiraling up from the oven door. An overturned pan of cookies lay on the tile like a toppled monument.

"Mrs. Claus?" Bobkin called as he switched off the oven, then, more quietly, he whispered "Margaret?"

"Over here!" Snaggle shouted.

The elves gathered around a smattering of red spots that ran across the floor and out the door.

"Blood," Grimdark muttered.

"We should wait for Santa in the workshop, right?" squeaked Winky.

Bobkin shook his head, "Santa's too far away. Margaret, I mean, Mrs. Claus, can't wait that long."

Grimdark frowned, "Isn't there an emergency procedure that says…"

"To gingerbread with the procedures! There isn't a moment to lose!" Bobkin shouted.

Winky and Grimdark took a confused step back. Snaggle, on the other hand, was unphased.

The old elf cleared her throat, "If we're going to rescue Mrs. Claus, we'll need to protect ourselves. The workshop has tools we can use as, as…" the old elf faltered.

"Weapons," Bobkin finished darkly.

•

In the workshop, Bobkin wandered over to a rack of mallets and ran his hand along the rubber heads. These tools were used to manufacture toys that brought joy. The thought of using them to injure someone sickened the elf. But his heart hardened when he thought of the fiend that had taken Margaret and killed Frostflower. He would do what had to be done.

Behind him he heard a click, click, whoosh.

Snaggle had fired up an acetylene torch.

"That may be a bit much," Bobkin said nervously.

After staring at the blue flame for a moment, Snaggle switched the blowtorch off. "Fine, I'll find something more 'practical.'" Snaggle made air quotes with her fingers.

Checking that Grimdark and Winky were still on the opposite side of the workshop, Snaggle reached out and squeezed Bobkin's shoulder. "Don't worry, we'll rescue Mrs. Claus."

The tips of Bobkin's ears quivered. "What are you implying?"

"Nothing, I just know you care for her deeply."

"Do I need to remind you of Rule #12931, no fraternization between elves and employers? In the 300 years we've worked for the Clauses no elf has ever broken that rule."

"Of course, of course, I didn't mean anything by it," Snaggle replied.

Fortunately, a distraction arrived at just that moment.

"Bobkin, should we bring the RELFs?" Winky called.

"No!" Grimdark shouted.

"Yes, we need all the help we can get," Bobkin said, ignoring Grimdark's sour look.

"Don't worry Grimdark, I'll keep them away from you," Winky said.

Bobkin asked, "Does everyone have something to defend themselves with?" The other elves, each holding a hammer or a screwdriver, nodded.

"Then we're ready," Bobkin said.

•

The kidnapper clearly wasn't worried about leaving a trail of cookie crumbs and blood for them to follow. Like a winding mountain path, it led them from the kitchen, through the dining hall, past the exercise room, into the library, through the recreation center, and ended at the old workshop.

"Why go there?" Winky wondered.

"It's abandoned. No one has been in there since last March," Grimdark replied.

Plastic draped the workshop's benches and tables, like a shuttered museum that hoped to one day reopen.

The RELF's clanking steps halted in front of another, half-finished RELF cocooned in bubble wrap and propped up in the corner. Together, the RELFs beeped imploringly at their unresponsive comrade.

Winky patted RELF 1 on the shoulder and explained, "I had to stop making robotic elves. Some people had, um, concerns."

The RELFs looked at Grimdark.

"You should have never made the first two," Grimdark replied defiantly.

"She doesn't mean it," Winky reassured the RELFs.

"Yes, I do!" Grimdark shouted.

The RELFs twittered sadly.

Snaggle cleared her throat. "They went in the Monitoring room," she said, jabbing a bony finger at the black door that was slightly ajar.

Winky whimpered. "I can't go in there."

"It'll be okay. It's not as bad as you think," Bobkin reassured the other elves as he resolutely swung the door open.

Banks of gray, dead, television monitors lined the walls, a throwback to a bygone age. Before high resolution satellite imagery, GPS, social media, big data, artificial intelligence, and all the other modern conveniences that now made identifying and tracking naughty children as simple as getting an alert on a smartphone, Bobkin had spent decades in the Monitor room.

A shiver ran up Bobkin's spine as he recalled reviewing thousands of hours of video and corresponding with endless parades of witnesses to build airtight cases against each naughty child. With each successful case, Bobkin knew some child's Christmas dream was dashed.

A cruel fate, to awaken on Christmas morning to nothing but a lump of coal, yet Bobkin took heart in knowing that most learned their lesson and mended their ways.

Still, he had been thrilled when Santa declared the Monitor room obsolete and shut its doors forever.

"This way!" Bobkin ordered. Reluctantly, the others followed.

Reaching the end of the trail, Bobkin pulled up short. "Oh no."

"What's the matter?" asked Snaggle.

"It gets worse."

The elves gathered in front of a rusty iron ladder that descended into a dark shaft.

"The coal mine," Grimdark croaked.

The elves stared into the gaping maw for what felt like hours but, according to Bobkin's watch, was only two minutes.

On the wall beside the ladder hung miners' helmets with huge, cyclopean headlamps. Bobkin silently handed one to each elf.

In the nineteen sixties Santa stopped leaving real lumps of coal and started handing out plastic nuggets. It was, he explained, healthier for the children and the elves. No one had been in the mine since.

The descent down the ladder was hair raising. The rungs creaked with each step and the ladder shook as if it would topple over at any moment. The elves were relieved to reach the bottom.

They stood in a chamber with tunnels branching off every which way, like spokes of a bicycle wheel. The headlamps strained against the shadows, barely lighting a fraction of the room.

Snaggle said, "I don't see any clues as to which way they went. It's going to take a long time to search the entire mine."

"We need to split up," Bobkin said.

"But what if one of us runs into the murderer?" Winky asked.

"We'll just have to be careful. If you spot something, come back here and get help," Bobkin replied. The other elves looked dubious. "We're running out of time!" Bobkin exclaimed, his voice echoing alarmingly.

"I guess we could separate into pairs if we use the RELFs," Snaggle said.

"I'm not going anywhere with a RELF!" Grimdark protested.

Snaggle held up her hand. "I was talking about Winky and I. You and Bobkin will stay together."

"Good idea," Bobkin nodded. "Each team explores a tunnel, then reports back here."

The others nodded in agreement.

Bobkin and Grimdark started down their passage, which

224

quickly became narrow and cramped, eventually ending in a dead end.

Running his hand over the smooth wall, Bobkin said, "One down."

As they retraced their steps, Bobkin heard shouting.

"Winky!" Bobkin said. The two elves tripped and stumbled up the uneven path. They staggered into the chamber to see Winky shaking RELF 2 by the shoulders.

"What happened? Where's Snaggle?" Winky cried.

The RELF didn't respond. Its head was dented and askew. One of its ears was missing and an eye was cracked and dim. Its left hand clutched Snaggle's cap.

Grimdark snatched the hat away and examined the damp, matted material in the light of her headlamp. A single, dark drop fell to the floor in a perfect, crimson, circle.

"The RELFs killed Snaggle and Frostflower! It was the robots all along!" Grimdark shouted.

"That's impossible..." Winky said.

With a sweeping swing of her mallet, Grimdark knocked RELF 2's head from its shoulders. The silver skull skittered across the floor like a hockey puck across an icy pond. Instinctively, Winky chased after it.

"Grimdark, stop!" Bobkin commanded, but to no avail.

Grimdark brought her hammer crashing down on RELF 1's scalp. The robot's ears sprung off and its eyes bounced out of their sockets. The robot tottered, gave a short, despairing warble, and collapsed into a pile.

"Now we're safe," Grimdark said in satisfaction.

"Bobkin, you have to do something," Winky pleaded as he cradled RELF1.

But Bobkin was no longer paying attention.

"Do you smell that? Not cookies but…" he took another deep breath of the sweet, flowery scent. How had he missed it? "Lilacs! Santa gives Mrs. Claus that perfume every Christmas. This way!"

He charged down the nearest passageway, not caring if the others followed. Only Margaret mattered now.

Occasionally a fork or side branch appeared but Bobkin followed his nose, never wavering from the main passage. With each step the smell of lilacs grew stronger.

The tunnel emptied in a circular cave. Margaret lay in the center, a lantern beside her head.

Thick green ribbon bound her wrists and ankles and a wide strip of wrapping paper had been used as a gag. Her tight, immaculate bun had come undone and white curls draped her bruised face. Coal dust stained her velvet dress.

Behind him Bobkin heard gasping as Grimdark and Winky caught up.

"Margaret, can you hear me? Are you hurt?" Bobkin asked urgently as he removed the gag.

"Behind you," Margaret warned.

A giant of a man blocked the exit. The hood of his blue parka was lined with fur and he wore white snow pants and heavy black boots. Grey stubble dusted his jaw like fresh snow on a mountain peak and deep angry lines crisscrossed his forehead like crevasses in the polar ice. A few red and white candy cane crumbs dotted the front of his jacket and Bobkin smelled peppermint in the air.

But what really caught Bobkin's attention was the pistol in the man's blue-mittened hand.

"Frankly, I always assumed there would be more of you," the man said matter-of-factly. "All the illustrations in the picture books show an army of elves working for Santa. Just another lie, I suppose." The man's voice was smooth and mellow, the sort of voice Bobkin could imagine listening to on an audiobook.

"Jasper Sparks?" Winky said in a confused tone.

"Who?" asked Grim.

"Jasper Sparks," Winky repeated. The other elves looked at him blankly. "The famous arctic explorer? He's spent the last forty years crisscrossing the North Pole, making all kinds of new discoveries. I keep telling you all to watch his documentaries. He's famous."

"That's not all he is," Bobkin said, "He's also the naughtiest child ever."

"Ha!" Sparks whooped, "I doubt that. There are a lot of dictators and serial killers in the world."

Bobkin shook his head. "Not like you. Jasper Sparks, the only child to make the naughty list every year. Ever."

"He's *that* Jasper?" Winky's voice shook.

"Yes, *that* Jasper," Sparks's nostrils flared. "Year after year, nothing but coal. My parents were so ashamed they even refused to bring me home from boarding school, yet somehow that fat bastard Santa always found me."

"Every year? No one is that bad," Grimdark said.

"Blowing up frogs with firecrackers, stealing lunch money, bullying orphans, kidnapping a blind woman's guide dog—

there was nothing Jasper wouldn't do. Nothing he wasn't capable of," Bobkin replied.

"Bah, the system was rigged against me," Sparks replied. "I even got coal my very first Christmas."

"You bit your mother's nipple off when she was breastfeeding you!" Bobkin shouted.

"Ridiculous, I didn't have any teeth!" Sparks replied.

"That," said Bobkin coldly, "is what made the crime so heinous."

After a moment, Sparks grinned and shrugged. "Well, the bitch had it coming. Just like all of you. Arctic explorer? Ha! My whole life has been a search for this workshop. And now that I've found it, Santa's going to pay."

Winky spluttered, "You'll never get away with this. Villains never win!"

Sparks laughed. "Have you ever been in the real world?" Seeing the elves' confused expressions, Sparks chuckled. "Never mind, it was a rhetorical question. Let me explain a few things. The good die young. Whoever has the most toys wins in the end. And no one believes in Santa Claus. Oh, and one more lesson."

Grimdark growled, "What?"

"Don't leave explosives lying around. They might fall into the wrong hands."

Bobkin had been in such a rush to reach Mrs. Claus, he hadn't noticed the old plunger detonator sitting near the entrance. Two yellow wires ran from the box up into the darkness of the ceiling.

Sparks snorted. "Ridiculous, really, I feel like I'm in a cartoon.

But you work with what you have." He pressed down on the detonator's handle.

The click of the handgrip being driven home was followed by a howling screech, like a blizzard wind knifing through a mountain pass. Something heavy struck Bobkin's shoulder, driving him to his knees. He coughed and choked as coal dust swirled and enveloped him. Before he could rise, more rocks pelted him, knocking his helmet from his head and sending him tumbling into unconsciousness.

When Bobkin opened his eyes, he was lying on his back. It was so dark that for a brief, panicky moment he thought he was blind. Gradually he noticed a faint glow emanating near his feet, probably from his lost helmet.

Every time Bobkin moved his head the tip of his nose scraped the flat slab over him. Clouds of coal dust kicked up with each breath, flooding his lungs and burning his nostrils. He could move his arms and legs, but only a few inches before encountering unyielding rock.

Bobkin was buried alive.

He panicked. Beating his fists and kicking his feet, he yelled and screamed for help, but only succeeded in nearly suffocating in the ensuing shower of coal dust.

Quickly exhausted, Bobkin stopped thrashing and lay limp and sobbing. There had been no response. He was going to die alone in his black tomb.

Bobkin closed his eyes. There were procedures for everything, he reminded himself, including cave-ins. Stay calm. Check for contusions. Call for help. Wait for assistance.

And if there was no assistance to be had?

The procedure didn't cover that, which meant Bobkin had only one choice.

The elf swallowed hard. He would have to abandon procedure.

Wiggling and squirming like a circus acrobat, Bobkin recovered his helmet. In the weak light of its cracked lamp, he began to dig his way free. Every bit of stone he pried free provoked ominous creaks and groans from the boulders overhead. He expected to be crushed at any moment, but didn't stop.

Time lost all meaning. Had he been digging for minutes? Hours? Days? It was impossible to tell.

Finally, he removed a stone and was greeted by a fountain of crisp, fresh, air. Weeping with relief, Bobkin dragged himself out of the hole and collapsed on the pile of rubble.

He was free!

And alone.

The debris from the roof nearly filled the entire chamber. Through sheer luck, Bobkin had emerged mere feet from the exit.

"Margaret? Winky? Grimdark?" Bobkin's voice echoed. Glancing fearfully around, Bobkin half-expected Sparks to lunge out of the darkness. All was still.

Closing his eyes, Bobkin listened for tapping, or shouts, or any signs of life. There was nothing but silence.

Even if he had heard something, there wasn't much he could do. He didn't have a shovel or a pick, and one elf was not going to make much of a dent in the pile of boulders.

He needed help. Instinctively, Bobkin glanced at his watch.

To his surprise, it was still ticking and showed only thirty-six minutes until Santa's return.

Bobkin had to warn him. But how?

After a moment's thought, Bobkin knew the answer. The beacon.

•

Bobkin retraced his steps up the tunnel, through the Monitor Room, and onward. With each limping step, Bobkin felt certain Sparks was going to grab him. Yet there was no sign of the explorer anywhere.

Growing anxious, Bobkin stopped outside the library and tore the bells from his clothes, violating Rule #21312. It was strange not jingling with each step, but he felt safer.

Reaching the workshop, Bobkin heard voices.

"Tell us where the jewels are, baby doll," Sparks said, but with an odd, gangster accent.

"No, no, I'll never tell," came a squeaky reply. It took Bobkin a moment to realize that this new voice was also Sparks.

With a puzzled frown, the elf risked a peek inside.

Sparks had his back to Bobkin, but the elf could see the explorer was holding an adorable teddy bear and had a dolly trapped in a vice.

"I'm afraid you leave me no choice," Sparks made the gangster bear say.

Bobkin heard a familiar click, click, whoosh.

"Noooooo!" Sparks squealed in his doll voice. Bobkin turned away as the torch's blue flame melted the toy into a gooey, plastic puddle.

The torch snapped off. "Well, Mr. Claws, what should we do

now?" Sparks asked the teddy bear.

"There's a whole shelf load left. Maybe one of dem will talks," the teddy bear replied.

"I like how you think, Mr. Claws," Sparks laughed as he ambled toward the rear of the workshop.

Bobkin seized the opportunity. Ducking behind tables and chairs, he limped across the workshop as quickly and quietly as possible and slipped out the exit into the freezing cold.

•

The storm Mrs. Claus predicted had arrived. Bobkin leaned into the wind, clutching his hat to prevent it from being torn away. Frost joined the coal dust encrusting his eyebrows and eyelashes and icicles dangled from the tip of his nose.

The gale knocked him backwards and sideways and spun him around. Bobkin lost track of where he was in the sleet and hail. The wind whistled and howled like a banshee, but Bobkin thought he heard banging, like someone had left the barn door open.

And then, like a vision, the blizzard parted and Bobkin saw the throbbing blue light of the beacon tower. No matter what the weather, Santa could always use it as a guide to a perfect landing.

"But not tonight," Bobkin muttered. He had to warn Santa, tell him not to land, tell him to get as far away from Sparks as possible. Bobkin just had to reach the beacon's control panel.

The wind tore Bobkin's hat from his head, but the elf took no notice. Bracing himself, he pushed forward through drifts that were as high as his waist until finally he reached the base of the tower. Miraculously, he still had his keys and he unlocked the steel box that contained the controls.

The number of dials and switches were overwhelming. The beacon could be programmed to pulse in any color visible to man, elf, or reindeer and in any pattern desired, including Morse code.

Bobkin grabbed onto the side of the instrument panel as another sharp gust threatened to topple him. How did one even spell murder in Morse code? Bobkin began crying, his tears freezing on his cheeks.

"Come on, think, what would Snaggle do?" he admonished. Snaggle would laugh, which was not helpful, and then she would point out that an elaborate message wasn't necessary, which was. If Bobkin just made the beacon flash red, Santa would realize something was wrong.

The wind shifted and the scent of peppermint washed over him.

Sparks shoved Bobkin away from the consoles. The elf stumbled and fell to his hands and knees.

A teddy bear was tucked in the breast pocket of Sparks's parka.

"Funny, I thought Mr. Claws was pulling my leg when he said we were being watched. Guess I owe him an apology."

The steel toe of Sparks's heavy boot caught Bobkin in the ribs. As the elf struggled to breathe, another kick struck his face. Bobkin coughed and choked. He tasted blood and felt pebbles, no, teeth, rolling across his tongue. He had to get up, but couldn't remember why, or what he was doing out in the snow, or why the slow, winking blue light of the beacon seemed so terribly, terribly, wrong.

"I don't know, Mr. Claws, seems like someone is trying to ruin our party."

"Yea, da dirty snitch was gonna rat us out."

"And you know what we do with snitches, don't you, Mr. Claws?"

"Yea, snitches get stitches, right boss?" came the growling reply.

"Afraid not, Mr. Claws."

"No?"

"No, I think something more permanent is in order. The fat man is due any minute and we can't have any loose ends."

Strong fingers dug beneath Bobkin's fur collar and wrapped around his throat. The elf tried to pry them loose, but the pressure only increased.

"Heh, heh, I gets it, he's gonna sleep with da fishes."

"Silly bear, there are no fish at the North Pole."

"Oh, right, sorry boss."

Bobkin's eyelids fluttered. The world was going dark. On the horizon the elf saw familiar twinkles flickering and glittering in the night sky.

Santa was coming home.

The List
Tim McDaniel

Editor's note: This story first appeared in
Asimov's Science Fiction, 2011.

The front door—that's where they would come through. The house did have a back door, in the kitchen, but there were piles of bricks, scraps of wood, and collapsed cardboard boxes filling that entranceway, as if one of the former tenants had raided demolition sites and tornado leftovers and piled his takings there. God knew why. If anyone came that way, it'd cause a lot of racket, and the junk would slow them down, give Kurt time to blow them to hell.

Kurt sucked the life out of his last cigarette and threw it to the ground. It had been a long night, and there was really only one way it could end. At the time—when he'd pried the list out of Hunter Martinez's bloody grip—he'd thought he'd finally struck paydirt, silver and gold, the end of all his troubles. Instead, robbing the dead Mexican had bought him a ticket to nowhere good.

Someone had boarded up the windows, so Kurt couldn't see the outside sky. But he knew the sun wouldn't be up yet. The house was cold; the fire he'd had going in the little fireplace had burned itself out. Kurt dragged his dainty wooden chair closer to allow his back to benefit from the remnants of heat escaping from the ashes. Winter. If he survived the night, he'd go somewhere where winter never happened.

His eyes grew heavy again. Too long with no sleep, but if he dropped off now he would miss whatever small chance he would have when they finally came for him.

He looked down at the list. Just a bunch of names, and not just kids either, with notes after each one. But he knew it was unlikely he'd ever have the chance to use it. Everyone else—everyone, from Big Red to the corner pot dealer—wanted that list, and eventually they would figure out where he'd gone to ground, and come for it.

Who originally had obtained the list, Kurt didn't know. Big Red ran a tight outfit, and things like this didn't normally slip through his fat fingers. Sure, it must have been an inside job—maybe The Dentist, maybe another of the Little Crew—but once let loose in the world, the list had changed hands more times than he could count.

Hunter, he knew, had got it off of Nucifora, and chances were good Nucifora had got it off of Rusty Ippolito and the Fake Belgian. And then after Kurt got it, he'd had to dodge Yuri, hanging for once with Lemon Lee. Talk about odd couples.

He wouldn't have to worry about them anymore, but he figured Emiliano would be coming along with Lowlife. Emiliano. Why would he hang with a guy whose name no one knew? Then again, Emiliano had no standards. He'd turned on Kurt after the chop shop bust fast enough.

Or maybe Big Red himself would be coming for it. God knows he wasn't a stranger to getting his own gloves dirty, and he had some pretty serious home-cooked custom-made shit.

The list. He'd given it a quick once-over. Some kid had

pulled the arms off his sister's Barbie. Some girl had lied to her boyfriend. But good stuff, too. An embezzling CEO, cheating husbands, even murders. Things people would pay him to keep to himself. The money would roll in. He would roll in it. He would—

Shit. His eyes jerked open. He must have fallen asleep; the fire's embers had died out completely, nothing but cooling ash in the fireplace.

But he thought he saw a sliver of light under the door. Daylight? Was this long night finally ending? And if he had survived it—well, another day. Another chance to get out. If he kept his head, he could choose one, maybe two off the list, get them to fork over the cash and unload the list on them, let them take the coming truckload of crap. He wouldn't get greedy. That's what caught all those guys. They didn't know when to quit.

Another hour. He'd wait another hour, and if it was all still quiet, he'd slip a board off a window in the back, get to the parking lot at the train station, and steal a car. He'd drive until the gas ran out, then find a payphone in whatever town he ended up in, choose a name from the list, and make the call.

Yeah. He could *do* this. If Emiliano had known where he'd gone, he'd have come already. And Big Red had connections all over, but even he couldn't see everything. An hour, when the parking lot was filled, then he could run. The train station was maybe ten minutes away, if he moved slow and careful. Once in the car, he'd stop for nothing.

Kurt swallowed. Yeah.

From behind him, a soft sound—just some bit of soot or something falling into the ashes in the fireplace.

Tim McDaniel

Kurt looked again at the door. No one there, and it was almost time to go. He opened the gun, checked to make sure it was ready. He checked it twice.

A presence behind him. Kurt started to swing the gun around, but a meaty, gloved hand closed on it, inexorable. But how —

Damn. The fireplace. He'd forgotten about Big Red's thing with chimneys.

"Ho, ho, ho, asshole," was the last thing Kurt heard.

The Battle of Hitchens' Bridge

James Blakey

I wiped frost from my glass and spied a brown figure floating against the morning sky. I squinted. No shiny red nose.

In O'Hair we had the best cavalry commander on either side, but even she couldn't screen a flying enemy.

A gunshot pierced the silence. I lowered the glass. A soldier rested his rifle on the breastworks, aimed into the air, and fired again.

"It's too high for you, Private," I said.

"Sorry, Colonel, sir. With us being on half-rations, thought one of those flying freaks might make a decent meal." He smiled with pale, sunken cheeks. The gray uniform sagged on his bony body.

Our army was wasting away.

I raised my glass and reacquired the interloper. It flew a lazy circle above our position. "I appreciate the sentiment, son. But we don't have the ammo to waste."

From an entrenchment down the hill, a few futile shots rang out. The spy in the sky took offense at our greeting. It executed a quick pivot over Apostles Creek and retreated higher. The reindeer became a brown dot against the gray clouds until disappearing from view.

It would report back. General Kringle would know we were cold, hungry, tired, and waiting for him. With superior numbers

239

and secure supply lines, the Jolly General, the Xians, and their Merchant allies had pushed us up the valley. The bulk of our Skeptic Army was boxed in against the mountains.

When would they come for us?

•

"Colonel, report!" General Christopher "Hitch" Hitchens barked. The Third Brigade commander looked to be in ill-health with bulging eyes and a pasty white face. Sweat dripped from his forehead even as frost clung to his cap. A cigarette dangled from his lips.

I saluted. "They know we're here, sir. Eye in the sky. Not more than twenty minutes ago."

"Bollocks! Nothing I'd enjoy right now more than the taste of roasted *rangifer caribou*.

"Sir?"

"The reindeer, Colonel."

I nodded. "Some of the boys had the same idea."

"Good men." He smiled, displaying crooked teeth. "Call a few of them up here."

The captain of "H" Company pulled a dozen men from a trench. They formed a semi-circle under a leafless maple.

Hitch reached into the pocket of his tattered coat and retrieved three packs of unopened Newports. "Here boys, spread them around. General Order Number One: Smoke'em if you got'em."

As the cigarettes were distributed, he slipped a shiny flask from his inner pocket, took a swig, and passed it along.

"General, sir, do you think they'll attack today?" a private asked, struggling to light his cigarette against the wind. "I mean it's Christmas Day."

"Of course, they'll attack." Hitch nodded and exhaled tobacco smoke. "It's the celebration of the birth of their Savior. Peace on Earth and all that rot. Their Savior died for *their* sins. Yet they choose not to emulate Him. Instead, seeking to kill us for what they perceive as our sins." He tossed the butt on the ground and stamped it out with the heel of his gum boot. "Bloody hypocrites."

He chatted with the men, asking about hometowns and sweethearts. And he earned chuckles by reciting a round of dirty limericks. My favorite featured the Grinch and St. Peter.

He lit another cigarette. "Okay, boys. Back to it. The festivities could start any time now." He saluted, and the men returned to the trenches.

Hitch pulled me aside. "Colonel, the retreat is going poorly. There's one narrow, ice-covered road to Darwin's Gap and it's ill-suited for the wagon train. Complicating matters, a storm is expected to dump another twenty centimeters of snow tonight." With his baton, he scratched out a map in the half-frozen clay. "Covering your left flank, upstream, is the 13th under Voltaire. Downstream, guarding the ford, is Dawkins' 32nd Regiment. And your 51st is overlooking the bridge. Evaluation?" He handed me the baton.

I exhaled, my breath as thick as the smoke from Hitch's cig. "That's the only bridge over Apostles Creek for twenty klicks in either direction. Despite the name, that's not a creek. It's a river, deep and fast-moving, where it hasn't iced over. But the ice isn't safe, yesterday 'D' Company lost a pair of riflemen who tried skating. Kringle won't bother to ford downstream, he'll come right at us."

Hitch nodded. "I've moved two batteries of six and eight pounders to the hilltop." He looked across the creek to the treeless, snow-covered fields. "The enemy has no good placement for their artillery. We'll have firepower superiority."

I drew lines in the clay. "I've got ten companies dug into a maze of connected entrenchments, twenty to sixty meters up. Their field of fire contains the bridge and approach. Kringle will have no cover. We'll see them on the valley turnpike long before they come into range." I paused. "If they choose to attack, it will be a killing field. But they have the numbers and they have faith."

He looked at me with tired eyes. "Our orders are to prevent the Xians from crossing that"—he jabbed with his cigarette —"bridge. If the fat bastard in the red suit hits our flank while we're retreating across the mountains, this war is over."

I nodded. Our orders weren't to do our best and bug out. We were to stay. A bloody battle to the end.

•

"They're coming!" a voice called out from the trenches.

Wooden soldiers. Not a present for a child. Walking death manufactured by inventive elves in Kringle's armament factories up north. These ghastly constructs were four-meter-high giants armed with bayonets, marching in unison, five abreast up the valley turnpike. I estimated three hundred in total. Through my glass, I observed their black eyes and painted smiles.

Above and behind, a cannon boomed. A shot landed short of the column, bounced off the ground, and slammed into the lead soldier's head. The wooden head was there one moment and gone the next. The decapitated soldier marched on, maintaining perfect rhythm.

Another shot smashed and splintered an enemy's leg. It toppled to the ground, the remaining leg propelling the disabled enemy in an endless circle, as it lay in the snow.

Not slowed by our artillery barrage, the monstrosities closed on the bridge. At five hundred meters out, I gave the order for the rifles to attack. Gunfire erupted from the trenches. Bullets chipped black hats, red coats, and blue pants. They kept marching, our rifle fire not rising to the level of annoyance.

"Aim for their legs. Focus on the one closest to you!" I shouted.

Bullets whittled away at soldiers' legs until they became splinters. Legless wooden soldiers littered the sides of the road. While the tactic was effective, we couldn't concentrate our fire quickly enough. The wooden army advanced to within one hundred meters of the bridge.

A cannon rumbled. This one sounded different, more of a low boom. The shell struck a goliath in the front row and it burst into flames. The conflagration engulfed its companions on either side. Another direct hit! The inferno enveloped a full row of our inhuman adversaries, reducing them to piles of ash.

The remaining automatons marched on, oblivious to potential destruction. A line of four strode across the stone bridge, covering its forty-meter length with a few strides. We raked them with bullets, but failed to slow their assault.

A skirmisher emerged from his bolthole, tossed down his rifle, and raised his hands. "Check your list!" he yelled. "I've been nice, not naughty!"

James Blakey

The Brobdingnagian foe thrust its bayonet through the chest of the boy. His cries cut short, and the giant tossed him aside.

"Everyone, aim for the one on the left!" I ordered.

Volleys of fire struck the behemoth as it crept up the hill. The torrent of bullets knocked the enemy off balance. It fell to the ground with a great thud. The foe rolled down the hill with increasing speed and splashed into the creek.

With their freakishly long legs, the other soldiers struggled to navigate the snow-covered slope, presenting an easy target. Concentrated rifle fire reduced the three to mere wood chips.

Haze made it impossible to see past the creek. I ordered the men to cease fire. The artillery went silent. When the smoke cleared, pieces of wooden soldiers littered the bridge, road, and fields. None stood.

"We whooped those SOBs good!" someone shouted.

A great cheer went up from our trenches. We had repulsed their first attack, suffering just one casualty. While morale was high, I ordered the company captains to take a quick inventory. The results were sobering. We used more than two-thirds of our ammunition, repulsing the offensive. With the wagon train on its way to the pass, we could expect no resupply.

Kringle had pulled a hell of a tactic, trading his troops to deplete our stores.

We weren't beaten yet.

I ordered bayonets to be fixed.

•

244

We heard the ringing of the bells.

Then came the singing.

Onward, Christian Soldiers!

Marching as to war,

With the cross of Jesus

Going on before.

Into view marched the blue-coated members of the Salvation Army, the shock troops of the Xian forces.

Our artillery remained silent. All shot and combustible were expended against the goliaths. A small supply of canisters remained. Deadly at close range against infantry, but if the enemy advanced that far...

When they reached half a klick from the creek, the Salvation Army broke formation and dashed for the bridge. The believers offered a tempting target. Five hundred meters was the effective range of our rifle companies. But if we started firing, we'd have nothing left when they reached the bridge.

I watched through my glass. Four hundred meters out... Three hundred... Two hundred... One hundred...

"Fire!" I commanded.

"Fire!" The company captains relayed my order.

The first volley dropped a dozen blue-coats. The second felled a dozen more. But their numbers were too great, an unstoppable wave of pious blue. In a minute, a score crossed the bridge. Our skirmishers charged them with bayonets, only to be cut down in mid-stride.

The enemy breached the breastworks and poured into the first line of entrenchments. All the while, they sang.

At the sign of triumph

Satan's host doth flee;

On, then, Christian Soldiers,

On to Victory.

"They're across the ford!" the messenger shouted, wide-eyed and out of breath. The owl insignia on his uniform identified him as a member of the 32nd. "They've overrun our position. Moving on your right flank."

"Who?" I demanded.

"Blue smocks!"

Blue smocks! Sam Walton's men. Veterans of the Black Friday Massacre. Walton, a genius at logistics, ensured his forces were well-fed and supplied. I dispatched "A" and "B" companies to reposition and cover our flank.

Our final few canisters rained down on the blue-coats' inexorable climb up the hill.

Christ the royal Master,

Leads against the foe;

Forward into battle,

See his banners go!

A private next to me tossed away his gun and scrambled out of the trench. "No atheists in this foxhole!" he yelled.

"Get down, you fool!" I climbed out and grabbed him by the shoulder. As I dragged him back, a shot tore away his face. A shower of flesh and blood blinded me. My knee exploded in pain. My leg collapsed, and I tumbled into the trench.

I landed with a thump. I cried out, but no words came, the wind knocked out of me. Twisting my body into a sitting position, I whipped out my knife and sliced away my pant leg to reveal a gaping hole where my left knee should be.

"That was a damn fool thing to do, Colonel," Hitchens said.

Instinctively, I made to stand, but throbbing pain stopped my feeble attempt.

Hitch knelt and slipped his baton between my teeth. I bit down as he tied a tourniquet around my thigh.

Our artillery was silent now. Rifle fire sporadic.

The general took back his baton. "This war is over for you, Colonel."

"And you too, sir."

He shook his head. "My orders are to prevent the advance, giving time for the rest of the Skeptics to escape." Hitch grabbed the panicked soldier's rifle and fingered the bayonet. "A good commander doesn't ask his men to do anything he wouldn't be willing to do himself." He coughed. "Plus, I've been smoking these bloody things so long" —he tossed the cigarette to the ground —"I'm already a dead man."

He handed me his sidearm. "When they find you, make sure those bastards die for their sins."

Like a mighty army
Moves the Church of God;
Brothers, we are treading
Where the Saints have trod.

He frowned. "I think it's their self-righteous sanctimony I hate the most."

He shouted to the other men in the trench. "Come on, boys! Gather round."

Seven or eight answered his call and knelt around him.

"It is a great honor to serve with free thinkers as yourselves." He paused to make eye contact with each man. "The battle, our battle, is not just against ignorance, superstition, and intolerance. It's a fight for the liberty to think, to question and to doubt. It's a war for who owns the most valuable real estate in the world." He lifted his left hand and tapped the side of his head.

Hitch grabbed the rifle and raised it high. "Those bastards believe in Hell. Let's go send them there!"

The men roared. With bayonets in hand, they scrambled out of the trench. Hitch turned to me and I raised my hand in salute. The general smiled, returned my salute, and clambered away.

•

Big fluffy flakes drop from the sky and cover me in a blanket of white.

I'm more numb than in pain.

Nearby, footsteps crunch in the snow.

I prop the pistol on my remaining knee, aiming where the trench meets the sky.

Thirsty, too. Could use some hot coffee.

In the distance music plays.

The smell of molasses fills the air. Gingerbread men! Must be close.

My hand wavers. The gun slips from my grip.

Can't pick it up. My arm won't move.

I hear singing. It's the Mormon Tabernacle Choir.

Silent night,

Holy night.

I close my eyes and wait for the end.

All I Want for Christmas
Joshua Harding

Ben had never slept well on Christmas Eve.

Never a wink. No visions of sugarplums; no long winter's nap for Ben.

It wasn't the giddy anticipation of a ten-year-old cataloging possible presents. For Ben, it was always the anxious cataloging of potential holiday hazards. Had he unplugged the Christmas tree? (Dry trees and mini lights accounted for approximately two hundred house fires each year.) Had he locked the front door? (Burglaries jumped more than eighteen percent over the holidays.) Had that Gingerbread Yankee Candle been left burning all night? (He hated that thing.)

Except for this year.

This year, for at least part of the night, Ben seemed to have slept like a manger full of baby Jesuses.

He awoke sometime around 3:30 am. His head was fuzzy and he must have slept in a weird position because his face was completely numb. He sat up in the small twin bed and struck his forehead on the low hanging eave that he'd forgotten was above the headboard.

He rubbed his head and looked around, trying to remember where he was. Madness and Cutting Crew posters stared back at him from the yellow wallpaper of his old bedroom. As he reached over to switch on the bedside lamp he knocked his high school tennis trophy onto the floor.

He'd been dreaming he was back at dental school attending a class on oral tissues. The lecture hall was packed and he sat in the front row in only his boxer shorts. His professor said, "Ben, please tell the class about the inscribers of incisors." Then he woke up.

The lamp didn't work.

He explored around inside his mouth with his tongue. The numbness prevented him from getting a good notion of the condition of anything. He stepped to the bathroom to look in the mirror and discovered the lights were out there too. He leaned towards the mirror in the darkness but could only make out a black stain on his chin and down the shirt of his pajamas.

He stumbled onto the stair landing, wondering which fuse he'd have to replace, and felt like kicking himself for not visiting his mother more often. She hadn't been taking care of herself—letting the house go, not taking her meds. Nothing had been the same since Dad died. Ben stuck a probing finger between his numb lips to get an idea what was going on in there.

And there it was.

Or, rather, there they weren't.

His upper incisors—numbers eight and nine—were missing.

"Whatha fuck?" Ben whispered to himself.

"Ben? Honey? Is that you?" his mother's voice rang through the dark. It came not from her bedroom down the hall behind him, but from down on the first floor.

Had he been sleepwalking? He thought. Had he fallen and knocked his teeth out? How long ago? Where were they? How would he find them in the dark?

Or was he dreaming?

"Mom?" he called down the stairs.

"I'm down here, honey. By the tree."

The only light in the living room was coming from the Christmas tree. The same white, artificial tree his mother had brought home from Kmart when Ben was five.

She was sitting by the tree, sipping coffee, and wearing her Mary Engelbreit dream wear bathrobe. The pattern had faded over the past twenty years, but Ben could still make out the inspirational quote that was embroidered throughout, "*It's those little moments that make life special.*"

She was holding one small wrapped gift in her lap. Ben sat on the couch, still convinced he was dreaming.

"Oh! Good morning! Merry Christmas, Sweetie!"

"Merry Chrith-mith, mom. I... I muth've been thleepwalking. I think I fell and knocked my teef out."

"Here! The first gift of Christmas!" She handed him the small present.

"Thankth, but, mom, I need to go to da ER."

"I got you the one thing you were saying you wanted."

"I don' haff mush thime, Mom," Ben said as he took the gift uneasily. "I needa find my teef, rinth them, geth them in a glath of milk—dere's only a tirty minute window before da rooth beginth to die."

"Go on, open it. It's all you wanted for Christmas—you were even singing about it in the shower yesterday."

Ben opened the box to find two front teeth resting on blue satin inside. The enamel restoration job on the number eight incisor let Ben know the teeth were his own.

He gasped and dropped the box onto the coffee table where it clattered next to a pair of bloody pliers.

His mother smiled at him. "I picked them out myself."

Ho-Ho-Nooo!
Shelly Lyons

Moments before the ship crashed on November 24, 1992 at 7 pm, Tony Flores, 43, hot-glued the final Velcro strip to his latest invention, an Alzheimer's smock for Uncle Fred which he planned to trademark as "Where's My Stuff?'™. The strips meant Fred would never lose the TV clicker again. The half-dozen pockets were for cigarettes and doodads; there was even a small foldable tray to hold grilled cheese sammies and sodas.

Tony was crackling on four rails of meth, so the metallic shriek followed by a boom could just as easily have been him grinding his teeth. But Uncle Fred drew him over to the window, pointed across the freeway towards Southaven County Park, where a glow underlit the canopy of trees. "Something crashed."

"What? No way. What crashed?"

"Spaceship."

On surrounding streets, police lights strobed as they raced to the scene. Smoke burbled up through the foliage. Tony fought encroaching memories of a napalm aftermath, clutching his head to squash images of smoldering ashes in the shapes of cows and villagers.

"Anthony." Uncle Fred shook him by the shoulder. "Let's try on the Where's the Stuff?"

"Where's *My* Stuff."

"I don't know. Let's go."

Tony smiled, guided Uncle Fred's arms through the smock, then Velcro'd the back closed.

"Stand still. We'll do a demo."

Uncle Fred held his hands out to his side. Tony tossed a lighter festooned with Velcro strips at the smock and it stuck! The TV clicker followed, landing on Fred's hip.

Uncle Fred clapped, so delighted to pull the clicker off the smock and turn on the TV.

Nothing on the news about the crash.

Tony knew he had to get some sleep before the Santa dry-run tomorrow and couldn't be strung out. Helicopter sounds cut through the night air. An occasional spotlight swept past his window. If he smoked or poked his shit, the noises and lights would have sent him over the edge. Luckily, he preferred humpty bumping up the schnozzle.

Occasional power surges blacked out the apartment, meaning that the clocks were fucked and his alarm wouldn't go off at the right time. He had woken up by nine to make a ten o'clock appointment. As with every Wednesday before Thanksgiving for the last decade, Long Island Santas would meet and socialize at the park before two vans dispatched them to various malls and department stores across the island for Santa service dress rehearsal.

But how would a meeting be possible with all this ruckus?

•

Being a Spencer's Gifts Santa sucked balls. Three weeks into the gig and he already felt the hella vise of responsibility, clocking in, accountability. They'd squished Tony into the corner on a big chair wrapped like a Christmas gift, with green and red bunting draped between candy cane stanchions. A sign read: "Spencer's Gifts: North Pole."

Tony, swimming inside an oversized Santa Suit, his meth teeth the color of old papyrus behind the shock of white beard and moustache, had been Spencer's Santa for going on six years. He was too skinny for JCPenney or Sears, and not a beloved community theater actor, so Macy's was out of the question. Also, since he once crashed the North Pole Choo-Choo, he'd never get a gig in the central mall area or even the food court.

A man's hand reached over Tony's shoulder to grab a lava lamp from the display. Tony didn't notice. His dark eyes twitched with thought as he pretend-listened to the little boy in his lap, but actually fretted that his friend Mike's life might be in danger.

His focus shot back to the kid summarizing his top three Christmas gifts: A Haro Sport BMX, a Talking Barney and the Boys 2 Men album.

"You know what you should ask for?" Tony's pinwheel eyes lasered in on the kid. "A math tutor. That way you can invent things. I'm an inventor."

The kid's mouth dropped open.

"I made the world's biggest disco ball. It's in the basement of my building." Tony shifted his legs, made a whistling noise and nodded at the Skinny Elf Chick, who snapped her fingers at the child.

"Come down here, child. Santa has heard you. Did you hear Santa?"

The kid blinked and shrugged, but she was speaking to his

mom, who smiled a *yes*. "Then show your love, momma." She nodded to a tip jar with cotton balls stuck all over it.

When the Skinny Elf Chick put up the "Back in 15 Minutes" sign, Tony bounded off his throne, pushing past the candy canes and the stragglers still in line, and vamoosed out the back door into the hallway network that ran behind the stores.

Tony plopped his skinny ass on the top of the three stairs, lickety-split pulling from his Santa pockets a Spin Doctor's CD, balancing it on his knee, and a tiny triangle of folded magazine paper which he opened enough to dump a bump. He chopped it with Uncle Fred's driver's license, basking in the tingling waves of expectation. Soon, he'd know clarity of purpose and the delight of a well-planned, well-executed project. He couldn't find a dollar so held the case up to his nose and zwooooop!

"Time to save Mike Cheebers!" his voice echoed down the hallway.

•

It's all so fucked up, fucked up, he thought as he clomped down the concrete hallway, chewing gum, snapping the bubbles. Fucked up. But Tony was certain he knew how to save Mike. He hadn't with Larry and Jesse, those poor fucks. But when he discovered the answer, he'd saved Ben.

"Gum, gum, gum is done," Tony sing-songed as he veered right along with the corridor. "Gum. Gum. Elastic lump of resin, of wax, of elastomer. What's it called what I'm chewing on? Gum. No. What's the actual ingredient?" At a fork in the hallway, he took the left tine without hesitation. This was a familiar journey.

Shelly Lyons

Few people got to see this employee transpo network. He'd made it to Sears in four minutes once, but on that journey he wasn't wearing the suit. Since he had only 15 minutes, he didn't bother with civvies. Meaning he had to keep a low profile because if the Smith Haven Mall boss Gerald saw two Santas together in the same place... Gerald compared it to meeting a version of yourself from a parallel universe, eye-eee, it cannot happen and one of you must die.

"Polyisobutylene! Yes! Polyisobutylene and sugar." He spit out his gum so forcefully it stuck to the wall. "Touchdown!"

Tony popped another piece into his nasty mouth. Would he make it to Sears's Santa's Village before Mike Cheebers exploded? Mike was a cool guy, part-time electrician, part-time dad, and, like Tony, a part-time Santa. He used to ride the speed rails to crazy town, too, but Mike went clean last Christmas-in-July. It was a rotten thing Tony was gonna demand Mike do. But if his theory was correct, it would benefit mankind.

He hooked a left into another long hallway that smelled of grease traps and bleach. Down at the end, a woman smoking a cigarette sat on steps leading up to the back door of Wicks and Sticks candle shop.

As he got closer, grease and bleach smells were replaced by candy apple perfume and menthol cigarettes. Helena. Helena, who only fucked Tony during Christmas in July and the official holiday season, and then only when Tony wore his Santa suit.

"Hey, Santa," Helena said in a chain-smoking middle-aged woman's baby voice. "I let my relatives buy candles with employee discounts, so I guess that puts me on the naughty list." She unfurled crepey legs so he could see up her skirt. No underpants. Schwing!

Not now, he told himself.

"I need a favor. First I gotta use the—" a jerk of his head and a three-part whistle indicated the bathroom inside the store.

"Sorry, the mamaws shopping for Christmas candles are in no way prepared for your stank."

"Fine, I'll wait till Sears. What I really need is some of your Dexatrim."

"Why do you need a diet pill? You seem to be doing okay."

"I need extra. For Mike Cheebers. If he doesn't—listen, woman, I don't have time to explain, but I need about five, please."

"Okay, you owe me." She dug through her fanny pack, pulled out a silver sheet with three pills encased in plastic. "That's what I got."

"Thanks." He made fish lips at her until she stuck the menthol in his mouth. After a long, sexy drag, he told her on the exhale: "Stay away from Sears today."

"Yes, Santa."

"Don't be naughty. Seriously, Helena. Not on this one."

"Jeez, whatever, fine."

And laying his finger aside of his nose, he winked, then split.

•

Sears were dicks about keeping their doors locked, except behind the Notions department, which was sort of like Spencer's gifts, minus the whimsy.

Tony burst inside, acclimated himself. The low hum he always heard at Sears threatened as usual to make him buggy. "Gotta get to Mike," he repeated to himself as he jogged over to the escalators.

Children clapped and cooed as he passed. Several parents frowned at the raggedy ass Santa mumbling to himself.

Tony perceived nothing except the path he had to take to get to Mike Cheebers. But his thoughts circled back to when he first saw Them, to what They could do, and how They might be defeated.

•

When the Santas gathered outside the park at 10 a.m. on Wednesday, November 25, wind gusts and clouds swirled through air still choking on smoke. The official word was that a small plane had missed the nearby Brookhaven Calabro airport and crashed into the park. The unofficial word cited a UFO or a research something-or-other being test-flown by the nearby Brookhaven National Laboratory.

Tony had no opinion, content to enjoy the reunion with his fellow Santas, most holding bottles of choice whiskey he could sample to dull the edges of his adrenaline. Nobody was around to tell the Santas that drinking in public was a no-no.

Queer movement in the bushes caught Tony's eye, but he chalked it up to the floaters he'd sometimes get in his eyes—until it got too frenetic to ignore.

When Jesse hit the punchline on his yearly joke—"...and she says, 'Hey Santa, you gonna *come* down my chimney?'—Tony slipped away from the group for a closer look.

Hovering before him, maybe four inches tall, was a group of critters resembling earwigs with pincers on their bellies. They unfolded membranous wings, rising in group formation above the apex of his velour Santa hat, then above the street lamp. A low hum intensified, giving him shivers, and then the creatures swooped towards the Santas, fanning out for one-on-one assaults —at which point Tony yelped.

A creature flew into his mouth. Its pincers scraped down his throat, and he felt it swimming into his stomach. No amount of gagging or coughing stopped its journey into the intestines. Once there, Tony felt it enlarge. Or was it just flapping its skin wings?

All the other Santas were bent over coughing and retching. But within a minute, every one of them straightened up, dazed. Nobody had an explanation or a theory. By this time, the two vans had arrived.

The ride to the mall was quiet, tense. Tony, stomach grumbling, and running a low temperature, thought the locusts or whatever the hell those things were had made him sick, so he kept himself clean from that day all the way until December 4, when he gave in and scored some good stuff from a food court janitor. The stomach issues weren't going away, so why not, he'd thought.

Armed with his new score, he skulked into the handicapped stall where he chopped and refined two rails on top of the toilet tank. He snorted the first bump, but instead of euphoria, felt a massive rumbling in his intestines. A rip and a stab. A toot out the poot, followed by a mightier cheek flapper and light blood spray. As a finale, something nearly a foot long tore out of his rectum and plunked into the toilet. "Ow, ow, ow!"

Tony jumped off the seat, reached for the flusher. That motherfucking earwig-looking exoskeleton with pincers had gotten bigger in the last week. But the most remarkable change was how its face had become less insectoid and more a gooey, nascent version of Tony's.

"Holy fuck!" Tony flushed, but the swirling water only buoyed the creature! Pincers clambered up over the seat and the wings flopped the body onto Tony's second rail.

"What? No!" came the crestfallen wail of a tweaker losing his stash.

Smoke billowed out from its underside as the creature spasmed, before tumbling dead onto dirty tiles. A strip of exo-skeleton was still burning where it'd landed on the rail.

At the time Tony didn't make the connection. More than a week later he heard about Jesse's body tearing apart when a creature expelled itself from its human cocoon, through organs and flesh. The police had no idea what to call it, so the story became 'spontaneous combustion,' and Jesse, a lonely alcoholic without kin, was cremated. Tony noted that Jesse didn't do speed. It was when Tony heard about clean-living Larry having a similar end to Jesse's, with a similar story from the authorities, that his hypothesis developed: The alien bugs no bueno'd speed.

Tony tested his theory on Ben Jackson by suggesting a two-dude party that included a snort or eight. Somewhere around 2 a.m., Ben's face got wonky and he sprinted into his bathroom.

Five minutes of moaning and crying passed before Tony put his ear to the door. "You okay, pal?"

Stomping sounds were his reply; then a pale, sweaty Ben peeked out. "Come look at this."

Splattered on the bathroom rug with a boot mark on its belly was an ailing insect critter.

"I had one of those. Smaller, though," said Tony.

It raised its tiny head, showing a face covered in mocha-colored flesh matching Ben's, and the same spate of black freckles. "We are coming. We grow inside you. We grow into you."

Tony flicked some speed at its body, sizzling it like a slug covered in salt. "I'm telling you, Ben, speed saves."

•

"Psst, psst, elf, elf..." Tony crouched behind a Christmas tree near Santa's Village where Mike had no less than 25 kids and their parents waiting in a line that snaked from Santa's throne all the way over to Kitchen Essentials.

The elf, a jockey-sized man with a shock of red hair, shushed him.

"Dude, you gotta send Mike on break."

"You can't be seen here," the Elf hissed.

"It's life or death!"

A few parents rubbernecked. A kid pointed at him and cried, "Santa!"

Other small children noticed Tony and clamored. Gerald, who like every movie psycho had a near-supernatural knack for appearing at the exact wrong moment, spotted him all the way from the vacuum displays and barked, "Flores!"

So caught, Tony went for it. "Mike! Mike! I need to talk to you!" He ran up the line, smacking away the groping hands of children on his way. "It's a matter of life or—"

Store security grabbed him by the back of his suit. But they couldn't lock on to Tony's body, which still propelled forward, bursting through the front of the suit—which Tony had redesigned in Velcro so he could tear it off when Helena was on the Naughty List. In underpants and Santa boots, Tony squirmed through the security guard's meaty hands and popped to his feet.

The crowd gave him a wide berth as he charged up the candy cane path, yelling, "Speed is the answer, dude! Speed is the answer." He tried and failed to hurdle the snow-topped gates to the Santa area, smacking face first into a herd of plastic reindeer.

Mike Cheebers, using his decades of community theater experience and his most sonorous voice, told the kids and families: "Please everyone, some elves are naughty elves and try to pretend to be Santa. But Santa will deal with this one, and it'll all turn out okay. If everybody returns in half an hour, Santa promises to listen to all your wishes."

Those were the final words Mike Cheebers ever spoke. In the next second, the poor bastard detonated, spraying everyone with red velour and chunks of flesh and innards.

A three-foot tall version of himself emerged from the entrails. Naked, shiny with viscera, it squawked at the crowd: "You are vessels!"

A din of outcries glutted Tony's ears as he extricated himself from the reindeer. Too late for the Dexatrim, he thought, pulling out his magazine paper triangle and wondering how much he'd need to shake over the new Mike Cheebers, who darted through the crowd, squirting earwigs out his ass. The legions of babies spread their membranous wings and shot into the noses of parents, kids, elves, Gerald, and Tony himself.

"It's gonna take a lot of meth to save these poor fuckers," were Tony's thoughts as he pinched a bump straight up his nose. Meanwhile, the Mike Cheebers thing tried to ascend the Down Escalator, shrieking in frustration.

With all the mayhem blinking and screaming around him, Tony Flores might have been staggering through the burning village after a few of his compadres lost their minds and became vengeful gods of democracy.

He entered bathrooms behind the Missus section changing rooms. Here, he'd wait for his ass to burp out the monster while deciding which authorities should be informed of his discovery: that only methylamphetamine could stop the aliens from body-snatching the world.

About the Contributors

Sam Agro
Artist, "Harry and Samir Are Still Asleep", "Have a Holly, Jolly Nuclear Winter", "The Holly King", "I Still Believe in Santa Claus", "The Santas", and "Snowman"
Sam Agro is a cartoonist, writer, illustrator, and sometime performer. He creates storyboards for both live-action and animation media, including such projects as Paw Patrol, Bunsen is a Beast, Fly Away Home, and several instalments of the SAW movie franchise. He also dabbles away at the fringes of the comic book industry, writes short horror fiction, and is a frequent essayist on pop culture subjects. Sam makes his home in Toronto with his wife, Beth, and their neurotic cat, Little V.

James Blakey
Author, "The Battle of Hitchens' Bridge"
James Blakey lives in the Shenandoah Valley where he writes mostly full-time. His story "The Bicycle Thief" won a 2019 Derringer Award. When James isn't writing, he can be found on the hiking trail—he's climbed forty of the fifty US state high points—or bike-camping his way up and down the East Coast. Find him at www.JamesBlakeyWrites.com.

Rhian Bowley
Author, *"Frankenclaus"*
Rhian Bowley is a Welsh writer, runner, gardener and cat slave, not in that order. She sees you when you're sleeping and she knows when you're awake. Find more of her fiction at www.rhianbowley.com

266

Warren Brown
Author, "The Night Before X-Mas"
Warren Brown is a dual Canadian/American citizen and currently lives and writes fiction and poetry in Tulsa OK. He has published fiction in *OMNI, F&SF, Amazing, The Book of All Flesh* (with Lana Brown) and other venues, and poetry in *This Land, Nimrod, Dear Leader Tales, Speculative North, Smoke in the Stars,* etc. His novel, "What Happened in Fool the Eye" is available on Amazon and Barnes and Noble websites. He is a member of SFWA and SFPA.

http://warrenbrown.synthasite.com/

Carson Buckingham
Author, "The Child"
Carson Buckingham knew from childhood that she wanted to be a writer and began, at age six, by writing books of her own, hand-drawing covers, and selling them to any family member who would pay (usually a dime) for what she referred to as "classic literature." When she ran out of relatives, she came to the conclusion that there was no real money to be made in self-publishing, so she studied writing and read voraciously for the next eighteen years, while simultaneously collecting enough rejection slips to re-paper her living room… twice.

When her landlord chucked her out for, in his words, "making the apartment into one hell of a downer," she redoubled her efforts, and collected four times the rejection slips in half the time, single-handedly causing the first paper shortage in U.S. history.

But she persevered, improved greatly over the years, and here we are.

About the Contributors

Carson Buckingham has been/is a professional proofreader, editor, newspaper reporter, copywriter, technical writer, novelist, short story writer, book reviewer, editor, blogger, and comedy writer. Besides writing, she loves reading, cooking and gardening; but not at the same time. Though born and raised in Connecticut, she lives in Kentucky now—and Connecticut is glad to be rid of her!

Chris Campeau
Author, "All Alone on Christmas"
Chris Campeau is a senior copywriter and author of short horror fiction and creative nonfiction. His work has been featured in the *Globe and Mail, 34 Orchard, Parhelion Literary,* and more. He lives in Ottawa, Canada, and is an affiliate member of the Horror Writers Association. Find him at chriscampeau.com.

Sarah Crabtree
Author, "Boat on the Bay"
Sarah Crabtree is a UK based writer. She has two books of short stories for adults, and two children's picture books available on Amazon, along with a non-fiction light-hearted guide for aspiring writers. Sarah is currently working on another short story collection for adults.

Jon Hansen
Author, "The Yuleist"
JON HANSEN is a writer, former librarian, and occasional blood donor. He lives about fifty feet from Boston with his wife, son, and three pushy cats. His short fiction and poetry have appeared in a variety of places, including *Strange Horizons, Daily Science Fiction,* and *Lady Churchill's Rosebud Quarterly.* He is, like so many these days, working on a novel. View his website at www.logicalcreativity.com/jon, or share your opinions at him on Twitter (@jonmhansen). He likes tea and cheese.

Joshua Harding
Author, "All I Want for Christmas"
Joshua Harding is an award-winning novelist and short story writer. His fiction is featured in *Writer's Digest, Acidic Fiction,* and *the museum of americana.* He's been a nuclear missile mechanic, an environmental lobbyist, a cemetery restorer, freelance artist, puppet master, set designer, actor, carpenter, mortuary officer, garbage man, you name it. The only thing he's done longer than anything is write. He lives in a four-person artists' colony in the woods north of Chicago.

C.L. Holland
Author, "A Night of Many Months"
C.L. Holland is a British science fiction and fantasy writer, and has been published in magazines and anthologies such as *Daily Science Fiction, Cats in Space,* and *Nature Futures.* When not working or writing she can be found playing computer games and tabletop RPGs, or reading about history and folklore. Sometimes she serves as furniture for her cats and has the scars to prove it. She can be found browsing Twitter as @clhollandwriter, and her website is https://clholland.weebly.com/.

Stephen Howard
Author, "Satan's Whispers"
Stephen Howard is an English novelist and short story writer from Manchester. His work has been published by Lost Boys Press, Scribble, and Ghost Orchid Press, among others. He now lives next to a graveyard in Cheshire with his fiancée, Rachel, and their demonic cat, Leo.

Brandon Ketchum
Author, "Heart of Christmas"
Brandon Ketchum is a speculative fiction writer from Pittsburgh, PA who enjoys putting a weird spin or strange vibe into every

About the Contributors

story, dark or light. Brandon is a member of the Horror Writers Association. His work has been published with *Air & Nothingness Press, Perihelion, Mad Scientist Journal,* and many other publications, and has won Writers of the Future contest honorable mentions. Brandon leads the Pittsburgh Writers Meetup Group, and coordinated the 2019 PARSEC Short Story Contest.

John Lance
Author, "The Naughtiest"
John Lance lives in New England with his lovely wife and daughters. He enjoys spending time with his family, reading, writing, and working in his garden. His stories have appeared in *Crunchy with Ketchup, Raygun Retro,* and *Misunderstood.*

Y Len
Author, "Deer Santa"
Y. Len is the pen name for a beginning author who, as a child, spent more time reading than talking. Nowadays, reading often gives way to writing, fishing, cooking and/or eating, while talking remains the least favorite activity. In 2020, Y. Len received an honorable mention from the Writers of the Future contest and, in 2021, sold the first story to the TdotSpec magazine.

Alice Loweecey
Author, "Red Grow the Rushes, O!"
Baker of brownies and tormenter of characters, Alice Loweecey always celebrates the day she jumped the wall (code for kicking the habit of a nun). She grew up watching Hammer horror films and Scooby-Doo mysteries, which explains a whole lot. As herself, she has 9 mysteries in her "Giulia Driscoll P.I." series and several anthologized short stories. As her alter-ego Kate Morgan, she has 3 stand-alone horror novels.

Shelly Lyons
Author, "Ho-Ho-Nooo!"
This Hollywood townie wrote a bunch of marketing verbiage and horror screenplays before reinventing herself as a narrative prose writer. Her horror/sci-fi novel, "Like Real," will enter the world via Perpetual Motion Machine Publishing in 2022. She would be delighted to discuss old made-for-TV horror films and thrillers with you.

Andrew Majors
Author, "The Island in the North"
Andrew Majors is a writer of fantasy, sci-fi, horror and weird fiction. Apart from the story in this collection, he has also been published in tdotSpec's *Strange Religion* anthology with the story "The Gods Also Duel", along with stories to *34Orchard* and *Cirsova*. He lives near Boise, Idaho. You can find his work at andrewmajors.wordpress.com.

Marco Marin
Artist, "The Battle of Hitchens' Bridge" and "Red Grow the Rushes, O!"
A Fantasy Painter and a Creature Breeder, those are the titles I want to be remembered for. I have a driving passion to create worlds, creatures and characters, bringing them to life through artistic visualization. I am passionate about videogames, card games, movies, cartoons, books and anywhere where the ringing bells of fantasy echo. Working with likeminded people gathering in teams and putting our energy together to flush out worlds and create universes of wonder is my desire. I want to meet people whose talents and driving passions can complement, challenge and nourish a wonderful narrative. If you are looking for someone who is passionate, borderline obsessive, incisive and with a loving approach to teamwork, look no further. I am your Fantasy Painter and your Creature breeder. https://ulmo88.artstation.com/

About the Contributors

Tim McDaniel
Author, "The List"
Tim McDaniel teaches English as a Second Language at Green River College, not far from Seattle. His short stories, mostly comedic, have appeared in a number of SF/F magazines, including *F&SF, Analog,* and *Asimov's.* He lives with his wife, dog, and cat, and his collection of plastic dinosaurs is the envy of all who encounter it. His author page at Amazon.com is https://www.amazon.com/author/tim-mcdaniel and many of his stories are available at Simily.co.

Dexter McLeod
Author, "The Holly King"
Dexter McLeod is an author from Kentucky who writes in the darker shades of Southern Gothic, folk and cosmic horror, science fiction, and the New Weird. His writing is available at *The Other Stories* from British publisher Hawk & Cleaver, and in *Upon A Thrice Time*, a fairy tale themed anthology from Pittsburgh's Air & Nothingness Press. You can follow him on Twitter at @DexterMcLeod.

Donna J. W. Munro
Author, "Santa's Little Helpers"
Donna J. W. Munro's pieces are published in *Nothing's Sacred Magazine IV* and *V, Corvid Queen, Hazard Yet Forward* (2012), *Enter the Apocalypse* (2017), *Beautiful Lies, Painful Truths II* (2018), *Terror Politico* (2019), *It Calls from the Forest* (2020), *Gray Sisters Vol 1* (2020), *Borderlands Vol 7* (2020), *Pseudopod 752* (2021), and others. Check out her first novel, "Revelation: Poppet Cycle Book 1." Contact her at www.donnajwmunro.com or @DonnaJWMunro on Twitter.

Rio Murphy
Author, *"The Selfless Gift"*
Sometimes described as "zany pathos", Rio Murphy's writing is grim, dark and yet always invested in what is impossibly human.

Rio Murphy has written several non-fiction articles over many years in feminist and Zen Practice publications addressing social and wellness issues, including a short memoir for *Sister Writes, the Work Issue,* in 2019.

Thanks to isolation and having a great view from her lock down move to a 15th floor condo in Pickering Ontario, the home of the Nuclear Power station, she has been writing science fiction and speculative short stories, several finding happy homes in publications like *Polar Borealis* and *Outsiders*, a one-shot anthology of speculative fiction, and *Wight Christmas*, a collection of horror stories about, you guessed it, Christmas.

She is a member of Toronto Science Fiction and Fantasy Writers, the East End Writers Group and Sister Writes.

Martin Munks
Author, "I Still Believe in Santa Claus"
Martin Munks is a short fiction writer, though mostly he works in advertising. He hopes to one day see the Earth from space.

Stephen Oliver
Author, "Daddy and Mommy and Me"
I'm an ex-software engineer who switched to writing after closing down my computer company in 2012 and returning to the UK from Switzerland. I look after my mother, who's my greatest fan, at present, even when she calls me "weird"! I spend the rest of the time writing, editing, revising, submitting, and thinking about being an author.

About the Contributors

My genres include self-help, science fiction, space opera, fantasy, urban fantasy, magical realism, horror, fairy tales, fairy stories, slipstream, interstitial, noir, detective fiction, action, thriller, humour, YA, and children's stories (often more than one genre in any particular story). In the last 9 years, I've written over 1.2 million words. In the past year alone, I've seen the publication of my first science fiction novel, as well as over a dozen short stories. I'm awaiting the imminent publication of a dark urban fantasy anthology, too.

Kara Race-Moore
Author, "A Christmas Cake"
Kara Race-Moore's first exposure to the horror genre was through Nickelodeon's Are You Afraid of the Dark?, leaving her wondering how to join the Midnight Society. Ms. Race-Moore resides in Los Angeles and is currently working on a variety of other short stories and novellas of multiple genres, working to be a part of the push to move those stuck in the margins to the center of the page. She has published short stories in science fiction, horror, and historical fiction and is always on the lookout for new ideas. She can be found at: https://kararacemoore.wordpress.com

Jude Reid
Author, "(Everybody's Waitin' For) The Man With The Bag"
Jude lives in Glasgow and writes dark stories in the narrow gaps between full time work as a surgeon, wrangling her kids and trying to wear out a border collie. She likes tabletop RPGs, running away from zombies and climbing inadvisably large mountains.

David F. Shultz
Author, "The Santas"
David F. Shultz writes from Toronto, Canada, where he is Lead Editor at *Speculative North*. His 80+ publications are featured through publishers such as *Augur*, *Diabolical Plots*, and *Third Flatiron*. Author webpage: davidfshultz.com

Matt Singleton
Author, "Harry and Samir Are Still Asleep"
Matt Singleton lives in Toronto.

David Tallerman
Author, "A Study in Red and White"
David Tallerman is the author of numerous books: the historical science-fiction drama "To End All Wars," thrillers "A Savage Generation" and "The Bad Neighbour," fantasy series "The Black River Chronicles" and "The Tales of Easie Damasco," and the science-fiction novella "Patchwerk." Next out will be "The Outfit," an account of the true-life Tiflis Bank Robbery and the part played in it by future leader of the Soviet Union Joseph Stalin, due from Rebellion in early 2022.

David's comics work includes the absurdist steampunk graphic novel "Endangered Weapon B: Mechanimal Science," with Bob Molesworth, and his short fiction has appeared in around a hundred markets, among them *Clarkesworld*, *Nightmare*, *Lightspeed*, and *Beneath Ceaseless Skies*. A number of his best dark fantasy stories were gathered together in his debut collection "The Sign in the Moonlight and Other Stories."

He can be found online at www.davidtallerman.co.uk.

About the Contributors

Karen Walker
Author, "The Twelfth Day of Christmas"
Karen writes flash fiction and prose poetry in Ontario, Canada. Her work is in *Unstamatic, Reflex Fiction, The Disappointed Housewife, Retreat West, Bandit Fiction, Five Minute Lit, Sundial Magazine, Potato Soup Journal, 100 Word Story*, and others.

Olin Wish
Author, "Have a Holly, Jolly Nuclear Winter"
Olin Wish currently resides in Kentucky, but travels around a lot. He has four kids, two full-time jobs, and enjoys day drinking. Aside from being lost in the woods, Olin is a regular contributor to *Drunk Monkeys Literary Journal, Kleft Jaw,* and *Unfading Daydream*, among others. His debut novel "The Last Minuters," a story about suicide, ninjas, and fine dining is available on Amazon.

Rainie Zenith
Author, "Snowman"
Rainie Zenith is an Australian writer with a penchant for pieces that fall broadly within the gothic fantasy realm. Her work has been published in numerous literary journals and short story anthologies, including *Tales of Blood and Squalor* from Dark Cloud Press. She was the winner of the 2020 Monash Short Story Competition and the Fountain 2020-2021 Essay Contest. Rainie was a judge in Iron Faerie Publishing's 2021 Betwixt Writing Competition. She is also a singer-songwriter. Find out more at facebook.com/rainiezenith

Printed in Great Britain
by Amazon